BROKEN IS BEAUTIFUL

JANE SHEARER

3Eyes Publishing

Published 2023
by 3Eyes Publishing

ISBN 978-0-473-66988-1 (Paperback)
ISBN 978-0-473-67678-0 (International Paperback)
ISBN 978-0-473-66989-8 (Epub)
ISBN 978-0-473-66990-4 (Kindle)
ISBN 978-0-473-66991-1 (PDF)
ISBN 978-0-473-66992-8 (Apple Books)
ISBN 978-0-473-66993-5 (Audiobook)

Teacup artwork from all-free-download.com

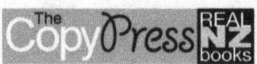

Designed and distributed in New Zealand by The Copy Press, Nelson, New Zealand.
www.copypress.co.nz

For Mum and Dad, who gave me my love of
books and words, and so much more.

1

5 MARCH 2020

"HELLO, I'm Julia and I am obsessed with broken things." Phew, it's out there. I am breathing hard, my palms are sweaty, and I can't raise my eyes to look around the circle of people. Is there a hush? Or are seconds pretending to be minutes, without giving time for people to react? Finally, "Hello Julia," choruses back to me and I let myself relax.

Ten of us are seated in a circle of brightly coloured plastic chairs in the middle of the Sumner Surf Lifesaving Club common room. I should be listening to the next speaker, but I am so relieved to have completed my turn that I can't hear a word and my eyes are drawn to the view outside the room. Small waves roll in from the ocean onto the sandy beach where silhouetted figures brave the water in the evening light. God-rays are illuminating the sea as it stretches away from us. I combine God-rays with rainbows in my head and imagine pots of gold where the rays touch the sea. I could do with a pot of gold right now.

By the time my concentration returns to the room, I have missed half the other introductions. I hope I said "Hello" to the other people in automaton fashion. When I raise my eyes above the parapet of my lap, no one appears to be staring at me so I can't have behaved too badly in my lapse. The person opposite me in the circle is speaking.

"Hello, I'm Matthew and I'm obsessed with tattoos."

I join in, "Hello Matthew."

Genius is not required to detect that Matthew is obsessed with tattoos; tattoos cover all the visible parts of his body. It's a good-looking body if you like a coating of ink. I estimate Matthew is in his early forties, with a physique suggesting exercise is a regular part of his life, along with tattooing. His shaven head allows an excellent view of the tattoos colouring his skull which extend over his face – the only exception being his eyeballs – and on under his black t-shirt. There are glimpses of tattoos between his t-shirt and blue jeans and above his Allbirds shoes. However, what is particularly noticeable about Matthew is that his tattoos are all brand names. I read Nike, Breville, Apple, Panasonic, Birkenstock, Red Band; there are brands I cannot make out from three metres across the circle. I realise I should stop staring and quickly turn my attention to the next participant.

"Hello, I'm Monique and I'm obsessed with eating plasterboard."

"Hello, Monique."

Monique is addicted to eating plasterboard? Really? Is that a thing? Is eating plasterboard how Monique, who must be in her fifties, stays so slim? She has expertly dyed long blonde hair and is wearing it in plaits. Monique is one of those people who dress apparently effortlessly in a style you want to emulate. Her clothes are unusual, but they look perfect on her, like her plaits which would make me look like an ageing child. She is wearing long khaki shorts with knee-high cream socks and beautiful tan leather ankle boots which match her leather bomber jacket.

I look at the corners of Monique's mouth to see if I can spot crumbs of plasterboard (yes, ridiculous, she would be on her best behaviour given this is our first group session). I scan the room for aspects vulnerable to a plasterboard addict and spot a few exposed corners on which one could have a quick nibble.

The last person in the circle is Greg. "Hello, I'm Greg and I'm obsessed with collecting Teenage Mutant Ninja Turtle paraphernalia."

"Hello Greg," we warble back. Everyone is now feeling more comfortable given Greg's is the last introduction.

Greg is a guy you wouldn't notice on the street, or anywhere else. He has mid-brown hair not yet markedly receding or greying and could be anywhere from mid-thirties to early fifties. He is wearing a brown t-shirt with a brown jacket and blue jeans. Greg's only claim to noticeability is his footwear. He has Doc Martens adorned with Teenage Mutant Ninja Turtles. It seems inappropriate to flaunt your obsession. However, Matthew is flaunting his obsession, and could hardly help but do so.

Fran is the last person to introduce herself formally. Fran looks casually stylish in a turquoise shirt and jean jacket with dark curly hair cut at chin length. When we arrived, she welcomed us into the room, checked our names off her list and sat us all down. She explained this session would start with introductions which must include us stating our obsessions. We would then do a group trust exercise. Fran had sent out the emails letting me know the time and date of this session. How large is the bureaucracy behind Obsessives Associated, or 'OA' as it's referred to in all the information she sent? Where in New Zealand might their central office be? How much information do OA already have about me, what additional information are they storing away, and how much of that information can my bank discover?

"Hello, I'm Fran and I'm obsessed with helping people in need."

"Hello, Fran."

What, are we all here to feed Fran's addiction? Could Fran be the entire bureaucracy of Obsessives Associated? Has she set up OA to get an obsession kick together with an income? Surely my bank, who required me to attend a support group as a condition of extending my home loan, will have investigated the background of the entity offering the services? It must be time to get on with the trust exercise, but I am not feeling very trusting.

Fran says we will have a social break first. She has brought vegan, sugar-free, gluten-free, additive-free cookies for us to have with a drink. It's hard to imagine what ingredients might be in such an everything-free cookie, spinach? However, the cookies taste remarkably good, so I eat three with my cup of peppermint tea, because I forgot to eat lunch in my anticipation of the meeting.

Fran tells us we bring snacks on a roster, in reverse order of our first names. J is in the middle of the alphabet so I know I will come after Monique and Matthew, and I still have three names to learn so my turn might be further delayed. That's a relief because I have little idea how to bake anything edible that apparently has almost no content of interest.

Fran lays out the exercise. I fear a group exercise will try to trick us into revealing something about ourselves we don't want to share. However, it turns out this exercise won't challenge me too greatly on an interpersonal level. We have to build the tallest possible tower out of spaghetti strands, some tape, some string, scissors, and a marshmallow to be placed at the top of the tower. To create a sense of competition, we are divided into two groups, and I am with Matthew, Monique, Greg, and an older guy called Barry. I'm going to have to discover Barry's obsession next week as he spoke before me, when I wasn't listening.

Fran starts an egg timer, and we have fifteen minutes in which to complete the tallest possible freestanding tower.

Barry is a man in a suit and tie who likes to be in charge. The rest of us are happy for him to take the leading role. Barry announces we should make an inventory of our construction materials. He grabs all the pieces of spaghetti to count them whereupon two pieces crumble. Barry puts on a 'doesn't matter' face and says with emphasis that we now have sixteen pieces of spaghetti where, seconds ago, we had ten.

Monique fiddles with the tape. I hope she won't accidentally stick bits of tape together, so they are no longer useful. It's green masking tape which is good for creating sharp paint lines when painting trim, but it isn't strong.

I pick up the string, which is old-fashioned brown twine, like Gran used to tie up plants. While I ignore Barry, who is telling us to brainstorm, I break a fingernail trying to straighten the string out where I have accidentally knotted it.

Telling people to brainstorm is as sensible as telling cats to sit. People's brains immediately do something other than the mandated brainstorming. We look at the fifty-centimetre tower the other group have already created, then Fran appears from behind us to redirect our attention to our own non-tower, as we guiltily return the things we've been engaging ourselves with.

Greg says, "Just a possibility, we could make triangles out of spaghetti and tape because triangles are strong. But it might be a bad idea."

"What should we do with the string?" asks Barry.

"We don't have to use everything. The string could be a deliberate distraction," says Monique.

"Could we use it to hang the marshmallow?" suggests Matthew. He tries to poke a hole in the marshmallow with a spaghetti strand which breaks into tiny fragments. I sit quietly, picturing my garden with its wild profusion of flowers and leaves and considering the pointlessness of spaghetti towers.

As the last grains of sand fall, we accomplish a ten-centimetre teepee of taped-together spaghetti pieces, collectively poked into the marshmallow. Our teepee wavers, then crumbles into a heap as we enviously observe the fine construction of our opposition. Their tower stands proud and tall with a pink marshmallow balanced upon its apex. Our group of four look like losers. Is the point of the exercise to make us feel like four losers in a losing alliance, rather than the individual losers who entered the room? This strategy is not making me look forward to next week.

Fran asks us to return to our circle and participate in a karakia prior to departure. I am dubious about prayers so am happy to find this karakia bears more resemblance to gardening than church.

The sun has set upon our gathering for the day.
The birds are silent.
The worms are still.
The world is at rest.
The night has arrived my friends.
So, tie up the waka.
Have we landed?
We have landed.

I shoot a glance at Matthew's broad shoulders and Monique's bony knees as they exit onto the wooden deck, chatting animatedly, and pick up my handsewn shoulder bag to make my solitary way home.

2

MY home is twenty minutes of relaxed walking from the Sumner Surf Club. I prefer the route by the sea, rather than through Sumner Village, enjoying the sounds and smells as the waves hit the stone armouring in front of the pavement. Longboarders and paddleboarders play on the waves and there is a holiday feel, although the summer holidays are long gone by March. Dreadlocked Europeans in wetsuits scurry back and forth with surfboards or carry bags of rubbish to sneak into the spilling bins along the street. Wafts of conversation fuelled by beer and coffee drift past. Backpacker vans lining the street are a new normal over the last few years as tourists look for free places to stay. A few vans were bearable, but the constant hordes now impact on my quiet enjoyment of the sea.

I turn away from the sea down Head Street, only two blocks to home now. My home is my haven, left to me by Gran when she died two decades ago. While I took care of Gran at home for the five years prior to her death, I got to know and love her house even more than I had as a small child. Gran's house was a refuge when our fey mother forgot to put food in the cupboards or the fridge.

Mum always had something to do that she regarded as more interesting than looking after children. She had many groups she loved attending more than she appeared to love us – pottery, book reading, Buddhism, Baha'i, Quakers (she was agnostic about religion), yoga, meditation, macramé, weaving, welding, EST (an awful group that occasionally met at home and who yelled out all the things they didn't like about each other), Save the Whales, Save Lake Manapouri. Mum didn't attend any group for long and flowed between them in loose, colourful caftans and scarves. She generally didn't wear shoes because she said shoes are bad for feet – did I know how many women need their feet operated on because they wore high-heeled shoes?

Our mother claimed she wanted to be a flower child but came to the party late, therefore she had lots of parties at our house to make up for that late arrival. When Johnno and I came home from school and there was a large bowl of brown and effervescent liquid on the table, referred to as 'punch', it was time to head to Gran's if we wanted to get any sleep. Guests would come and go, eat, drink, shout at each other, start kissing on the sofa, get pushed off the sofa by someone else who wanted to sit there, have a little sleep on the floor, and then start eating and drinking again. There were generally a few guests scattered around the house in the morning if we crept in to retrieve a forgotten piece of school uniform.

If there was one thing I was sure about as a child, it was that when I grew up, I wasn't having a house full of coming and going people. My house would be mine and it would be a lucky and worthy person who came over my doorstep.

Gran allowed my dream of a home of my own to come true. Gran always knew what we wanted and tried to make it happen, within her means. She inherited her house from her parents, who built it in the early 1900s. Her parents, Ma and Pa Stout, moved from Christchurch City to Sumner Village, which was growing in popularity as rich Christchurch people built mansions near the beach. Gran never said how they got the land; perhaps someone gave them their scrubby patch of low-lying sand, which appeared undesirable in comparison with the sun-drenched slopes of Scarborough and Clifton Hill with views of the Pacific Ocean and Southern Alps.

Pa Stout was a carpenter and Ma Stout cleaned and cooked. When they first moved out of town, Ma Stout got a job at the Café Continental, but it burned down after only three years. After the fire, she found work in the houses of the people she had served in the café. Pa Stout built new houses for the rich while the two of them lived in a canvas tent on their section. He slowly built their own house from construction scraps he scavenged at the end of his building jobs. As a result, Gran's house has always looked slightly askew, built with different weatherboard shapes on different aspects and windows at different heights because there wasn't a plan, just a flowing creation. The oddity never bothered Gran, and it hasn't bothered me either; 29 Head Street is mine and that's what makes it the best place in the world.

I arrive at my poppy-coloured front door, guarded by a central brass knocker with a lion's head, and feel happy before I even get inside. The door is painted with leftovers from a can one of my clients gave me. It's the only part of the house exterior that is currently well covered with paint. I have been meaning to paint the outside but it's a big job and not an appealing one. How would I avoid standing on the plants? I don't think painting is that important. Gran's house survived the Canterbury earthquakes, and it isn't going to fall down now for lack of paint on the walls.

I am craving a cup of tea that doesn't taste like a peppermint postage stamp, so I head straight to the kitchen. To be truthful, I can't head straight to the kitchen because there are a number of boxes to negotiate along the hallway. I notice one box has acquired five friends above it and the top box towers over my head, so I move the top box sideways to join a two-box-high pile.

I turn on the gas and put my burgundy kettle on the stove. I've always had gas and it served me well in the earthquakes when power went out for months at a time. The push button sparker on the stove stopped working years ago so I light the gas with a match. I pull out my cloisonné jar of Kenya Bold tea, lift the lid and inhale joyously. It is possible I am obsessed with Kenya Bold tea, but this is not an obsession the bank knows anything about, and I am not telling them. The worst thing about liking Kenya Bold is that the nearest place stocking Kenya Bold leaf is a nine-kilometre cycle ride away.

I make my tea in Gran's brown and cream Temuka pottery teapot with a matching cream and brown tea cosy. This tea cosy was the first knitting project I remember undertaking. Gran taught me how to knit and I find it peaceful. I can completely lose myself sitting in my garden and knitting for hours. Gran was very proud when I knitted a tea cosy that more or less fitted the teapot.

Johnno tried knitting too and cried because he'd dropped too many stitches, so his tea cosy unravelled when he attempted to pull it into shape. Johnno threw the cosy on the ground, stamped on it, and said it was a stupid activity for girls. Gran got cross with Johnno. She told him off for suggesting girls are inferior to boys and pointed out where his dinner had come from that evening.

I take my tea into the corner of the sitting room to drink it, weaving my way back between the hallway boxes. I carry the teapot, and my gold filigree bone china teacup on its matching saucer, on my Indian inlaid wooden tray. This is my favourite tea-drinking set, the set with which Gran and I drank tea. We had two filigree teacups then and it is possible I still have two, but I only need one at present given my lack of visitors.

I drink tea in the corner of the sitting room because my little problem now occupies most of my sitting room. Not that the room is large, but all the space is taken up with … well … with … things … broken things. That's my problem, you see. As I said in the meeting tonight for the first time ever, I can't let go of broken things.

Broken things make me sad. I want broken things to be fixed. I believe I am the person who can fix broken things. Gran taught me a lot about fixing and I have subsequently had plenty more practice. However, I have discovered there are many broken things needing fixing in this world, even in this city. After a series of earthquakes Christchurch was full of broken things requiring repair. These broken things are accumulating in my house, and they appear to be getting the upper hand.

I read a good simile for my feelings about broken things in a book about a girl who lived in the frozen north of Canada. She found a lost mitten and felt absolute empathetic despair with the mitten. There was a terrible sadness in the loneliness of the knitted mitten that would never be reunited with its fellow mitten. It had been a singular pair of mittens, knitted by hand by someone's loved parent, or grandparent, or child. No other mitten could be a replacement, that particular pair of mittens uniquely belonged together. The mittens had kept the loved one's hands warm, until a forgetful moment meant there was only one mittened hand, one cold hand, and a lonely red mitten abandoned out in the snow.

3

12 MARCH 2020

TODAY is important because I have a potential client coming to visit, the first for many weeks. I haven't been welcoming of late when people have expressed interest in my services. Most clients come through word of mouth, although I do keep flyers on the notice boards at the Sumner Supervalue, by the Bohemian Bakery, and at the Woolston New World. However, my bank now requires me to attend my weekly Thursday OA group *and* demonstrate I am increasing my income.

I stopped having clients come into my house some years ago. People were tripping over my boxes, and I don't want the contents scattered all over the floor. The simple solution was to have clients visit in my garden. My garden is a wild thing I have let run deliberately loose. Many of the flowers which now cover the paths remind me of Gran. I have no issue with plants growing on paths as long as they don't complain when I walk on them. We have reached a reasonable accord, primroses, poppies and petunias, granny's bonnets and gerberas, marigolds and marguerite daisies, nasturtiums and nigella, all frolic together in a riot of colour in the spring and summer. Jasmine and honeysuckle scent the air while disguising the fence, and clematis and wisteria climb over the veranda.

Gran's house is unusual for its era in that Pa Stout built a veranda on its north side to keep the house cool in summer. The house is on a corner with roads to the west and south sides, so the norm would have been to build the veranda facing the long southern axis. Pa Stout wasn't wealthy, but he was smart and brought Gran up to be smart too.

My vegetables grow happily between the flowers. Rocket and sprouting broccoli seed themselves. Potatoes I miss at harvest time provide the next year's crop. Pumpkins sprout up from the compost piled by the fence. Bean plants grow from old pods. At this point in late summer, vegetables are outcompeting the flowers.

I move some pumpkin vines off the mosaic sofa seat I designed with my china, which shattered in the February 2011 earthquake. Almost everything breakable broke, so I had plenty of scope to adorn a concrete sofa. It's a mosaic of a taniwha, fish, sea, and seaweed, swirling blues and greens and creams, with bright rays of mirror sun glinting through the water. My sofa is the perfect art piece to give clients confidence that 'Broken is Beautiful' can do something special with their offerings.

'Broken is Beautiful' is the name of my business. In my twenties I prosaically named it 'Julia's Repairs', when I was more focused on fixing things than on creative reconstruction. I never had a 'normal' job – I liked the look of Gran's life. Gran worked hard for other people but always called her own shots because she never worked more than a day a week for any one client. Gran would say she couldn't clean today because she had a meeting to attend when her meeting was with her own garden. "Why is my garden less important than their dirty toilet?" was her catch phrase.

Gran taught Johnno and me how to fix and make things, from those days of knitting tea cosies and before. On rainy days when we were little, we would make pictures to put on our dressers by cutting images out of magazines, melting a layer of candle wax into the bottom of one of Pa Stout's old tobacco tins, carefully placing the image onto the warm wax and then melting another layer of wax on top. If you weren't careful the image would go askew in the wax and stick out the side. Then you would have to heat the tin up so the wax would melt and start the process over again.

We tried everything we could to find materials to make and improved our skills over time. We folded hundreds of origami paper cranes to hang in our windows to remember the people of Hiroshima. We embroidered samplers for our rooms with our birth dates and city, although Johnno took his down just before his tenth birthday party, in case his mates deduced he had done the embroidery rather than his sister. There were pieces of Pa Stout's wood stacked in the corner of the property which I used to make a kindling box for the fire and Johnno made into a beautiful ladder for climbing into the roof space.

We darned our socks and sewed buttons on our school uniforms, put up hems and lengthened them again, as fashions changed. We rewired light switches and plugs. We moved on to repairing appliances, carefully disassembling then reconstructing them. It was so exciting when the appliances functioned. Before he left home, Johnno took a whole car engine apart and put it back together. Gran was annoyed because some parts lived in the sitting room for several months. Almost all the parts went back in; the three left over can't have been important as the engine worked well. Gran was over her crossness once the engine was refurbished because there was no more mess in the sitting room. We were exceptionally proud of Johnno and toasted him with spiced tomato juice made of tomatoes harvested from our garden.

By the time we were close to finishing high school, Mum took herself out of our picture. She headed north to Takaka, or thereabouts, with a new boyfriend who was running a yoga school somewhere in Golden Bay, in the northwest corner of the South Island. Mum asked us what we would like to do, go with her, or stay with Gran. Did Mum ask Gran first? It is quite possible she didn't. Johnno and I voted wholeheartedly for staying with Gran. Johnno had his sights set on learning more so he could earn lots of money and get out of Sumner, out of Christchurch and out of New Zealand. I was starting to get worried about Gran, who was falling over a lot more often than she ought to and getting confused about which day of the week it was. So, Mum wafted off north with Bruce and has remained in Golden Bay ever since. Golden Bay suits her well, although Bruce didn't suit her for long.

When we finished school, Johnno applied his mechanical skills at the University of Canterbury. I took my skills and applied them to fixing things for other people, while helping Gran. Gran was always keen for me to further my education, but I couldn't see the point; I could learn as much as I wanted to know by reading and experimenting.

When Johnno entered his second year at university, he used his student allowance to go flatting. He came home sporadically, needing a free feed or his clothes washed, but his visits became rarer, until we were surprised when he turned up. We knew Johnno had visited when the fridge was empty and the cupboards largely bare.

By then, I was getting a reputation as the local fixer-upper and was pleasantly surprised I could earn a decent cash income that supported me and supplemented Gran's pension.

I was accidentally introduced to the possibilities of creative repair when I came across a book on kintsugi in the Sumner Library. The book was on the 'staff picks' display stand. The cover showed a beautiful ceramic bowl with irregular threads of gold woven through it. How did they do that? I got the book out and read with fascination and awe. Kintsugi is a four-hundred-year-old Japanese art form which glues broken pottery pieces back together, then highlights the cracks with gold. Kintsugi's concept embraces flaws and imperfections to build something more beautiful than the original item.

Doors in my mind flew open, filled with possibilities of how to repair broken things and make them better than they ever were. How to embed the story of an object, its fragmentation and re-amalgamation, into its whole. With kintsugi there is no need to hide the breaks, one celebrates them. I could go beyond repairing a toaster so the electrical circuits worked again, I could paint an artwork on the exterior. How about a toaster with flames shooting up the outside, though that could be frightening. Or a pair of hands warming themselves on the metal? Or an amalgam of random shapes in attractive colours that make you want to get up in the morning to put stale bread in your exciting appliance? Those daydreams were where 'Broken is Beautiful' originated, a synthesis of ancient Japanese art and imaginings of ornate toasters.

4

THE potential client dropping round today is Robbie from Coffee Culture in Sumner. I am hoping Robbie might have items I can creatively repair in exchange for him painting the outside of my house. I could also engage in creative accounting to satisfy the bank if he pays me for the items and then I pay him for the painting. Robbie said he likes solid outdoor work as an antidote to designing little flowers on cups of coffee which will vanish in seconds down someone's throat.

Robbie will end his shift at 4pm and cycle here. He's a Scottish backpacker who has worked at Coffee Culture for the last few months. Robbie hitchhiked from Auckland up to Cape Reinga then started the Te Araroa walk down the length of New Zealand on a whim. He was a hiking newbie who says he loved his new-found freedom of getting up and walking every day and seeing where he ended up. Robbie got his job because he happened to meet the owner of Coffee Culture Sumner in a bar in Bluff over a beer, as the two finished Te Araroa simultaneously.

I feel a little stressed because my OA session is at 5.30pm, I can't be late, I don't like to arrive flustered, and I must get my attendance scan. I need to leave by 5.10pm and it is already 4.20pm. I generally avoid having deadlines or concrete time frames insofar as is humanly possible, but I have no option in my mandated OA attendance.

The letter that dropped a bombshell into my world arrived on a Thursday. I was looking out the window when the post-person pulled up at my mailbox in their red, electric toy car. I get as few letters as visitors so that was a surprise. Afterwards I felt foolish for imagining it could be a nice surprise. Something in the mail ... perhaps Johnno had finally got off his rear end to send me an early birthday present for my birthday in April? I opened the envelope eagerly, to then be puzzled by its contents.

The letter was from Bank Aotearoa, who I thought a perfectly adequate bank, up to the moment I started reading that letter. They wanted to inform me I was in arrears on my mortgage payments. I should have known I was in arrears. It is possible I did know I was in arrears but was successfully blocking the knowledge away from the knowing part of my brain. I am very good at segmenting off information I don't want to know about from the remainder of my brain.

I should never have taken a loan out on Gran's house, and I knew it when I signed the papers. Gran never owed money on her house and taught me lack of debt equates to freedom. Now I know, more than ever, how correct she was. The incentive for taking out the loan was getting extra work done on the house when it was repaired after the Canterbury earthquakes.

The Canterbury earthquakes were bad in a whole lot of ways. There is nothing like living through large numbers of earthquakes to make you understand them properly. We had earthquakes when Johnno and I were little. The house shook for a while and Gran told us to stand under the doorframes as the safest place to be. Nothing of consequence happened and, after my childhood, I couldn't remember when I felt an earthquake until September 2010.

Everyone in Christchurch knows the dates of the earthquakes – 4 September 2010, 22 February 2011, 13 June 2011, and 23 December 2011.

September's earthquake hit west of the city on the Canterbury Plains and sent liquefied mud into houses around the Heathcote and Avon

Rivers in Christchurch. However, east of the city in Sumner we got a big shake but nothing more.

February was disastrous. One hundred and eighty-six people died in the city centre when two big buildings collapsed, and brick fronts fell off heritage buildings onto passers-by. February's hit Sumner hard, then June's smacked us again.

The earthquakes made one in ten Christchurch houses uninhabitable – through rock fall, liquefaction, sinking foundations, brick houses losing all their bricks. Nearly every house in the city had some damage. Also, this wasn't just four earthquakes, there were literally thousands of smaller earthquakes between the big ones, so you were woken up every night for months.

The outside of Gran's house weathered earthquakes well as its flexible wood framing, wooden weatherboard cladding, and light iron roof wriggled around a lot but didn't break. The lath and plaster coating inside did not fare so well. The walls became full of cracks, which widened as earthquakes continued so plaster fell on the floor and filled the air.

In September, the brick fireplace chimneys in the sitting room and bedrooms fell down. The bricks dented the roof but luckily fell into the garden rather than into the house.

In February, my hot water cylinder ripped itself out of its fixings and fell so water spouted everywhere, including into all the holes in the walls. The water to Sumner got shut off quickly and didn't come back on for a month, but it still managed to do a lot of damage.

It wasn't only my hot water cylinder that was damaged, by 23 February 2011 I no longer owned many breakable objects. By a complete miracle, Gran's teapot and two filigree teacups and saucers survived. I used them at breakfast then placed them in the sink to leave the kitchen tidy. The hand towel hanging under the cupboards fell into the sink and saved them from banging together.

Isn't it funny how we call good and unlikely events miracles, but we don't use the same word for bad and unlikely events. There was a man in Redcliffs, the suburb west, whose wife asked him to pick raspberries for dessert. The earthquake struck while he was picking the raspberries and a boulder fell and squashed him. It was most unlikely, but bad, therefore cannot be called a miracle.

The insurance claim process for the earthquakes was a nightmare, rather than a miracle. I filed twelve insurance claims because I had to make separate claims for the house and the contents and the land. I couldn't keep track of them and nor could the insurance system. I remember one horror of a call when I wanted to know the results of an inspection. The person on the other end of the phone (always a different person) assured me Gran's house had not been inspected. I told her it had been inspected because I had been there. We went back and forth in this style for over an hour until she belatedly discovered the inspection had been filed under a claim for June and I had given her the claim number for February.

Another part of the insurance saga was how Gran's house repaired itself, according to the insurance company anyway. When the house was first inspected, the report said the house would have to be demolished. I was shocked and upset – the house was reasonably habitable, and it was far too precious to ever demolish. Luckily, the assessors rethought their report, and the next news was they considered the house repairable. By the fifth inspection, the house was considered only slightly damaged. I was sure Pa Stout didn't build a magic, self-repairing house. However, by the fifth inspection I was too tired to argue with the bevy of men who strode through, acting as if they knew everything and I knew nothing.

Like all things, including very bad things, after thirty-six months, the insurance deliberation process eventually ended in late 2014. I was informed the house would be fixed by Fleecer Construction. I would have to stay somewhere else for three months while repairs were carried out, but Fleecer promised it would be all like brand new.

Charlie from Fleecer visited and asked whether I would like the builders to do anything extra while they were working on the house. Now I know I was upsold, but I was in too fragile a state at the time to notice.

Charlie pointed out the house wouldn't be exactly like new because insurance would only cover repairing and painting walls with specific earthquake damage. Nothing had happened to most of the window paint, so the windows would be looking tired against relined and freshly painted interior walls. All the wooden floors were scarred but there was only major damage in the kitchen, where my plates had embedded little shards in the floor. Charlie suggested painting the outside as well – insurance considered the paint was too worn prior to the earthquakes to be covered – but that was one cost too far for me.

Charlie was sure I could get a loan to improve the house and Bank Aotearoa were indeed happy to give me one. I signed the mortgage papers, the repair went ahead, and the inside was substantially improved, including insulation and heat pumps to replace the broken fireplaces, making it warmer in winter. My mortgage didn't feel excessively large at twenty thousand dollars with repayments at fifty dollars a week, equivalent to only one extra up-furbished toaster. Except, unfortunately, that wasn't how things worked out. There's something else huge here that changed everything, but that I avoid thinking about, which is how Amanda died.

5

AMANDA was born on my fortieth birthday, 20 April 2011, and I thought myself the luckiest person in the world. It didn't matter my house was a mess because I hadn't finished tidying from the February earthquake. It didn't matter that the walls were torn and crumbling. Amanda instantly became the star at the centre of my world.

When I was a child, I never imagined I would be a mother. Mum wasn't a motherly role model. She had twins (at least she didn't make the same mistake twice) at age twenty-two. I don't know who our father was. When we asked, Mum said there were several guys who could have been our father, but all were eminently forgettable. The way men came and went in Mum's life it was quite possible she had forgotten our sperm donor by the time she knew she was pregnant.

In New Zealand in the early 1970s there was nowhere official you could go to get an abortion and back-street abortion was risky. If Mum had become pregnant in the mid-1970s, when the first abortion clinics were opening, Johnno and I wouldn't have existed. However, at the time, she was at the apex of her flower power phase where anything was possible and communal raising of children seemed an excellent idea. Mum lived in a perpetual shifting commune in a derelict house at the back of Redcliffs. She still has the belief she followed then – if you go with the flow, everything will work out all right. So Mum figured raising twins would be no problem. If Gran hadn't helped, raising twins would have been a substantial problem. However, in Mum's world view, Gran was a symbol of the world falling into place as it should.

After being actively uninterested in progeny, wanting a child hit me like a bolt from the blue when I was thirty-eight. Over a small number of months, a part of my brain I never knew existed woke up and told me I wanted a baby, my baby. This part of my brain also told me my time to have a baby was running out fast. However, the lack of men on my scene to contribute to baby-making was a challenge, not that there were women on my scene either. As a teenager, my interest in the opposite sex and sex in general was limited and things haven't changed too much. I tried sex out as an experiment. It was okay, but it wasn't exactly earth shattering. Sex was messy, sometimes painful, and there was the fear of getting pregnant accidentally. I didn't want to end up like Mum.

Wanting a baby when there wasn't an available sperm donor was inconvenient. However, I read an article in the paper explaining *in-vitro* fertilisation and how every woman in New Zealand is entitled to one try at it, paid for by the government. My problem had a solution; I called a fertility clinic in Christchurch and arranged an appointment for the next month. I was screened for eligibility for free treatment, which meant I had to quickly invent a partner called Raymond from whom I had recently separated, and with whom I had never managed to get pregnant despite considerable effort.

The process to acquire a baby was arduous, almost as arduous as earthquake repairs, but a great deal more invasive. My stomach turned into a bruised pincushion of injection sites, and I felt like a black hole had swallowed up my brain. However, I turned out to be a lucky IVF recipient. My body dutifully produced lots of eggs, almost all the eggs fertilised successfully, and I became pregnant on the first insemination. I chose a sperm donor from the three options offered without feeling much angst. Any baby would have an unpredictable mix of my and his qualities, I wasn't going to try to constrain a child before it was even born.

Finding out I was pregnant sent me over the moon and beyond. I floated through three months of sore breasts and morning sickness, propped up by the knowledge I would soon have the child I wanted. I spent little time considering practicalities. How would I continue my business and support a child on my own? What did I know about raising children? I left those questions for a later day. Sometimes I can be more like Mum than I care to admit.

I did go to the suggested antenatal classes as a sop to doing things the right way, ten kilometres from home so I wouldn't accidentally meet people I knew. I developed my stories of Raymond – my improved Raymond left me briefly but returned when I told him I was pregnant. It was a tiresomely long bike ride as I got larger with pregnancy. Raymond became an observer on offshore fishing vessels, doing six-week shifts and then being asked to extend his stint because the boat hadn't yet caught its quota. Everyone was concerned and asked whether Raymond would be onshore by our due date. I smiled and said I was sure he would make it back.

For once Mum did something useful and came for Amanda's birth. I had no friends to whom I was close enough to expose myself to such a degree of vulnerability. I wrote a letter to Mum, as she considers electronic devices like computers or cell phones aura-damaging, and possibly gut flora-damaging.

To my surprise, Mum replied saying she would love to see my baby born. I surprised myself further by writing back to say how much I would love her to come. I missed my connection with Gran, though she died long ago, and Mum was my remaining link to Gran's support.

Mum arrived from Takaka a week before Amanda was due, which was plenty long enough. Gran's house is small so I could hear every time Mum turned over in bed.

"This bed is horribly uncomfortable, Julia. You should think about your guests and buy a new one."

"I hardly ever have guests. If you have that much of a problem with the bed, why don't you go and buy a new one. I certainly can't afford to."

"Julia, I don't have much money either and *I* wasn't left a house to live in but have always had to make my own way in the world."

"You might have made your own way, but you didn't look after your own mother, did you? I cared for Gran while she was peeing the bed, but you *never* came to give me a break."

"Well, Julia, you owed a lot to Gran for putting up with you when you were a tiresome teenager."

"You have to be kidding me! Gran looked after me and Johnno because you were *too lazy and selfish to do so*."

We needed time out after that set-to. Mum went to see a mate of hers in South Brighton for a couple of days and, by the time she returned, Amanda was ready to make her appearance.

I wanted a home birth but, after fourteen hours of labour pains with no progress, hospital with painkillers sounded like a good option. The midwife arranged an ambulance, and I was carted into hospital for another day of labour until, somewhere in a blur of pain and confusion, Amanda entered the world.

I would like to say it was love at first sight, but my first thought was, how did I produce something that looks like Gollum just crawled out of the swamp? Mum was a lot more impressed by Amanda and bawled her eyes out as she got to her hold her for the first time. For me, it was love at second sight, though. Once we were both cleaned up and I got to hold her in my arms, I knew I had exactly what I wanted, a daughter.

We all went home from the hospital by taxi and the next few weeks were tough, but some of the best of my life. I focused on one thing, and one thing only, Amanda. I slept when she let me sleep, I fed her when she wanted to be fed, and I carried her round with me in a sling when I needed to do chores.

Mum returned to Takaka once I figured out how to feed and change Amanda and considered I could survive on my own. She was keen to get back to an upcoming yoga camp and I was keen to reclaim Gran's house. We both surprised ourselves by crying and agreeing she would return for a family Christmas celebration. I couldn't remember the last time we had a family Christmas with Mum. Johnno and I usually went to Gran's for a traditional roast dinner and Christmas stockings with oranges and chocolate in their toes.

I had told my clients I would have a break from work, and they all understood. Business had picked up substantially during the earthquakes and I had quite a queue of items to repair. Everyone in Christchurch had broken things needing fixing and 'Broken is Beautiful' had become the business of choice to create a new object from the shards of the past. I was featured in the *Press*, heavily pregnant with Amanda, showing some of my favourite repair creations and explaining my mosaic sofa concepts. I look like I have so much energy in that photo, I can hardly believe it was me.

The biggest problem with my queue of repair jobs was that people didn't want to keep broken things in their own houses so asked me to look after their possessions until I had time to carry out repairs. That was where my box problem originated. I was too keen to say yes and too convinced I could help everyone. I started numbering boxes and putting them in my garden shed. I quickly realised this was a mistake because number one was in the back corner, and I would have to remove fifty-three boxes to get to it. But what next? I was running out of space.

I shelved the problem to focus on Amanda and we settled into a routine. Then the June earthquake struck Sumner and struck terror into my heart. Never had I been responsible for another human being, and this one was so small and felt so fragile. Mum tried to convince me to be tough from the start and put Amanda to sleep in her own bedroom. I wasn't ready. I'd prepared her room but couldn't bear sleeping separated from her. Although it seemed that everything that could fall in the house had already fallen, and everything that could break had broken, if an earthquake struck, I wanted to be able to pick Amanda up in seconds to stand under Pa Stout's solid door frames where we'd be safe together.

6

HOW could I have forgotten the mirror? The heavy mirror with its ornate gilt frame had been fastened to Gran's bedroom wall for as long as I could remember. I regarded the mirror as a permanent fixture because the wall paint colour licked around it, showing it hadn't moved in years.

When I looked at the mirror I could see my childhood-self reflected in it. We were not allowed to enter Gran's room without asking, but it was the only mirror in the house. So, every morning we stayed at Gran's on a school day, our ritual was to check ourselves in the mirror while our pre-departure cup of tea was brewing in the Temuka stoneware teapot. I would go first and Johnno second. We would check our ties were straight and there were no spots on our white school shirts. I would stand straight and tuck my tummy in and then turn round and look sideways to see if my tummy was sticking out without my being aware of it. Then we would have our cup of tea in which a spoon could stand up, before being ready to face the world.

One of Gran's clients gave her the mirror because the bottom corner was a little tarnished. By the time I was looking at my reflection in it, all its edges were substantially tarnished. The mirror was a repair job we never got around to because we couldn't figure out how to detach it from the wall. Gran's client's handyman had brought the mirror round. She said he fixed it on the wall because it was so heavy, he didn't think she could lift it. Gran laughed, "Of course I could have picked it up, but if the silly man wanted to put it up for free why stop him?"

I cared for Gran in her bedroom as she became frailer. She got confused about which day it was, then the time of day. She woke up in the middle of the night and demanded to put her clothes on and go to the supermarket. Some days she repeatedly asked when Johnno was coming home. Gran had gone back to when we were children coming in after school and, she hoped, staying the night. I realised Gran felt she had failed Mum but was committed to raising Johnno and me, giving us all the love we needed. We filled up Gran's house, giving her a purpose she had struggled to find as she aged.

The worst thing was when Gran started wetting the bed and I had to change the sheets and comfort her while mostly wanting to get back to sleep. It was a godsend when the doctor recommended an incontinence nurse, and I learned about adult nappies. Nappies stretched our budget, but Gran was eating little, and I was tired of washing bedclothes every day.

Gran's doctor, Jessie, would visit Gran on her way home rather than making her attend the clinic. Jessie asked whether I wanted to keep caring for Gran, or whether she should move into the nearby Edith Cavell rest home. I told Jessie this was Gran's home, Gran wanted to die in it, and I would do everything in my power to make that happen.

By the end, Gran's breathing was getting weaker by the day, and I could barely persuade her to take a sip of water to moisten her dry mouth. One evening I kissed her goodnight and headed off to my room as normal. I heard nothing in the night, but when I came to see her in the morning, she was lying with her head sideways; she could have been asleep, except she wasn't breathing.

On Gran's request, I had built her a casket from the last of Pa Stout's wood in the woodshed. The top was kauri, and the sides were rimu. I inlaid fragments of shells from Sumner Beach in spiralling patterns in the kauri. I made a padded interior covered with material with patterns of intertwining flowers, although I kept that in my cupboard so mice wouldn't get at it. Gran loved the casket, giving it a friendly pat and smiling at the thought her last resting place would be tied to her house and Ma and Pa Stout.

When Gran died, I discovered it is challenging to move the dead body of an adult, even the tiny adult Gran had shrunk to. I quickly found I couldn't lift Gran into her casket because I couldn't keep hold of all her limbs. In the end I wrapped her up in a sheet and swivelled her sideways down into the casket on the floor, then pulled the sheet out and tidied up her dressing gown.

Once Gran was secure in her casket I went to the kitchen, pulled out the cloisonné tea caddy, made a pot of Kenya Bold in the Temuka teapot and brought a cup for each of us in the gold filigree cups on the inlaid Indian tray, just the way she liked to have tea. I put Gran's cup beside her on the floor and slowly drank mine, sitting in the upright chair that backed the wall, opposite the mirror. When I finished my tea, it was time to call the undertakers because Gran was ready to go.

I found it very hard to move into Gran's room. It felt wrong taking it over. Johnno and I had always slept in twin beds with sagging springs in the second bedroom. When Johnno went overseas, I stayed in 'our' room where we'd had turns telling each other bedtime stories to help us go to sleep. When I was sure Johnno wasn't coming back any time soon, I moved his bed into the shed. When the mattress became a home for mice, I got it taken to the rubbish dump. Not that I mind mice, but they were eating Gran's pumpkins, stored for winter. I stayed on in that room for two years after Gran died.

Until I was ready to shift into her bedroom, I left Gran's room as it was. I left her clothes hanging in the wardrobe and her shoes in the chest at the foot of the bed. Gran's clothes were mostly blues and greens, with bright blue her favourite. When I finally brought myself to move Gran's clothes out of her room I was struck by her socks, many of which had more darning than sock. I took her clothes to the Salvation Army Store in Sumner and dropped them by the desk, rushing out before the store attendant could tell me they didn't want them.

The reason I finally moved into Gran's room was because it has the best view of the garden, rather than the rock faces of Scarborough Hill visible from the second bedroom. When I moved in, I thought about shifting the mirror but rediscovered it was fixed firmly and invisibly to the wall. Was it nailed on with the holes painted over? I changed very little. I put my clothes in the wardrobe and my shoes in the chest at the end of the bed. I did take down Gran's prints from the walls, as they had faded to a murky blue with their images now indiscernible. I hung prints of my favourite artists, including Hundertwasser and Klimt as I love metallic paint, to hide the plaster rifts insurance wasn't yet fixing.

Once Amanda was born, I shuffled furniture to make space for her crib. The shoe chest had to go, and the wardrobe shifted to the opposite side of the window, so her crib could stand directly in front of where I slept, and she could get a view of the garden. Her crib blocked my sightline to the mirror but that was okay. It was Amanda I wanted to look at, not my own reflection when I was not looking my best.

The twenty-third of December was to be celebratory. Mum would arrive on an afternoon bus from Takaka. I was excited for Mum to see Amanda who had, of course, grown unbelievably from the tiny baby Mum last held in May. I sent pictures in the mail when I remembered, but pictures are not the living, breathing human.

However, Amanda had been restless all day. She was teething and not sleeping well at night. I was waking multiple times to pick her up, feed her, soothe her, and put her back down. I knew this was against all the advice in the books, but I was determined to bring her up the way that felt best to me.

Amanda was cranky, I was knackered, and Mum was going to turn

31

up tired from a day of travelling. A rest would be the best thing to give us the best first evening together. I put Amanda down in her crib, lay on top of Gran's quilt and closed my eyes, just for a second. Some uncounted numbers of seconds and minutes passed, as Amanda and I slept.

I awoke with a start as a sledgehammer hit the end of the bed and a huge 'crack' sounded from within the room. My limbs felt weighted, and the world ran in slow motion as the mirror detached from the wall and fell lengthwise onto Amanda's crib, smashing it to the ground. According to the ambulance staff who came back and visited me a few days later, I lifted the heavy mirror and threw it sideways across the room. However, my superhuman effort was to no effect. The mirror's impact had already bruised Amanda's brain beyond the point of no return.

7

IT'S 5pm and Robbie hasn't turned up, so I leave. It would be quicker to bike to OA, but I like the peace of walking. I might drop into Coffee Culture after the meeting to look for him, or maybe I won't because it could be embarrassing.

The sky is overcast, a strong north-easterly is blowing and the sea is a surly grey. A couple of keen paddleboarders stalwartly battle the gusts and spray. The grey sky mirrors my mood as the state of my finances comes to mind, together with how many repairs I need to do to cover my bills, let alone pay off my loan. I will have to attend OA forever in the unlikely event Bank Aotearoa is that benevolent.

When I read the scale of the payments required to get me out of arrears in the letter from Bank Aotearoa, I knew there was no way I could possibly repay the required amount in any immediate future. My income dropped to a trickle as my enthusiasm for work dwindled after the earthquakes. I coped immediately after Amanda's death but my interest in work withered quietly, while broken items requiring repair piled up around me.

At first, I felt I had more than normal energy. I motored through Amanda's burial, organising Mum, who had turned into a soggy mess of a human being. She cried her way through the days and flopped around the house in her most faded caftans. She didn't help with anything: organising, cleaning, cooking, or talking with the people who came by

33

to say how sorry they were. I ignored Mum while being a whirlwind of action and looking like I was coping amazingly well.

Once the action died down and people stopped supplying us with meals, I suggested to Mum it was time she wrung herself out or got back on the bus. She called me hard-hearted and bought a ticket to Takaka the next day. Since then, we send each other birthday and Christmas cards and have the occasional landline call but we don't communicate much. It's hard to know where to ring Mum as she moves around. And we don't have much to say; there's little point in tracking someone down for a long-distance call about the weather.

After Mum left I got on with my creations. I was bubbling with energy and the house was overflowing with earthquake-damaged memorabilia and dented appliances. I wired and soldered and hammered and painted. I started on my mosaic sofa. I created the concrete shape and then used plaster for a curved finish. I became completely lost in time-consuming mosaicking. My taniwha grew claws and a tail and spun in its surrounding surf wash while fish swam merrily around it.

I noticed I was low on friends when I finished the sofa front and wanted to celebrate. I poured myself a cup of tea in the gold filigree cup and sat on the sofa in the sun. There was no one I could invite to share the afternoon sun because there was no one I kept in contact with. This felt like a loss, but a distant one that I had no impetus to redress. I could have taken that feeling as a signal to action, but instead succumbed to it as a sign of the inevitable.

People kept coming by, dropping off items to be fixed, while I acted like fixing things was something I still did. I had half cleared the shed in my high-energy phase, but now items were arriving far faster than they were departing. I listed the jobs in order on a whiteboard but, as the queue got longer, I draped an attractive piece of fabric over half the board so the list looked practical. At some point the fabric slipped to cover the whole board. That was a relief.

I tried to dissuade people from leaving their items, saying weakly I had an awful lot on and didn't know when I would get around to their job. However, I wasn't emphatic enough because I wanted to fix those broken possessions. I knew that, in their owner's minds, the broken pieces were still a whole possession that just needed to be reunited with itself. I knew I could make broken things better than they were before. I could … but I didn't. Boxes of broken things expanded from the shed through the house.

By the time Bank Aotearoa's letter turned up, I was forcing myself to repair two appliances each week so I could buy food and bare essentials. I would choose the two easiest items to repair, generally kettles and vacuum cleaners. Occasionally I rose above my gloom to paint a small flower on a kettle or a dinosaur on a vacuum cleaner, but mostly I just made sure the appliance worked before calling the owner and leaving it outside the front door. I asked people to leave cash for the repair in a box on the doorstep when they collected their item.

Every so often I thought about applying for the benefit, but I have no qualifications and have never been employed by anyone else. I don't *want* to work for anyone else so the government requirement to be looking for work if you get a benefit seemed like an impossibility.

The letter from Bank Aotearoa decreed I would have a meeting with my 'customer relations manager' at my home, at a time of the bank's choosing. The letter pointed out I had been sent three warning letters and had chosen not to respond therefore this was the next step in their process. I had not paid the interest on my loan for one year and had not repaid any capital for three years.

I had no memory of three prior letters, but I had mislaid a few things of late. It was possible I had collected the mail, absent-mindedly placed it in a box on my way through the house and never retrieved it. The current letter explained the meeting at my home was necessary to check its state in the event the bank needed to foreclose on my loan and retrieve its money. It simply hadn't occurred to me the bank could sell my house to pay off a twenty-thousand-dollar debt which was a fraction of the home's value, but it appeared that was the case.

Terrence turned up on the duly appointed day and time, together with his building inspector, Darrell. I let the pair in the door and realised that, while there was room for a thin woman to squeeze past the hallway boxes, it was a challenge for men with sizeable stomachs. Terrence sent Darrell to check the outside of the house while he surveyed the inside. I mutely sat in my tea-drinking corner of the sitting room and waited for the outcome.

Terrence went out to join Darrell; they sat deep in discussion on my mosaic sofa. That made me mad. What right did they have to sit on my beautiful sofa when they were proposing to take the house, and the sofa, away from me? They flicked through sheets on a clipboard. The process may have only taken thirty minutes, but it felt like hours.

Terrence knocked on the window and suggested I come outside. I pulled over a log round to sit on beside the sofa. Terrence put his foot on his knee in a dominant triangle and laid out the situation. "Either you show you are increasing your repayments on your loan, or Bank Aotearoa will foreclose on your mortgage, as explained in your letter.

"I am concerned about the state of your house, which I will report back on. It certainly couldn't be sold as it is at present, it looks derelict. The outside needs painting and the trees and shrubs chopped down or cut back. In the event of a sale, the bank will deduct the cost of preparation from the sale price."

Fully realising Gran's house could be sold from under me broke through my relatively impervious exoskeleton, on which there had been little impact since Amanda's death. Gran's house is my home and my memories. I *cannot* lose it, however derelict it appears to the Terrences of this world. Tears started leaking out of the corners of my eyes and I slumped on my log, feeling helpless and pathetic.

Terrence's demeanour changed little. I imagine my reaction was identical to that of most people in arrears when confronted with their debts and he was wearily accustomed to such behaviour.

He got on with the next part of his spiel, putting his shiny, black-shod foot back on the ground so the creases in his well-ironed trousers both pointed at me. "Bank Aotearoa is generously giving you a chance to keep your house but there are two requirements. Within six months you must be making payments which cover the interest on your loan. If you achieve this target, the bank will consider giving you a further twenty-four months until you have to cover capital repayments as well as interest."

Covering interest payments seemed vaguely possible, if challenging. There must be some way I could re-enthuse myself to earn income, in the interests of saving Gran's house. I could definitely pretend it was possible, in the interest of saying "Yes" to Terrence.

"Bank Aotearoa also requires you attend an ongoing course or support group that will help you achieve your repayments. We have found there is usually an underlying issue when people aren't paying loans. We want to be able to help." Terrence looked meaningfully at my piles of boxes. "Of course, we wouldn't want to force you to go to a group that isn't relevant to you, so we let you choose." He smiled brightly at me, like he was giving me a great opportunity I mightn't be properly recognising.

"What sort of thing do you want me to attend?"

"Here's the list of options. As I already explained, you get to choose the course. However, a budgeting course might be a good idea."

I scanned the list of courses which had the course name, its location, meeting day and time. Most courses were in the city centre or further west, a long bike or bus ride away. One location jumped out at me, the Sumner Surf Club; attending a course there would have the least impact. The course name was 'OA'. I knew that 'Overeaters Anonymous' rebranded as 'OA' a few years back, presumably to take the stigma of gluttony out of their name. It had to be the same organisation. They advertise on the board outside the Sumner Supervalue, saying they can help people eating too much, too little, or the wrong thing. I've thought at times about going to a meeting because I've had problems eating properly forever, and far worse problems over recent years.

"That one." I pointed at OA on the list.

"That's appropriate." What did Terrence mean? I'm thin, but not unusually so.

It wasn't until the first information arrived from Fran that I discovered what this OA group was about. By then it was far too late to say I'd signed up for a group to which I didn't want to admit I belonged.

8

I arrive for my second OA meeting early. Fran welcomes me and tags me in on her phone, which puts a record of attendance on my phone also. Bank Aotearoa want evidence I attend all but two meetings a year unless I make a special request for non-attendance to be excused. Terrence made it sound like being excused from meetings was not likely to happen.

Seven attendees are discussing something animatedly. I join the knot of people to discover everyone is talking about the 'Chinese disease'.

"China's building huge hospitals in a couple of weeks," Matthew says.

I have a vague feeling I've heard about a new disease. Is it primarily in China? Or is it from China? Or both? I pay little attention to international news because it is mostly more upsetting than uplifting and there isn't anything I can do about events in countries to which I have never been and to which I am never likely to go.

I have never owned a television; Gran didn't like them. Like her, I prefer listening to the radio, mostly More FM which has tunes I recognise, with some National Radio thrown in so I don't feel like I am completely abandoning my intellect.

Gran always had the radio on, and we would sing along with her favourite songs. Gran particularly loved Dolly Parton and the Beatles. I don't know how many times we sang 'Islands in the Stream' and 'Eleanor Rigby'. Johnno had a lovely voice and Gran often said she wished he would take lessons, but he was more interested in riding his bicycle.

I listen further to the group conversation. "Yes," says Monique, "Chinese industry is amazing. I wish New Zealand could be that proactive."

"It's here now too," chimes in a woman whose name I don't know. "It arrived last week."

"Sure did," says the guy standing so close to her that they must be a couple.

They look like those older couples you often see walking a small and fluffy dog on the beach. The guy will be half-heartedly holding the lead like the dog belongs to someone else who he is searching for; if he had a dog, it would be much bigger and tougher. The woman is walking determinedly forward making sure everyone gets a reasonable dose of exercise on their outing. Her hair is stylishly cut with highlights, and they are both attired in smart casual clothes suitable for dog walking and post-walk lattés.

I prefer not to compare myself to such tidy people at the beach. Our lack of similarity is beyond tidiness, as I don't have a dog or a partner. My clothing preference is self-sewn pinafores with large pockets that allow me to walk, ride my bike, and carry my phone and money without needing a bag. My hair is greying and self-cut because I don't want someone else fiddling with it, and now I can't afford a haircut anyhow. Early in my cutting attempts I couldn't hold a straight line with the scissors and looked like a child's manky doll, but I have become proficient and swift.

"Actually, the virus arrived in New Zealand week before last," Monique corrects. "It's been spreading around the world since January and China has locked down Wuhan province where the virus was first found. In Wuhan no one's allowed to leave their house and thousands are sick, so they need the new hospitals." Monique appears to be a well-informed person who likes others to be similarly well-informed. "Northern Italy has declared a state of emergency, there are so many sick people queuing at hospitals. They have banned flights from China and blocked roads to the rest of Italy. People can only leave their houses to buy food or go to the chemist."

Monique's description sounds extreme. Can it be true? Media reporting can bend the truth. Surely New Zealand wouldn't keep people in their houses. This isn't a country where the government controls where people go, although I can believe it of China. While Gran was generally positive about people and the world, she always said China was up to no good and doing the no good quietly and strategically in its own best interests.

Monique continues, "New Zealand has already stopped flights from China and people who arrive from Italy and South Korea must stay at home for two weeks after they land."

"Hey, you guys are already behind the times." Barry sounds triumphant, he has news no one else yet knows and is reading it on his watch, with reading glasses. "The World Health Organization has just declared a global pandemic related to COVID-19, that's what the virus is called. There are more than one hundred thousand cases in one hundred and fourteen countries. Four thousand people have already died.' Today is a day everyone in the world will remember for a long time."

Everyone falls silent. This isn't news easily topped by further information or an anecdote. The atmosphere in the room changes from competitive to catatonic and Fran breaks in to suggest we all move to our seats and start the group session.

We assemble on our coloured chairs, sitting in the same order as last week but there are now only eight seats.

"Kia ora tatou," Fran calls us to attention with a greeting. "Welcome, everyone, to our second meeting. Our group has already reduced by two. I hope everyone else will continue to come to meetings. This group's purpose is to help all of us manage our obsessions, supported by each other. After our introductions we will do another group exercise as part of building the trust we will need to help each other."

What happened to the two people who have dropped out? Did they feel helpless in the face of the new virus and choose to live with their obsessions rather than fight hopelessly? I could give up now. I remind myself how good I feel when I enter through my red front door and strengthen my resolve to save Gran's house, despite it being me who is risking losing it.

We go around the group stating our name and obsession and everyone echoing a greeting. The first to speak are the couple whose names I didn't hear last meeting. They are David and Diana, and have a joint obsession, buying presents for each other. This sounds like a nice obsession as obsessions go, buying and receiving presents. Why is reciprocal present giving something they need to work on?

Barry turns out to be obsessed with cats and eating cat food. It's not clear which came first. Barry mumbles his speech at his lap, so Fran asks him to speak up; his confidence is sapped when he talks about his obsession. Barry is part of an organisation called 'Red Zone Cats' that supports people's pets, or more likely the offspring of pets, who were abandoned in uninhabitable houses following the Canterbury earthquakes. I wouldn't have picked Barry's obsession from looking at him – he's a new twist on mad cat ladies.

After our introductions we have our cup of herbal tea. I try tea with lime that tastes much better than peppermint, but nothing like Kenya Bold with milk.

Monique has brought today's food and presents us with beautiful vegan savouries with sprigs of herbs decorating their tops. Monique clearly intends to be a hard act to follow. Next week will be Matthew and then it will be me; I have two weeks to come up with something appropriate to cook and enact the cooking of it. Living on my own has not set me up well for cooking interesting treats for groups of people. I could do baking practise next week but that will eat into my budget.

Today's exercise turns out to be trust falling. This is a big step beyond towers topped with marshmallows.

"We will work through the exercise in steps, checking everyone is comfortable before moving on," Fran explains. "Let's start with everyone standing in a close circle, shoulders touching. I will be a pinball in the middle." Fran closes her eyes, gently tips on her heels and we take turns pushing her back to the centre of the circle. Then we do a half step back and try again.

Fran asks for a volunteer pinball and Diana steps forward. We collectively breathe an internal sigh of relief that it's Diana, who is petite, rather than Barry, who is large. Diana successfully pinballs around and then Fran takes us up another notch.

"Now we will stand in two lines of three, shoulder to shoulder. We will have three pairs, Matthew with David at the front, Diana and Monique in the middle, Barry with Greg at the back. The faller will stand immediately in front of the lines."

Huh? I'm not in a pair, am I doing the falling?

Fran is instructing me to fall backwards, with my body straight and arms crossed over my chest. "It's all fine Julia, the team will catch you."

I can't find a pause in which to object.

As I fall, I see Gran's garden. I'm throwing Amanda in the air. It's early morning and the kowhai are in full flower with bellbirds warbling in the branches. Amanda is growing fast but I can still easily throw and catch her weight. She yells with joy as she flies up and falls back down. Amanda trusts me to catch her, and I trust myself to let her fly and fall, fly and fall, over and over until we sink down on the ground and I press her joyous face to mine.

Next thing I know I am lying on the ground and Fran is asking, "Julia, are you alright?"

I am not alright.

9

17 MARCH 2020

I have opened a vortex into which I am spinning, and my previous semi-animate state was a far more desirable way of being. My brain is overwhelmed trying to decipher how I feel and how I got to this point. My vortex is becoming cluttered because information about COVID-19 in New Zealand and the world is pouring in from every direction. For someone who generally spends little time on media, I can't escape news of the virus.

As I head to the supermarket via the Esplanade, I wave hello to my neighbour Alan, who lives next door to Gran's, one house north. We generally wave in a bland, friendly fashion when we see each other; my vegetation mostly blocks that possibility. Today when I see Alan he rushes from his garden to the pavement and starts spouting about the need for New Zealand to lock down its borders right now to prevent more Chinese coming into the country and spreading their nasty disease.

"Have you heard the professor at the University of Otago on the radio? He's told the Government to slam shut our borders for the last month to keep COVID out. Most professors are too know-it-all. But this one might actually know something. I always thought Chinese are bad news and I don't like how this Government, led by that Ardern woman, is cosying up to China and selling them our milk so New Zealanders can't afford to drink milk. How can a woman be Prime Minister anyway?

44

When she has a baby to look after? How can her husband think he's a real man, staying home to look after the baby? I thought Clarke Gayford's fishing show was pretty good but now he's a sorry excuse of a man. You know Ardern was a member of the Communist Party? Once a communist always a communist."

Hasn't New Zealand been trading with China for quite a while before this Government? I am neither sure enough nor interested enough to debate this point. Is our Government communist? I don't think so, but I am not so clear on what 'communism' means. Is it when the government owns everything? What I am sure of is I don't want to continue this conversation because it is much better when Alan and I wave across the fence rather than talking. I don't know how Gran managed to keep on civil terms with him for the decades they lived as neighbours. Perhaps their shared dislike of China helped?

When I enter the supermarket, headlines scream at me however hard I try not to look. Every day new cases of COVID-19, or 'the virus', are reported in New Zealand, and countries all over the world are reporting cases. Countries everywhere are closing borders and forcing citizens to stay home. Our Government has announced everyone entering New Zealand must stay home for two weeks to check whether they are infected, which doesn't sound like a bad thing if it keeps the virus from spreading.

People are discussing COVID in the aisles and the queue. I hear COVID-19 repeated from every direction as well as emanating from the newspapers. The words crash inside my head, echoing back and forth to the point that I can think of nothing else, and the world starts shrinking to a narrow dot at the end of a dark tunnel. I leave the milk I was about to purchase, rush out the door to the carpark and gasp some air into my lungs.

When I'm stressed the best resort is to breathe with the waves on the Esplanade. On my beachward route I pass Coffee Culture and Robbie waves me in. Without asking, he makes me a coffee and puts it against his personal coffee allowance. I appreciate that a lot. I love the smell and taste of coffee but when you are in massive arrears to the bank, four-dollar coffees are a luxury you can't afford. The café is empty, so we sit on stools by the window; it isn't far back to the counter for Robbie if someone walks in.

Robbie has bright blue eyes, a cheery smile, and a way of listening to people that sucks you into talking to him. When he listens to you it feels like he listens fully, with every fibre of his being. He looks at you intensely, sometimes too intensely, and you never feel like he is going to interrupt you. He always leaves an extra pause at the end of your statement as if he wants to be sure you are finished saying whatever it was you had to say. When all you have to say is, "The coffee was great," a pause can seem awkward, but you are sure he means well. With all the intense looking it's a good thing he must be fifteen years younger than me so no one will think he is my boyfriend.

Did Robbie train as a counsellor? Was he taught listening skills? He seems much more interested in me than the counsellor to whom I went after Amanda died. The funeral director told me I could get ten free sessions with Family Works to help me through Amanda's death. It's not often you get something for free so, when I still had energy, I decided to try the sessions out. I thought Denise might be like Gran. Gran would say, "Everyone has their own stories to tell, and I like hearing them. Julia and Johnno, always remember the most important thing in life is writing your own story and writing it requires telling it too."

Gran loved every person she met, even Chinese people when she met them in the flesh. When Gran went to the supermarket she would come home and tell us about the people she talked with in the line, their lives, families, jobs, aspirations and hopes, as well as the age of the check-out girl's baby. Then she would start casting on a knitted purple teddy bear to give to the baby. "Everyone is different, and everyone is interesting."

The problem with going to Denise was that she didn't seem to want to hear my story the way I wanted to tell it, she just wanted me to talk about Amanda. I was scared that if I started talking the pain would begin all over again and, a second time around, I didn't think I could bear it. Denise would ask me questions about Amanda's death and then patiently wait. If I didn't respond, after a long, painful pause, she would ask the question a different way. Early on, when Denise asked the same question four times in a row only slightly rephrased, I wondered if she thought I was stupid and hadn't understood the question, or that I was deaf and hadn't heard the question.

When I was a child and Mum wasn't paying attention to Johnno and me, I worked out that the easiest way to get over bad things is to shut them away in a room in your head where you can't see them, just like boxes in a shed. Talking lets things spill out that no one wants to see. I would try to tell Mum about how someone was mean to me at school, or how disappointed I was in getting a C in my art class. Mum would say, "No point whining about life Julia. You just have to get on with it." What Mum said didn't seem to match up with what Gran had told us – Gran said we should tell our stories to people, but Mum said we shouldn't whine. I rationalised that people want to hear good things and the bad things we should keep to ourselves. So I created my mental box collection.

By the time I went to counselling, I was accomplished at storing bad things in my head. Initially I fought internally over not disappointing Denise when she asked questions to which she apparently wanted answers. However, with practise I found I didn't mind her re-asking questions or leaving long pauses. The quiet was pleasant. It became an interesting exercise; how long could I go without saying anything?

At our eighth session, Denise said, "I think today should be our final session."

"But don't I get ten free sessions?"

"Yes, you do. However, a counselling session involves the patient talking to help them resolve their own crisis and I have been the only person to talk in the last two sessions."

I didn't return.

Robbie and I chat about nothing in particular. He appears as keen to not talk about COVID as I feel. We started chatting a year back when I was still paying for my own coffees. I liked hearing his rolling Scottish accent and stories about Scotland and his travels.

Robbie comes from a small town in the north of Scotland. He spent his early childhood roaming the heather-covered 'muirs' and scrambling up rugged mountains where the weather can turn from beautiful to life-threatening in the blink of an eye. Then he got hooked on surfing and went with his brothers and friends whenever he could. His mother taught them all to swim in the cold Scottish sea; he tells me how she was keener on staying in the water than her children.

He tells me how Scottish houses blend into the landscape because they are made of rock from mountains nearby. "New Zealand houses stand out like blots on the landscape with remote farm buildings brick-red against their green surroundings. And houses here are so temporary, made out of wood," he says. "In Scotland they're made of stone and brick, to last. My brothers and I, we all trained in the trades, building houses. Malcolm did plumbing, Angus got an electrical apprenticeship, I did construction."

Robbie clearly misses Scotland and his family there, but never refers to wanting to go back to see them, it doesn't make sense. Perhaps there's something bad about Scotland that he's storing in a box too?

Today we don't talk of Scotland or Robbie's travels in Europe. We cover the weather, how high the tide is, and whether the wind will be good for surfing; Robbie adores surfing. "The water's so warm here. I remember surfing Scottish beaches when the waves turned to frozen slush at the edge of the sea. When we got out my pal and I would yank each other's wetsuits with hands feeling like flippers. His wetsuit wouldn't stretch over his head, and he'd yell he felt claustrophobic. I'd laugh so hard I'd fall over, and he would stumble around pulling at his wetsuit like a clumsy black walrus.

"You're looking a tad pale lassie," Robbie rolls out in his broadest accent, trying to get a laugh out of me.

I manage a weak smile and then deflect his comment, saying I must not have been out in the garden enough lately.

"We'll catch up about your house painting on Thursday, right?"

"Weren't you coming last Thursday?"

"No lassie, definitely this Thursday."

Oh, he wasn't late, I had the date wrong. I must start using my phone calendar to prove I am not a complete Neanderthal and stop relying on my brain, which might be like that of a Neanderthal's. It might be better if Robbie didn't come because this chat is sucking up my weekly quota of energy. However, my energy levels are so depleted I don't have the resources to put him off so say, "Great, as long as the weather is good, and we can sit in the garden without getting too cold."

"Sure, lassie. For a Scottish lad like me the weather must be grim before one cannae sit out in it."

I could almost look forward to Robbie coming round, except I haven't enough energy to look forward to anything right now.

10

19 MARCH 2020

ROBBIE arrives on time on the correct Thursday, and we have a nice cup of Kenya Bold in the garden. This is a significant step for the current me, offering someone tea. I even bring Gran's gold filigree cups out on the Indian tray.

Robbie admires my garden and investigates the remaining summer vegetables growing through the flowers. The nasturtiums are flowering beautifully; orange and red and yellow. "It would be great to have veges but I'm not usually somewhere long enough for them to grow," he says.

Robbie has three charger cables and a worn backpack that needs patching and its zipper replacing. I remind myself I need my house painted to impress Terrence, should he return, and summon up enthusiasm about the fixing jobs. The backpack has creative potential, which I need to exploit because one can't reasonably charge much for such small jobs. We discuss designs and colours Robbie might like on his backpack.

We debate using combinations of Scottish and New Zealand flags and whether to use the Māori flag rather than a Union Jack. I suggest an abstract appliqué of brightly coloured shapes covering the many worn patches as another approach. The creative part of my brain lurches into a degree of action it has not experienced for some time.

The hour passes surprisingly quickly, and I need to leave to go to my third OA meeting.

As I stride along the Esplanade, the sun is glinting on calm waves rolling in from far away. A pack of children is struggling with blue foam surfboards in the white water near the shore. One of the cohort manages to scramble onto their feet and ride a wave for five seconds before falling sideways in a deliberate, attention-grabbing plunge. The group yells triumphantly and all pump their fists in the air.

I feel oddly hopeful, despite the week's challenges. I can see glimpses of a future where I revive my creative business and earn enough money to pay off my loan, not just scrape together sufficient to meet the monthly interest payments. I allow myself to dream … I could exhibit work in a gallery. Before I had Amanda I aspired to being recognised as a creative artist, but it has been many years since I thought that aspiration sufficiently credible to allow it space in my thoughts.

At OA I smile at Fran as she tags me in, then my mood fragments back into shards spinning down the sides of my vortex as COVID-19 discussions close around me again.

"Have you heard?" Barry is holding forth. "New Zealand's closing its borders midnight tonight to all arrivals except New Zealand citizens and permanent residents. This is the first time in history our country will close its borders! People entering will have to quarantine for two weeks. Foreigners here on holiday are being encouraged to leave."

David and Diana look upset. "Our son's coming home from his OE with his Panamanian girlfriend the beginning of May. We haven't seen him in three years. Can he still come?"

"He can, but she won't be able to," Barry replies.

"How long will this last?" Diana says. "Surely they can't keep the border closed more than a few weeks."

Monique chimes in. "The Government have announced people can't meet in groups of over one hundred. My best friend Lucy is getting married at Easter and she has two hundred people booked to attend her wedding in the Marlborough Sounds. Her partner Richard and his best men will all cycle in on the trails and Lucy and her best women will paddle kayaks there. They've been planning the wedding for nearly two years, and I have sewn dresses for the best women. There's no way they'll call the wedding off. How can Lucy ring half the guests and tell them they are no longer invited?"

We all fall silent as we imagine choosing which wedding participants to uninvite. I can't envisage one hundred people I might invite to an event, let alone two hundred, so for me it would be easy to uninvite the majority of the invited. Why stop at one hundred? Why not take the number down to, say, five? Wouldn't five be enough to celebrate a wedding, for anyone who has the odd desire to get married?

Fran moves into her role as group facilitator, smoothing the waters over. "Let's not get too stressed. COVID could be like the 2003 SARS pandemic. That hit the news briefly, but nothing happened in New Zealand. Let's hope our Government is overreacting because they want to be cautious, and the restrictions will be rescinded in a couple of weeks. Our Prime Minister says not to panic or pay attention to rumours. She'll give a national presentation midday tomorrow, so we'll find out more then."

Barry isn't yet prepared to lose the floor. "My wife's friend returned from northern Italy last week and says it's mayhem there. She was on sabbatical from the University of Auckland for six months with her husband. They escaped on a bus because all the flights were full. They said the airport was a madhouse of arm-waving Italians mobbing the counters. It sounded like a scene out of a horror movie, all it needed was a few zombies to turn up.

"They got a bus to Austria, and astronomically expensive flights from Vienna to London then London to New Zealand. They reckon the trip home cost over fifteen thousand dollars. Now they're on the phone for hours to the insurance company who say they won't pay out because insurance doesn't cover global pandemics. But the pandemic was declared the day *after* their flight so, when they flew, they should have been covered because there was no pandemic. Insurance companies will wriggle out of payments any way they can; I think they have gotten worse since the Canterbury earthquakes."

The room quietens down. Once again, Barry's story is untoppable. Moreover, if everyone else is like me, we don't want the story to be true so aren't interested in more information backing it up. Fran takes advantage of the pause to get everyone seated on their coloured chairs.

We roll around our admissions of obsession smoothly in a practised fashion on this third recitation. Already, it doesn't feel as hard to say I am obsessed with keeping broken things. At least I am considering the planet in my desire to repair all things rather than throwing them away. I bet Diana and David chuck things in the bin without considering how to fix them, in their rush to buy presents for each other. They look like they have lots of money, given their branded leisurewear.

How does Monique repair her chewed plasterboard corners? Does she select a more edible filler so she can eat from the same locations? Does filler taste like plasterboard, or might it be off-putting so dissuade her from her habit? Does Monique wait until there is a reasonable amount of damage then call in a handyman to fix and paint her walls? Monique could make the handyman cups of coffee and scones and see if he would reduce his bill when she smiled nicely at him. How does she explain the wall damage to him? Does she blame the holes on a dog? Or a friend's dog that visits? To blame wallboard damage on a dog would require that she only chews the lower parts of the walls unless she is going to conjure up a Great Dane.

Matthew has brought vegan Afghans to have with our breaktime tea. There's a problem though; he forgot to bake the Afghans with gluten-free flour and Monique doesn't eat gluten. "I'm on a gluten-free FODMAP diet to manage my irritable bowel syndrome." Now that sounds like oversharing.

"That's a bugger, Monique," says Matthew. "What's a FODMAP?"

Monique flutters her eyelids at Matthew. "I understand Matthew, how could you know? If you're interested, I can explain food types for you after the session."

I know Monique's type because I had a semi-friend like her at high school. My semi-friend kept a flock of guys on call – close, but not too close. I wonder if she'll hook him in.

I have my cup of tea sitting with Greg. Greg feels like the safest person in the room to be around because he hasn't voiced any opinions about COVID, or anything at all yet. He is wearing the same clothes for the third week in a row. Should I ask him what the names of the Mutant Turtles on his Doc Marten boots are? I decide not to ask; no point in prodding at people's weaknesses and getting answers you don't want to hear.

Fran calls us back to order to participate in our activity. There is a unified sigh, which suggests we are becoming more of a group than we may intend to be.

"This week we'll play the telephone game. You might remember it, it's very easy. We'll all stand in a circle and the first person whispers a word into the ear of the second person in the circle. That person whispers what they heard into the next person's ear, and on around the circle. When the word gets to the last person in the group, they say out loud what they heard, and the first person says the word they started with."

That's a relief, Fran stepping down the intensity of the games after last week's fiasco. This game used to be called Chinese Whispers when I was at school, but it can't be politically correct any longer to have a game named after a particular cultural group, especially Chinese right now.

"Let's stand up and move away from the chairs to form a circle. I will start the telephone off." Fran steps over to Diana, who's on her right, and whispers a word in Diana's ear. Diana whispers into David's ear and the word goes around the group. I'm the last person in the circle and the word I hear and repeat, is 'COVID'.

"How odd," Fran says. "I said 'Pandemonium'. Let's try again."

By the third time around the circle, when Matthew starts the chain and David closes it, and the whispered word again turns into 'COVID', Fran says it must be time to finish. She thanks us for coming and we say our karakia together. There is little banter between the group as we pick up our belongings and head out the door. If we had known how long it would be before we would see each other in person again, would we have been more effusive in our goodbyes?

11

22 MARCH 2020

THERE is no possibility of avoiding thoughts of COVID-19 as new cases are reported all around the country.

I listen to our Prime Minister, Jacinda Ardern, on the radio on Friday, twenty-second of March, at noon when she announces a 'COVID-19 Alert System' and puts the country into Alert Level 2. She says there is likely transmission of the virus within the community, therefore older people and people with compromised immune systems should stay home as much as possible. The Government is also asking people to work from home.

Jacinda speaks calmly and clearly, and I want to burst into tears at the enormity of her words delivered in such an even manner. I attempt to calm myself with a restorative cup of Kenya Bold and go into the garden to drink it. If I can bring myself to work at least I have no problem working from home.

I feel like I did after the February earthquake, a couple of months before Amanda's birth. As if I am living in a movie and my brain is operating my body from outer space. That February day was also the twenty-second; ten years and one month ago today.

I was at the Sumner Supervalue, feeling heavy and unwieldy in the latter stages of pregnancy. With little warning, everything started swaying and items fell from shelves onto the floor and shoppers. People were screaming and everyone was crouching down. Crouching is challenging for someone pregnant, but I found myself on my hands and knees, jammed in against the chocolate biscuits. Did I need a packet of chocolate biscuits? Suddenly I desperately wanted to eat a chocolate biscuit. I reflexively tore a packet open, put a toffee pop in my mouth and several more in my pocket.

When the shaking stopped, stressed-looking supermarket staff encouraged us off the floor, out of the building and into the car park. Dust was rising from the cliffs and the fire brigade siren was in concert with sirens from locked cars. People looked confused and wandered vaguely in all directions.

As I waddled out to the street, I saw people pointing at the cliff diagonally opposite the shopping centre where a huge block of rock had fallen off. Had it fallen onto the Returned Services Association building or the car repair yard next door? I didn't want to know. I've never done a first aid course and pregnant women are no good at lifting rocks. Enough people were walking and running towards the area for me to be absolved of any guilt, so I turned left and headed home.

It took an inordinate amount of time for me to travel the four long blocks to Gran's house. People were on the street, pointing at the cliffs and their houses. Luckily, because all the brick chimneys had collapsed in the prior September earthquake, there were no bricks to fall from on high. Some houses had cracked windows and others were at odd angles to their foundations.

I passed an elderly woman sitting on her walking frame on the pavement. "Hi, my name's Julia, are you OK?"

"I'm Bettina, my daughter's going to collect me. She works in the city."

Bettina was wearing a thin top; the day was overcast, and she was shivering. "Aren't you cold? Do you need some warm clothing?"

"Yes, but I'm too scared to go back inside."

The Somerfield stone cladding on Bettina's semi-detached retirement unit lay scattered across her garden. I entered her door to be assaulted by items teetering on shelves and trying to join the chaos on the floor. I found a brown knitted woolly hat, with a pompom that reminded me of Gran's Temuka teapot tea cosy, and a heavy tartan rug, like rugs on which Gran, Johnno and I picnicked at Sumner Beach. I found a warm coat in the piles of clothes on the floor of Bettina's wardrobe.

When I went back out Bettina was in the same position. I helped her slowly put the coat on, pulled the blanket around her and put the hat on her head. "I hope your daughter comes soon."

Days later I wondered whether Bettina's daughter made it to Sumner, given the catastrophic damage in the centre of Christchurch. On the day of the earthquake, however, as soon as I walked on, she slipped from my mind.

A house was well ablaze further down Nayland Street. The fire crew hadn't yet reached it. Do fire hydrants still work when the power goes out? I became concerned about Gran's house, simultaneously wanting to be home and not to be home. I wanted to see the damage, but I didn't want to see the damage. My slow feet dragged along the pavement, and I chewed a toffee pop from my pocket without tasting the chocolate or caramel.

I was close to Head Street when a woman ran down the road towards me. "Got a cell phone? My house's been squashed by a rock." Which emergency service do you call when your house has been squashed by a rock?

"I don't think cell phones are working."

The woman ran on down the street while I continued my slow pace to Gran's house, my feet moving more sluggishly the closer I got.

From the outside little had changed. The chimneys were still in the garden and tarpaulins still covered the holes in the roof where chimneys used to be.

When I opened the front door, I found things were far worse than

I had hoped. My wooden coat stand had fallen across the entrance with coats, hats and shoes all tumbled on the floor. Water had run out of the bathroom door and along the hallway into the kitchen. A few prints hung askew on the walls, but most were on the floor in the water. The cream painted walls had cracks and tears across them and plaster dust coated the few empty patches of floor.

When I reached the kitchen things looked even worse. Every cupboard door was open and the contents either on the bench or the floor with packages broken open. Porridge, golden syrup, and oil mixed into an un-bakeable sludge under my feet. Tomato sauce was splattered across the table and chairs. The fridge contents had spilled out. The sitting room was better off as it housed fewer breakable items. However, one of Gran's red glass vases had shattered on the floor and flowers were wilting in more puddles of water.

My bedroom was the, by now, expected mess. My clothes were tangled on the cupboard floor like Bettina's. Dresser drawers had fallen and deposited their contents in my way. My cabinet of mementos, which I made from a tray that once held printing press letters, lay on the floor with its figurines, stones and keepsakes distributed through all the other debris. The only thing intact was Gran's mirror, determinedly reflecting my bulk in its tarnished surface.

What I desperately wanted to do was lie down on the bed and go to sleep. Aftershocks were rocking the house at regular intervals, but I felt entirely exhausted. I pulled myself together, thinking I should make a small part of the house functional. Clearly, what I needed was a cup of tea.

In the kitchen, I looked for the cloisonné tea leaf tin and spied it lying in the back corner of the room, under the table. If I got down on my hands and knees, I doubted I could get back up. Gran came to my rescue as her walking stick was still hanging on the back of her kitchen chair. I used the stick to manoeuvre the tin towards my feet, from where I awkwardly reached it.

Now I had tea leaves, but what about my teapot? That's when I found my miracle of the earthquake, the Temuka teapot and gold filigree cups covered by the towel in the sink. A ray of sunshine poked under the clouds and shone straight into the kitchen.

However, it was not yet plain sailing to the shores of a cup of Kenya Bold. Would the stove work? The next best thing after finding my tea set, was when the stove lit up so I could put the kettle on it. I always fill the kettle after pouring tea, to be ready for the next cup. My next cup of tea would be coming from the toilet cistern.

Thinking of the toilet cistern reminded me how often I needed to pee. Peeing would be in the garden for the foreseeable future, so Gran's stick would be an essential aid to ensure I could get back onto my feet.

I took my cup of Kenya Bold out into the garden to escape the havoc. My fruit trees and kowhai were still standing, the tomatoes were still producing fruit, hope was present in the face of destruction. I contemplated how a cup of tea had the power to right many wrongs, if only momentarily.

My mind shifts back to my present situation and COVID, a much less tangible threat than an earthquake. What can I do in the face of an unknown threat, beyond drinking tea?

I dedicate the rest of the afternoon to harvesting ripe produce as well-stocked food cupboards never go amiss in an emergency. I pick tomatoes and make tomato sauce to bottle for future pasta meals. I pick apples and quinces and wrap them in newspaper while the sauce cooks. The newspaper is from February, when COVID was barely a blip in our consciousness and the front page reported a forthcoming Rod Stewart fiftieth anniversary concert. How long ago February already seems.

12

25 MARCH 2020

NEW Zealand is closing down for at least four weeks and the Sumner Supervalue has run out of toilet paper, hand sanitiser and pasta.

When I was a teenager, I couldn't read enough dystopian fiction. I imagined myself as the heroine, moving through the storyline of the book. Now I know such fiction isn't accurate in its detail because there's nothing about people clearing supermarket shelves of toilet paper when they heard of a pending apocalypse. I have also discovered that, once you have experienced a civil emergency, the thrill wears off and you no longer want to be an apocalyptic heroine.

Supervalue staff have Sellotaped signs to the shelves including 'Only 2 packs of toilet paper per person'. I watch a dishevelled woman observing the packs of toilet paper in the shopping trolley of a woman dressed like she is going out for dinner, rather than the supermarket.

"You've taken three packs of toilet paper. You're only allowed two."

"Mind your own business!"

"It *is* my business because I want some toilet paper, but you've taken the last rolls."

"I wanted a twelve-pack, but these are four-packs, so I'm buying the equivalent of one twelve-pack."

"No, you're not." The dishevelled woman grabs a toilet roll pack from the dress-clad woman's trolley. They wrestle with the pack until it splits, and paper rolls bounce down the aisles.

Two days ago, Jacinda told us we would immediately move to Level 3 of the new alert framework, and we will move to Level 4 at midnight tonight, Wednesday, March twenty-fifth. Level 4 means everyone stays home, other than essential workers, unless they absolutely need to go out for food, medical assistance, or exercise. If we go out, we must stay two metres away from other people. When we go shopping, we must wear face masks to prevent breathing the virus in and medical gloves in case the virus is living on surfaces.

For someone who likes being on their own at home, I feel surprisingly upset. This scenario may be a case of 'be careful what you wish for', supposedly a Chinese proverb. Is China everywhere?

I missed the last rolls of toilet paper but think sufficiently laterally to purchase newspapers before other people realise newspapers are a toilet paper alternative. The newspaper headlines yell bad news at me so their use as toilet paper seems appropriate. 'Country to lock down for 4 weeks'. 'Stay home and stay safe'. 'NZ joins the 100 COVID case club'.

When I get home, I can't help myself and read more of the details in the papers before consigning them to the toilet. There is a graph of COVID cases in countries around the world. While most people were not watching, China's cases shot into the stratosphere then levelled out. Italy's cases are closing in on one hundred thousand and their trajectory isn't levelling off. Several European countries follow close behind – Spain, Germany, France, with Switzerland, the UK, Austria, and the Netherlands a little further in the rear. New Zealand is at the bottom left corner of the graph, just coming out of the starting gates. If we have low toilet paper stocks, how much toilet paper is there in Italy or China? Why the focus on toilet paper given that, of all the reported symptoms of COVID-19, diarrhoea is not highlighted?

There's an article on the symptoms of COVID, so you know when you might have it and should visit the doctor in your mask and gloves. What would the doctor do if I arrived with COVID symptoms? Put me in a room and talk to me through the door? There are a range of symptoms like those of a cold or flu: temperature, runny nose, cough, tiredness. The unique symptom is a loss of taste or smell. I check whether I can taste my cup of Kenya Bold. I don't normally actively consider the taste of my tea. Yes, I can definitely taste Kenya Bold, and I don't have any other COVID symptoms. I should find my thermometer so I can check my temperature if I don't feel well. I hope it's in the bathroom which only contains a few boxes of broken items so it shouldn't be too hard to find.

According to the papers, the whole world is shutting down travel and shutting its doors to everyone who isn't a citizen; I remember Barry's story of his wife's friend trying to escape Italy and their son stuck in Colombia. There are sad stories of people trying to return to New Zealand. Flights are being cancelled at a moment's notice and with no explanation. People don't have enough money to pay for expensive new flights. People with sad faces look out from the pages of the paper above their sad stories. Do photographers ask people to look sad and take the pictures repeatedly until the person looks sad enough?

There's a picture of our Jacinda, also looking sad. Does she think she picked a bad time to be Prime Minister? Her small daughter, Neve, was born in the first year of Jacinda being Prime Minister. Neve must be … I don't want to think about Neve. Lucky Jacinda, that she will get to stay home with her child if everyone in New Zealand must stay home. "Stay home, break the chain, save lives," Jacinda says. "We can be a team of five million, each person doing their part."

Combined with the Level 4 lockdown, New Zealand is going into a State of Civil Emergency. People from Christchurch know about Civil Emergencies because we were in a State of Civil Emergency after all four of the Canterbury Earthquakes. Declaration of a state of emergency makes things feel worse; it's like an official statement that the situation is dire.

Once I finish reading the papers, I consider what else I can do today. I realise, with a growing sense of panic, the only regular appointment in my week is OA group. OA group is on Thursdays, which is tomorrow, and no gatherings are now allowed. What does this mean about my loan? What does this mean about Gran's house? Terrence specified I must attend all but two meetings in the year and I need my attendance records to provide to Bank Aotearoa.

So far the bank hasn't asked for proof of my attendance, but we haven't been going long. What say an automated request comes out and I have no proof to supply? Have Bank Aotearoa considered the possibility of a nationwide lockdown? Is there a computer-driven process that will tip my mortgage into default if there is no documentation of my meeting attendance? Bank staff aren't going to be in the office discussing the situation or noticing when the default pops up. They will be at home like the rest of us, wondering where their next roll of toilet paper is coming from.

A tiny part of me feels concerned for the other OA attendees. Is Monique at home gnawing on her plasterboard in response to the stress of the COVID situation? It will be hard for her to find anyone to repair the bite marks during lockdown, so she could be acquiring a mouth guard at the chemist to keep herself away from her walls.

Is Matthew contemplating how to ink his own next tattoo? What would it be, Purex? If he lives with a tattoo artist, they could develop a more complex design; there were those dogs called 'Shar Pei' who have incredibly wrinkly skin that were used in toilet paper advertising. They are originally from China. That's another arrow pointing to China. If you tattoo a wrinkly dog on your skin, will it look good when your skin becomes wrinkly? Would it be better to tattoo a Shar Pei without wrinkles and let the wrinkles accumulate with your own age?

Monique and Barry will both be driving anyone they live with crazy by telling them lots of information they don't necessarily want to know. I imagine Barry, sitting at a computer, looking up information on COVID faster than he can read it and printing articles for later.

I don't have a functional computer at present. I have several computers in boxes that need repairing, though computers are generally beyond my level of fixing competence unless the problem is something as simple as a loose electrical connection. I did own a computer once, but it operated at slower and slower pace until my level of frustration outweighed its utility. I can do everything I need on the internet from my phone, but a computer could be useful for entertainment in a pandemic when you have to stay home.

If Barry doesn't live with someone else, he can tell his cats the latest news. I wonder if Barry is getting worried about his Red Zone cats? Does feeding cats count as an essential activity for which you can go out? If he cycles, he could say he is exercising. What about cat food? Will the stores have run out of cat food as well as toilet paper? Barry could be sitting at home, feeling desperate because his cat food supplies are low and neither he nor his cats can eat.

What is Greg doing? Is he reorganising his Teenage Mutant Ninja Turtle collection and looking online for more items to buy? What could have led him to be so interested in such a strange children's story?

Diana and David will be locked up together. They can hold hands the whole time and finish each other's sentences. They can buy each other presents online, if courier deliveries are still happening as an essential service. Lockdown could be difficult if they have little to do other than feed their obsession with buying presents. They could start present-buying wars where both are trying to buy the biggest present, or the most expensive present, or the most obscure present.

When I try to imagine what Fran is doing, I have no idea. She has told us little about herself in the process of facilitating our meetings. We know she is obsessed with helping people. Does she have a houseful of people to help so can spend her lockdown days continuously fulfilling her obsession?

My sitting room suddenly feels both congested and empty at the same time. I have gone to the furthest extent a restorative cup of Kenya Bold can take me. What tea cannot solve, a view of the sea might alleviate.

13

I exit my red front door and start down Head St towards the sea, when Alan-next-door collars me, because I am not looking out for him. I flinch internally from the expected tirade regarding the state of the country and the horrors of the Chinese. I try to counter that feeling by considering how he must be lonely given his wife died last year.

"Can you believe what Cindy is doing to our country?" Alan demands.

Who is Cindy? "What do you mean?"

"Locking everyone in their houses, putting people out of work, and there isn't even enough toilet paper to go around."

"People will most likely realise they don't need so much toilet paper soon. I bought newspaper instead."

"It's a travity, that's what it is."

What is a travity? A cross between a travesty and a pity?

"Cindy's on TV every day, telling us do this 'n do that. Wear masks 'n wash your hands and stay two metres away from people. She looks all sad but why would she be sad? She isn't losing her job, is she? She's sitting pretty, up there in Wellington, earning loads of dosh, together with all those other imbiots who pretend they know how to run a country."

"It's quite tricky, isn't it." I have deduced both who Cindy is and that I need to end this conversation. "Gotta run, Alan. I need to check whether the Supervalue has toilet paper in yet."

I stride rapidly towards the sea looking fixedly ahead. Few other people appear keen to start a conversation. The occasional pedestrians cross the road to give me the entire pavement to myself. A woman with three children gathers them towards her like ducklings under threat.

The sea is boisterous, full of energy and splash. The waves bounce off the rock wall and reflect offshore. The north-easterly wind adds force to the water and blows spray across my face. I can't walk along the sand, because it's covered by the tide, so I walk along the sealed surface of the Esplanade with its six metres of passing room for potentially COVIDy walkers.

I head towards Cave Rock, a local landmark close to Sumner Village and a favourite stomping ground of Johnno's and mine.

When we were young Mum was happy for us to run out to play after school; no one thought children playing on their own was a risky business. We climbed up Cave Rock from every side to a little building cemented into the rock at the top with a flag flying from it. We would race each other, climbing from opposite directions. The winner would yell, "I'm the king of the castle and you're the dirty rascal." There was a piece of pole down a vertical section of rock which we slithered along with feet dangling. If we were feeling brave and the lifeguards weren't watching, we would jump between mussel-clad rocks with sea lapping around them, daring each other to jump further away from the shore.

Occasionally I climb to the top of Cave Rock and sit there, remembering Johnno and wondering what he is doing now. I think he's in Singapore, working as a mechanical engineer. Johnno was offered a job with a multinational construction firm in Auckland before he graduated. They transferred him overseas where he moved up the corporate ladder. He was never good at keeping in touch when he was younger, and he hasn't improved with age. He used to send a text message on our birthday and another at Christmas saying something contentless like *Have a great day!* Some years ago those stopped coming; I'm not sure when.

I was hugely angry because Johnno didn't come home when Gran died, or before. She would have loved to see him again, even when she could barely remember anything. Johnno always said he was busy but would come as soon as he could. Soon never happened and so many years have gone by that I wonder if I'd recognise him if I passed him in the street.

I'm sure he will have a partner. He always had a girlfriend. On the rare occasions he came home for a meal in his last two years at uni, he would have a long-haired, long-limbed beauty in tow, but it was unusual for us to meet the same girl twice. Johnno will be forty-nine soon, will he have a party? He was always popular given his easy way with people. His easy way with people other than family, anyhow.

Thinking of Johnno reminds me of Mum. I should call her, given this whole lockdown thing. I hope she has somewhere decent to live. We have had our differences and she wasn't interested in us as children, but she is still my mother. I will call her once I get home and don't have to focus on staying two metres away from other people.

As I walk further along the Esplanade, I think one good thing about COVID is the disappearance of the backpacker vans. Presumably the backpackers have flown home to their families around the globe or are parked up somewhere in a camping ground, waiting out the lockdown. I hope they are paying exorbitant prices for camping grounds, given they were staying for free at my beach for months. Oh, there is a backpacker still there, resting on a bench with their belongings poked underneath. How do COVID lockdowns work if you are a vagrant? Do you get forcibly taken into a shelter or are you within the letter of the law as long as you stay two metres away from everyone?

When I get closer, I see it's not a vagrant sitting on the bench, it's someone I know – Robbie. "Hey Robbie, how are you doing?" comes out of my mouth before my brain computes Robbie probably isn't doing well if his belongings are stored under a bench. I also remember I have his cables and pack, which will be why his belongings are in supermarket bags.

"Hey lassie, how're you doing yourself? I'm just watching the sea."

"I thought you were in a shared flat near the beach. What happened?"

"COVID happened lassie."

"Well, yes. But what happened to you?"

"Lost my job. No job for a barista in closed cafés. My flatmates ran home to their mummies and daddies and my landlord wants the house for his family. So here I am. The beach is a fine place to be."

"It's a fine place to be when it isn't raining. What will you do when it rains? Or when it gets frosty in winter? You can't live on a beach forever!"

"London tramps'd be downright envious of me here. No snow. More sunny days than grey. For sure there's no tube stations when it rains, but I'll manage."

I'm not normally an impetuous person. If there is a cautious-impetuous continuum, I would be towards the cautious pole. However, as with my greeting, the words spill out of my mouth before I think them away. "Would you like to stay with me? There's only me in Gran's house, I mean my house. There's a spare room you could stay in. You've only seen the house from the outside but it's not bad on the inside. Staying with me would be within the COVID rules if you come before lockdown at midnight tonight."

"Midnight tonight's the drop dead? I'll make a call right now. Thanks, lassie, I'll say yes. But when you tire of me, throw me out."

I like Robbie calling me lassie, it makes me feel young with possibilities ahead of me rather than roadblocks.

I might have made a mistake in inviting him to stay because, since Gran died, no one has lived in Gran's house other than me and, briefly, Amanda. Now it's just me and my broken things. However, I needn't have worried because, in a house of broken things, Robbie fitted right in.

14

ROBBIE and I walk back towards Head St. He carries a bag and balances his surfboard across his bike while I carry the other bags. "Not so good for surfing today, is it?"

"Nae, but the forecast's good. COVID'll help me improve my surfing. And my gear will be safer at yours than under a bench."

"Might you have to go home to Scotland? Could the Government force foreigners to leave."

"I dinnae reckon. What'll they do? Drive round in buses and grab us like the Indonesian Government clearing the Jakarta streets?"

I wonder why the Indonesians did that, but I don't ask. I am remembering that I like living on my own because I like quiet. So we walk the last block in silence, past Alan looking from his garden with great interest.

"Stay two metres away from other people! And wear masks!" he yells.

Alan, you hypocrite. Only an hour ago you were telling me how you hated that Jacinda is saying what we can and can't do and now here *you* are telling me what I can and can't do.

"This is Robbie, Alan. He's living in Gran's house with me. We're allowed to be less than two metres from each other as we're in the same bubble."

Alan looks sceptical but I don't care. Robbie grins cheerily at Alan and waves as we head past the house to my red front door. Did Robbie wave a single finger at Alan as we disappear round the corner? Alan's eyesight is failing, so he likely won't have seen it.

I hope Robbie will admire my front door, but he follows me inside without a mention, as my mental concerns swell like a balloon. I wasn't inviting people into my house because it is cluttered. How can Robbie and I cohabit this space? I feel like I got new glasses while walking and my blurry house has moved into sharp focus.

There are boxes, and more, everywhere. The hallway appears threatening, with towers of boxes at every step in a seventy-centimetre-wide space, so it's preferable to turn sideways as you proceed to avoid dislodging anything. Do I take Robbie to the kitchen? Or towards the second bedroom? I choose the kitchen as the lesser evil because I know there is enough space to stand and make a cup of tea.

"Why don't we leave the door open and put your bags, board and bike in the doorway for now?" I say brightly. "We can have a nice cup of Kenya Bold. You do like tea, don't you?" Given that Robbie has been working in a coffee shop it is possible he doesn't like tea. That could be an issue.

"Tea's fine thanks, lassie. Are you sure about me stayin'?" Robbie eyes the boxes nervously. I hadn't seen Robbie as large, but I am not sure he'll fit through the hallway beside the boxes.

"Absolutely," I say with conviction I don't feel. "It's only a few boxes, we can, er … shift them."

Robbie shuffles sideways to the kitchen with his hands at chest height to ward off potential cascading boxes. In the kitchen, I realise there's room for one person to make a cup of tea but not enough room for two. Robbie wedges himself against a stack of boxes in the hallway.

I jabber on about nothing while boiling the burgundy kettle and searching for the second gold filigree teacup. I find it in the back of the spice cupboard, jammed between boxes of curry and jars of dried leaves so old they have turned to flakes of dust. The cup is filled with sesame seeds; the packet must have grown a hole and I didn't know where to put the seeds.

"Do you have milk in your tea?"

"For sure."

"Normal milk, right? Not oat milk, or almond milk, or cashew milk?"

"Cow milk is fine, lassie. This nut milking, d'ya reckon big nuts have nut babies before they lactate?"

We share a laugh and I pour the hot water into the Temuka teapot. Then we manoeuvre our return along the hall to the sitting room and gain it with all boxes intact. However, the sitting room isn't a great success because it harbours my tea-drinking spot, with the emphasis on 'my'. My chair sits resplendent with no further space around it.

I found the chair at a second-hand store, back in my enthusiastic fixing days. It has teak arms and legs which I refinished to a clean smooth surface and then lovingly oiled. I removed the faded green velour fabric, resprung the seat and covered it with a Marimekko print which has a design of large red flowers with orange centres. Like my front door, the chair makes me smile to look at it.

However, this room is not making me smile today. What felt like a cosy space in which to peacefully drink tea is now a cramped and dingy corner out of which a bat could fly or a large spider crawl.

I start gabbling. "There're a few things needing putting away so why don't we go outside, seeing as it's still fine, and have our cup of tea in the garden. It's a beautiful evening and of course you've been in my garden before, but it's my favourite place to sit."

We weave along the goat track between boxes and electrical appliances from the chair to the French doors that open out onto the garden. There are mixers and kettles and hairdryers and a few power tools. Their cords have developed an unhealthy interest in each other and turned into copulating tangles. Could that be why I have so many appliances, they reproduced madly and one appliance became ten? I hope the offspring aren't wild, like when stray cats have kittens who hiss at every human they see. What does Barry of OA do with the wild kittens?

We sit on the mosaic sofa and sip tea without conversation as I have run out of gabble and Robbie looks stunned. Kenya Bold has a partially restorative effect on my brain function. "Why don't you bring your bicycle and surfboard through the side gate into the garden. You can lean them against the shed. I'm sure they'll be safe; I've never had anything stolen out of the back garden and I've kept my bike in it for ever."

Robbie slips the surfboard between the pumpkin vines growing up the shed. He looks like he wants to say clambering through the overgrown garden to reach the shed makes it a difficult place to store his belongings. All he actually says is "Thanks," then props his bike against the wall of my bedroom, squashing granny's bonnets in the process.

There's still one major hurdle to overcome. I promised Robbie the second bedroom. As I sit on the mosaic sofa, the full challenge of that room solidifies in my mind. I haven't been into the room for three and a half years. The reason I haven't gone in is because the door no longer opens. The room was Amanda's, and no one has slept in it since Mum left after the Christmas I have done my utmost to forget

The one thing I had done in preparation for Amanda's birth was paint her room. I hadn't bought baby equipment, but restoration and beautification were my focus. I painted her walls as a rampant garden of peonies, lilies, bougainvillea, birds of paradise. I didn't worry about which plants grew together, just created a collage of the most colourful and beautiful flowers. Afterwards, seeing those flowers was a constant stab to my heart. The earthquakes wrought havoc on their beauty, with huge tears across sections of my plaster canvas, but the impression of bursting life remained painfully at odds with reality.

When Fleecer Construction repaired Gran's house, I refused to let anyone into Amanda's room and said I would fix it myself, or not. I locked the door to keep repairers out. I put the key in a safe place and then forgot that safe location over the six-month period the repairs took, well beyond the promised three months. I still don't know where the key is and being unable to go in the room became the easiest course of inaction. How will I explain this to Robbie?

The only way to explain a locked door, it turns out, is to say that it's locked, and the key is lost.

There are two options for entering the room. One is to kick the kauri panelled door until something breaks. The other is to enter through the windows on the south side of the house. I give Robbie the options with strong weighting in favour of the least breakage.

He asks whether I have a box cutter and a chisel. I could have many things; they just need to be found.

I direct Robbie to the garden shed and, in due course, faintly hear him fiddling outside the window. I have retreated to my Marimekko chair corner in the sitting room.

Eventually I hear Robbie clamber over the sill and move around inside. What's still in the room? Did I put Amanda's belongings there after Mum left? How can I not remember where her bassinet went and all her tiny clothes? The only toy of Amanda's I chose to keep was 'Keko', her blue and green swamp hen who now lives in my bed.

I hear Robbie lift his shopping bags off the front doorstep and post them through the window. He returns to the shed and I wonder if he is looking for a ladder to make his access easier. I hear sweeping and shaking noises.

After a while Robbie comes and finds me in my chair. "Thanks for the bed, lassie. I'm ready to sleep in it. Don't worry about sheets n' all, I've my sleeping bag."

"Great, see you in the morning."

Tomorrow will be a new day in which it could be that the many problems looming will have as fresh a look as my boxes did this afternoon. One can hope.

15

3 APRIL 2020

A week into lockdown, Robbie and I have found an equilibrium of sorts in which to live where he climbs through the window to access the bedroom. This is a good solution because he doesn't have to negotiate the hallway boxes and I don't have to see him all the time.

An unexpected issue is our different body clocks. I prefer to stay up till midnight, while Robbie gets up at an hour I don't consider to exist. I hear him creep out his window then I go back to sleep. We meet for a cup of tea in the garden after he returns.

Robbie goes for a bike ride or a run or a surf every day, his activity dependent on the weather and tides. It's amazing how energetic he is. Is it because he is so much younger than me? I don't remember ever being so active. My exercise consists of gardening, walking to the shops or biking to the further shops. Why would I deliberately raise my heart rate with furious activity? Robbie says he doesn't feel good unless he exercises every day; is exercise Robbie's obsession?

We have lunch together while listening to the latest Government COVID news on my phone. We eat outside because it's a perfect autumn with still, sunny, warm days. The universe must know we have to stay home so is being kind to us.

Our Prime Minister tells us to be kind to each other. We hear from her as she reports to the nation daily, along with the Director of the Ministry of Health, Ashley Bloomfield. I find myself sucked into absorbing more media than I am accustomed to, which includes these 1pm briefings in which we hear how many people have been diagnosed with COVID-19, as well as what our country is doing to manage COVID. Today there were eighty-nine new cases, the biggest number so far. Only one person has died from COVID to date in New Zealand, which makes it sound like COVID isn't dangerous

There is debate on the radio about whether lockdown is a good thing, saving lives, or whether it is a terrible thing and is destroying our economy for little gain. Anti-lockdowners say our economy will collapse therefore people will die of illnesses we won't be able to afford to treat. No doubt our economy will suffer because there isn't much to spend money on other than groceries and at the chemist. All the tourism money propping up the New Zealand economy has vanished; isn't it amazing how the whole world can rapidly change to that degree? As with the earthquakes, you can wake up one morning and everything is fine but, by evening, life as you know it has crumbled around you.

I look for interesting articles to read on the internet. I am picking up my phone during the day with increasing frequency. Any article is good that will distract me from checking COVID cases and death tolls in different countries. I have become reliant on accessing information and entertainment on the internet in a way I never have before. My favourite article today is one about a guy who stuck magnets up his nose and needed them removed by doctors at the hospital. This guy is an astrophysicist, studying where rockets might go. However, he can't be a rocket scientist as would anyone of great intelligence stick magnets up their nose?

The astrophysicist, Daniel, said he was using magnets to create a device that will set off an alarm when your hands get too close to your face, so you don't accidentally get virus particles near your nose, mouth, or eyes. I visualise little COVIDs, pictures of which look akin to small bombs with warts, crawling stealthily and determinedly up nasal passages.

Daniel's device wasn't working out, so he entertained himself by putting magnets up his nose – really? An adult sticking magnets up his nose? One of the magnets went too far up and Daniel then tried to remove it using other magnets on the outside. Unfortunately, magnets like being together so he developed a colony of magnets up his nostrils.

Daniel got some pliers to remove the magnets. The magnets magnetised the pliers, so his entire nose was pulled sideways as he brought the pliers towards his face. At this point Daniel knew his magnet situation was out of control. His partner was laughing hysterically but had to get herself sorted to drive him to a hospital where a doctor pulled the magnets out.

Daniel is shown in a hospital bed looking grim and regretful. Why did he let his picture be taken? If I was in hospital because I stuck magnets up my nose, no way I would want my stupidity advertised globally. On the other hand, the internet shows that many people on the planet have no trouble advertising their stupidity; it could be me who is the exception.

I remember a number of stupid things I did, luckily never broadcast internationally. I shoved toy animals down the overflow pipe in the bathroom sink to see if they came back up, a clothes hanger into a heater to investigate where the heat came from, and plasticine into my friend Marion's hair. Gran removed the plasticine with scissors then I had to apologise to Marion's mother. I don't know why I had to apologise because it was as much Marion's idea as mine.

While I am traversing memory lane, I hear shouting. The voices sound like Alan-next-door and Robbie.

"Hey you, you shouldn't be surfing."

"I dinnae ken ya, mate. Dawn surfing in quiet waves. The water's calm today."

"The Government says no surfing or swimming. You foreigners, you think you can do whatever you like in our country. If you get into trouble, the lifeguard and police will have to rescue you when they've more important work. If you've got COVID you could intagion your rescuers. You should get on a plane and go home, not be a burden on our country."

"Mate, I dinnae ken your problem. I paid my taxes right till lockdown stole my job."

"Don't call me mate, I'm not your mate. You go and 'mate' your bloody Pommy friends with their posh accents who are buying up Sumner houses so they're too expensive for real New Zealanders. If I see you with that surfboard again, I'll be calling the COVID-19 rulebreaker hotline, you watch out."

I dash out into the garden and call as loudly as I can, "Robbie the kettle's boiled and your tea is getting cold." I don't want escalating arguments or the police turning up on my doorstep and asking embarrassing questions like, "Did you know there is a ladder being used to climb in your window?"

Robbie thumps through the gate into the garden and drops his surfboard on the pumpkins. He strips off his wetsuit and throws it into his rinsing crate but doesn't bother to run water in to clean off the salt. Robbie has a compact, muscular figure. He could look good in a kilt playing the bagpipes, though those long socks bagpipers wear look stupid.

I go to speak to Robbie, but he strides back out the gate, around to the other side of the house and I hear him climb in his window. I suppose that means he doesn't want a cup of tea.

I make some Kenya Bold and take my gold filigree cup out into the front garden, but it feels like a cloud has come over the sun. I sit with my back to Alan's fence to ensure there are no further conversations with the neighbour today.

16

20 APRIL 2020

IT'S the twentieth of April and today is my forty-ninth birthday. It's a tolerable pandemic birthday because I received a letter from Bank Aotearoa delaying my loan repayment requirements *and* Jacinda has announced we will move to Level 3 of the COVID alert framework *and* Robbie has made me a birthday cake for afternoon tea, which he has carefully placed on a cut log in front of the mosaic sofa.

New Zealand won't move from Alert Level 4 to Level 3 for another week, but the reduction in alert levels indicates our COVID outbreak is becoming controlled. Case numbers have dropped to ten or fewer every day this week, well down from the high of eighty. There is light in the pandemic tunnel.

The Bank Aotearoa letter was in the mailbox three days ago, but I didn't open it until this morning because I haven't felt resilient enough to cope with bad news. A civil emergency can make you feel permanently fragile and unable to deal with anything of consequence. Since lockdown started, I have actively suppressed thoughts of what the bank might do. What they are actually doing is giving everyone a six-month interest holiday on loans.

I don't have to pay the bank anything for six months! Six months to restore my client base and start fixing items from the boxes. The letter doesn't specifically refer to OA attendance but says there will be a follow-up letter regarding any special loan conditions. This gives me a moment's concern but it's my birthday so I focus on positive thoughts and conclude there will be an OA deferral as well.

What might my fellow OA attendees be doing? I haven't seen any of them on my walks around Sumner, but there's no reason to think they are locals. At the next meeting, I must try to find out where they live. When will our next meeting take place? There's still no clarity around when New Zealand will move to Alert Level 2, at which meetings might be allowed.

A birthday cake is exciting as I haven't had one since before Gran became demented. When Johnno and I were little Gran made us amazing cakes. Gran enjoyed the creativity of making our birthday cakes. Johnno and I had the same birthday, but we did *not* want the same cake. That would have been a cheat.

Our fifth birthday was particularly memorable because it was Saturday, and we would have our first day of school on Monday. We were psyched about going to school, no more baby kindergarten for us. We had our school uniforms ready to wear and our little satchels ready to put our lunch boxes in. Gran must have organised all these things because I cannot imagine Mum being that forward thinking.

We went to Gran's early on Saturday morning after a long night of loud partying at Mum's house. We weren't supposed to see our cakes until our birthday party in the afternoon. Some kindergarten friends were invited, about whom I remember nothing. The prospective food was the big excitement. Gran allowed us to choose two types of party food each. Johnno chose cheerio sausages with tomato sauce and chocolate eclairs. I chose sausage rolls and pavlova with cream and strawberries. Gran would make everything, and I would help decorate the pavlova on Saturday morning.

When we arrived, Gran was snoring so loudly we could hear her from the front door (most likely she had been up late preparing the party food) and we giggled to each other. We headed for the kitchen to look for our cakes, but no cakes were to be seen. We examined the tins on the bench and found the eclairs and pavlova, but still no cakes.

We figured the cakes wouldn't be in our bedroom; they must be in the sitting room. We headed there, shoving each other in our excitement while Gran snored on. We looked under the couch and behind the couch. We found dust balls together with a multicoloured rubber bouncy ball and two marbles. No cakes in the fireplace or on the mantelpiece.

Finally, success! One cake was inside the radiogram and the other was on top of the wardrobe in which Gran kept all the best china, on wooden shelves she had built. The cake in the radiogram was mine, it was a Hansel and Gretel house covered in a multiplicity of interesting looking sweets. The cake on the wardrobe was Johnno's. It was a swimming pool with figurines floating on a sea of jelly and chocolate-covered biscuits creating the perimeter.

We balanced a chair on the coffee table to look at the cake on the wardrobe but didn't dare lift it down in case we dropped it. We snuck a single biscuit each from the edge and pushed the remaining biscuits towards each other, so the gaps weren't visible.

The cake in the radiogram was far more accessible. We stared at the sweets, our breakfastless stomachs rumbling. Surely one sweet each from the back of the house couldn't hurt? I chose a red jellybean and Johnno a liquorice allsort. One sweet didn't fill our tummies, so we chose one more, this time I got an Eskimo and Johnno a marshmallow. Then Johnno wanted to try the sweets I had tried, and I wanted to try the ones he had eaten, until the back of the Hansel and Gretel house was reduced to its cake framing.

At this point Gran came into the room. We hadn't noticed her snoring ceasing. There was a moment of horror, as Johnno and I stared at each other, and Gran stared at us. "Sweets for a fifth birthday breakfast is it, darlings?" We nodded mutely. "I had better get the spare bags of sweets for the party so we can build it back as good as before, hadn't I?"

Robbie's cake isn't a Hansel and Gretel construction but it's very welcome. He must have cooked it while I was out for my regular afternoon pandemic stroll by the sea. It actually looks more like a big scone than a cake. There is a large white candle in the middle; in pandemics one makes do with what is available, and I always have industrial size candles after living through the Canterbury earthquake power cuts.

I sit on the mosaic sofa and blow out the candle as Robbie sings 'Happy Birthday'. He slices the cake and I see it is indeed a large scone with promising mountains of jam and cream in the centre.

Robbie pours Kenya Bold from the Temuka teapot into the gold filigree cups and hands me a large chunk of scone on a gold patterned Crown Lynn plate he must have found by wedging open the obstructed wardrobe door in the sitting room.

"Here's to a better birthday next year!" Robbie says, and, without warning, a wave of sadness slams into me as I imagine all the birthdays Amanda never had and never will have.

Today would have been Amanda's ninth birthday. We could have made a cake in the shape of a piano, or a computer, or a bicycle, depending on what she liked to do best. We could have paged through Gran's *Australian Women's Weekly Birthday Cake Cookbook* looking for ideas and cake construction methods. We could have stirred the dough in the kitchen, eating morsels off the spoon to check the mixture. Would Amanda have preferred chocolate cake? Or carrot cake? Or traditional sponge cake? Would she have been a diligent baker, paying attention to the process and the cooking? Or would she have been a dreamy child, forgetting the cake once it was in the oven?

How many primary school friends would Amanda have invited to her party? Nine guests for a nine-year-old? Would Amanda only have invited girls, or girls and boys? Silly me, Amanda couldn't have had a ninth birthday party because her birthday would have been in the middle of a pandemic. Amanda being alive wouldn't have changed the course of world history. A bat in a Chinese wet market might still have conveyed the virus to a purchaser. A sloppy Chinese scientist could still have contracted a virus they were playing with in a test tube. Or did the scientist drop their test tube after receiving a call through the earpieces in their hazmat suit? "I'm sorry to inform you that your daughter was just run over by a bus."

Robbie is staring at me and shards of a gold filigree teacup pile at my feet. There are so many things broken here that I have lost count, together with my heart.

17

20 APRIL 2020–6 MAY 2020

"JULIA, are you okay?"

I mentally vacillate between an automatic and clearly inaccurate "I'm fine!" and "Isn't it obvious that I am not?" What comes out my mouth are hiccupping sobs as I shakily pick pieces of teacup off the ground.

"I'm sorry about the teacup, did it hold a lot of memories?"

The teacup had been overflowing with memories prior to its demise. "It was Gran's teacup and there are only two."

"Can you repair it? Sounds like you've had plenty of practice?" Robbie smiles hopefully at me; broken things can be repaired and the shattered made whole. His blue eyes go well with his red curly hair, which has become long during lockdown and springs in every direction from his head.

Looking at Robbie, repair seems possible. I cast my mind back to the kintsugi-inspired origins of 'Broken is Beautiful'. I can see the cup glued back together, in teacup form but with additional gold lines on its surface, highlighting the imperfections developed in its lifetime. "You could be right," I say slowly.

Robbie makes another cup of tea, giving me time to myself. He brings the tea out in a chipped, flowery mug I don't recognise; it could be someone else's mug waiting for repair. I sip tea and nibble the edges of the scone. The raspberry jam and cream filling taste delicious so I eat more.

"You know, lassie, I could help with the repair thing. I'm handy with tools and fix-it jobs."

Robbie is handy, huh? How come he gave me his cables and pack to repair? It's conceivable he needed someone else to do the pack repair work because it's best done on a heavy-duty sewing machine. However, he could have repaired his own phone cables. Does that mean he wanted to see me more, outside the café setting? My heart gives a little jump, a feeling I haven't experienced in a long time.

"Excellent. I have a few jobs backed up, as you can see." I smile back at him. "It would be nice if it was easier to get along the hallway, wouldn't it?"

"Then where do we start?"

That's a good question. Looking around with my increasingly unblinkered eyes, there are broken things in every nook and cranny of Gran's house. They live in the cupboards and drawers, under beds, on dressers and wardrobes, in plastic crates along the perimeter of the house, spilling out of the garden shed.

We start with the shed because it holds the oldest items, and we can move boxes easily to the garden to sort them. The boxes are stacked to ceiling height in random fashion; luckily none of the stacks have yet fallen and blocked the door.

I stand at the door and pass boxes to Robbie; he takes them and piles them in the garden. Some boxes are labelled, some are not. Some contents are labelled individually and some not.

Early in the shed disembowelment we find two tarpaulins and spread them in the garden. Labelled boxes go on the right tarpaulin and partially-labelled or unlabelled boxes on the left tarpaulin. Tools go under my bedroom window. We find more tarpaulins and Robbie rigs them up to cover the piles at the end of each day.

The next two and a half weeks are some of the best times I can remember in my adult life. Robbie and I settle into a routine of repair, exercise, and shared meals. The weather is a continuous succession of warm, blue and gold days as the sun shines and we sit outside in the garden to dine, remarking on the swelling pumpkins hanging from the shed.

I think Robbie is still surfing at dawn, but I don't say anything. I hope he doesn't encounter Alan-next-door, but I will leave that risk up to him. If surfing makes Robbie happy, and a happy Robbie wants to help me repair things, that's all good with me.

I do my normal middle-of-the-day walk to look at the waves. I almost want to swim and show Robbie I can go in the water too.

The shift from COVID Alert Level 4 to Level 3 lockdown doesn't change our lives much. Level 3 is referred to as 'Level 4 with takeaways'; the biggest changes are that construction firms can operate again as can online sales and courier deliveries, and cafés can offer takeaway food. As neither Robbie nor I have a job, we can't afford takeaways or online purchases.

The biggest change for us is that swimming and surfing are allowed. On April twenty-eighth, I go into the sea for the first time in several years to show Robbie I can do it. I proudly walk back to Gran's house along Head Street with a towel wrapped around me so it is clear that I went for a swim.

The shed clearing takes longer than it might have because I slow the process by getting stalled on particular items, remembering the people who own them. There's a large unlabelled Clarice Cliff vase in pieces that belongs to Bev from further down Head St. Bev is ninety and a keen surfer. I saw Bev on the beach with her surfboard and she told me I should try surfing. "Never too late. I started when I was only a bit younger than you, dear. Then I couldn't stop. My son said I should try standing up but the buzz from catching a wave lying down is good enough for me. I ride my bike to the beach every day to look at the surf. I walk back with my board if it looks good."

When we were chatting, I recognised Bev as my Sumner Primary School music teacher. Bev was an enthusiastic teacher, as enthusiastic about music as she is about surfing. Our class would play a range of instruments, attempting to sound like we were playing the national anthem while she accompanied us on the harmonica.

Bev is also a keen gardener and encouraged me to drop by and check out her vegetables and flower garden. I kept meaning to visit as she only lives a couple of blocks away. However, when I met Bev, I was already losing my energy for doing things, so haven't yet gone round.

One day she dropped by with this vase, which she said her husband Bill had given her shortly after they got married. The vase fell off their sideboard in the February 2011 earthquake. Bill is now losing his memory with Alzheimer's. He still remembers giving Bev the vase but is forgetting their story of buying it, then cycling from the city to Sumner with it on his handlebars.

Bev wants to help Bill relive memories. Objects triggering memories is one of the ways she helps him preserve his stories and sense of who he is. She had left the vase in the corner with most of its breaks hidden against the wall. When she heard I repair things she brought it round, hopefully. I feel a nasty pang of guilt; she brought it at least three years ago. I look at the vase's stylised flower pattern in reds, yellows and greens and have the spark of an idea about how to enhance it. I place Bev's vase at the front of the queue of items on the labelled box tarpaulin.

Robbie is very patient with my reveries over miscellaneous items. He continues to pull boxes out by himself or sits on a log scrolling through his phone. I notice he avoids standing anywhere he could be seen by Alan-next-door.

The internet reports people all over the country having semi-isolated parties at the ends of their driveways, separated by fences and roads. I often see them when I walk to the beach on a Friday or Saturday afternoon. Luckily that's not something Alan is going to suggest, as Siouxsie Wiles – one of the go-to scientists for the media – has recently told us the virus is too infectious for such behaviour to be safe. People should refrain from any socialising other than online, until we reach the heady heights of COVID Alert Level 2. While I am happy to have a valid reason to avoid Alan, I also feel like we are moving into a framework of state control I am uneasy about. Can the government tell you not to talk to your neighbours?

Alan falls into another category of person described in the media – the 'telly-offies'. Telly-offies enjoy telling other people what they should be doing even when the telly-offies are not doing the right things themselves. Telly-offies watch the behaviour of others in real life and also on social media. Apparently, some people record where they walk or ride, and other people have been commenting on their exercise being inappropriately long or far from their houses. Luckily, I have no interest in broadcasting my every action on social media so don't have to consider acceptability of my activities in the telly-offie age. Do people actually bother to share how much exercise they do and where they go all the time? It seems rather odd.

I wonder what or who Robbie is looking at on his phone. Is he checking out the exercise other people do online? Reading the news? Catching up with friends? He still hasn't been forthcoming about his home or family, mostly telling me funny stories from his travels. Should I try investigating him on social media to learn about his background? I would quite like to know more about him and, if he isn't going to tell me directly, I might as well use the resources the internet makes available.

18

7 MAY 2020

I have little practice investigating people on the internet in general or through social media. My use of digital technology has been limited by my lack of both a computer and enthusiasm for reading on a tiny phone screen. I mostly text when I need to communicate with people and occasionally use email. Most people I contact are my clients, given that I have apparently reduced my number of friends to zero, or one if I count Robbie. My clients use a whole lot of different messaging platforms which I can never keep track of. At least, I couldn't keep track of them when I did contact a lot of clients. I don't know why they can't all text, it would be much simpler.

Before investigating Robbie, I check my emails for the first time in several days. It turns out this is lucky because I find a week-old email from Fran.

Dear Thursday Group members,

I hope you are finding strategies for managing your lockdown experience successfully. We all hoped this lockdown would be relatively short, but now 5 weeks have gone by and we cannot yet predict the end. It is also possible the Government will continue to require meetings be conducted remotely once we enter COVID Alert Level 2. As a support group, it is important we maintain continuity in these challenging times. Therefore, I thought we should explore the possibilities of connecting via technology rather than in person.

I am hoping many of you will already have had the opportunity to use Zoom in your work or social lives. I propose we convene on Zoom at our normal 5.30pm on a Thursday, from Thursday 7th May. I will understand if you can't join our first meeting but let's see how many people can attend. At least we can be sure few of us will have appointments to go to outside our houses.

Looking forward to seeing you all again online. I will send a Zoom link in a following email.

Best regards

Fran

Today is the seventh of May. I will have to put my investigation of Robbie on hold while I figure out how to join a Zoom meeting. I feel surprisingly enthusiastic about catching up with the OA group given it was originally an unwelcome requirement foisted upon me. I feel interested in how the other group members are doing. Having Robbie around during lockdown has been nice and reminded me how good communicating with people can feel. However, I have not yet had 'the opportunity to use Zoom' and have no idea what it might be. 'Zoom' sounds like a three-year-old simulating a fast car, yelling excitedly as his toy races across the room to lodge under the corner of the sofa.

I google 'Zoom' and discover it's a company providing video conferencing services via the internet, on computers or tablets or phones. 'Zooming' requires a username and password to log into a 'meeting' online. To access Zoom I need an app on my phone. I need to remember how to get a new app for my phone, which is an ageing iPhone a happy client gave me in lieu of payment. The client, Rosemary, was annoyed by her phone having a significant crack across the screen and wanted a new phone, as well as being pleased by my re-creation of the mug she had brought for repair.

Rosemary is a trainee doctor from the United Kingdom, one of the many who have flocked into Sumner to meet the needs of the New Zealand health system while living somewhere with better weather than their home country. She was still in Sumner pre-lockdown because I saw her zipping past on a road bike looking very fit. Rosemary's Gran gave her the mug as a going-away present and Rosemary's flatmate had dropped a frying pan on it.

I re-created the cup, which was tall and thin with a William Morris design of roses around an angel. Rosemary said her ninety-year old gran has a garden full of roses which she determinedly prunes. She has prickle-induced arthritis from many years of pruning roses so every cut must hurt but for her, like my gran, gardening is an important part of her identity.

The mug was badly broken with the handle in tiny fragments. I re-created it with wings coming out of the angel's shoulders, forming a new way of holding the cup while the original pattern remained visible. I painted over the cracks with metallic rose-colour paint. Rosemary was thrilled when she collected it and brought me an iPad to fix that she said was running tediously slowly. I couldn't bring myself to tell her that mugs and iPads are rather different things and put the iPad in a box.

Robbie finds me on the mosaic sofa, muttering swear words under my breath at the phone, which are getting more lurid by the minute. It is cup of tea time, prior to box sorting. I am so engrossed in the frustrations of trying to do something on a digital device, I have forgotten to put the burgundy kettle on the stove. Robbie gets us both a cup of tea and we drink in silence while I calm down and try not to look at the infuriating phone.

"Want a hand?"

"No, I'm fine, just loading something."

"Another set of eyes wouldn't help?"

I cave. "Okay, I can't load the bloody Zoom app. I have restarted five times because the screen locked up and it keeps asking me for a password I can't remember."

"You want to Zoom on your phone? How many people? A phone screen's small for lots of faces."

"Our group has eight people. We usually meet on Thursdays and we're having a Zoom meeting because we're missing getting together."

"It would be better to use a tablet."

"Great idea, if I had a tablet."

"There was an unlabelled iPad in a recent box we went through. What's wrong with it?"

That must be Rosemary's iPad. She gave it to me over two years ago and hasn't called so she can't be missing it. Could I use it before returning it to her?

"Hmmm, not sure I can remember who owns the iPad. I think it was running slowly."

"That could be easy. Maybe a glitched app. Full memory. Corrupted operating software."

Robbie could just as well be speaking in Chinese for my level of comprehension of his suggestions.

"I'd be hugely grateful if you could fix it. Do you know how to make it do this Zooming thing?"

"For sure, lassie. I'll fix the iPad. Then we can sort Zoom together."

Robbie takes the iPad away and, half an hour later, returns to the garden where I have removed three boxes from the shed. I can see the floor now. This is good, but ominous, because the next step will be doing something about box contents rather than putting them in tarpaulin sandwiches. However, today is for focusing on Zoom.

"All go lassie. Let's hook it to your phone, load and run Zoom, then test it."

Hook the iPad up to my phone? That's another novel concept. How does one connect a phone with a tablet? Robbie shows me how to link tablet to phone using Wi-Fi to access the internet. This makes me nervous. My phone has limited data.

"Will I run out of data if I use Zoom?"

"Could be a problem, lassie. How about broadband on your home phone?"

"I don't have a home phone to save money."

"You could get naked broadband."

I shelve that piece of jargon for another time, along with dealing with box contents.

Robbie explains how to load the Zoom app, we run a video test, and it's much easier than I'd expected. Perhaps I am not as hopeless with technology as I thought? I enjoy sitting close to Robbie on the sofa while I hold the iPad and he makes suggestions when I don't know what to do next. I could get used to having someone so helpful and pleasant around the house long term. Little thoughts of something more than 'around the house' unfurl at the corners of my mind, like seedlings poking their heads above the soil, as I look at Robbie's attractive profile focused on the screen.

19

IT'S OA meeting time and I click on the appointment that magically transferred from my email to the calendar on the tablet when Robbie showed me how. I click on the Zoom link; the Zoom app pops up and a message tells me to wait until the host lets me in. I sit patiently until the screen fills with a big picture of Fran and little boxes above containing Matthew and Monique. Soon more little boxes appear containing Greg and Barry, then David and Diana.

"Hi Julia," Fran says. "Can you please turn your video on?"

Where's my video button? My eyes dart around the screen.

"It's on the bottom left," Barry says. It would be him telling me.

Most people are wearing headsets with microphones, which makes them look like experienced Zoomers. At least I can hear sound fine on the iPad and there is little happening in my sitting room for them to hear. I find the iPad is in much better focus when I push it away down my lap as far as my arms can reach. Does that mean I am going to need glasses soon? I'm not even fifty yet!

I look carefully at the boxes to see what people's rooms look like. Fran's box has a slightly wavering picture of a beach with palm trees that prevents one learning about her house. As I wonder how she did that, I realise I need to prevent the Zoom view of me including any of my boxes of broken things. The group knows about my need to collect broken things, but they don't need to see my boxes.

I swivel in the Marimekko chair so my box only shows the fabric and the off-white corner wall behind me. My walls are all Resene Quarter Truffle, other than the spare bedroom with its flowering walls that Robbie can see and which I don't want to look at. Fleecer Construction gave me a choice of paint colours, while requiring the whole inside be in a single colour unless I wanted to pay even more money. I chose Truffle as a warm white to make the rooms of Gran's house look larger.

David and Diana have their own Zoom boxes; I expected them to be seated cosily together on a white leather sofa. Instead, they are sitting in separate offices. Diana has a turquoise wall in her background, while David's wall is canary yellow. They have wood-framed windows with closed light-screening blinds. Diana's room is spartan with nothing visible on her desk other than a wine glass, while David's desk is cluttered with stacks of paper. A bookcase against his wall holds piles of books and electronic gadgets. He's got a glass that might be holding whisky and ice to his right.

Monique's room looks as stylish as Monique. She is sitting in a hanging cane chair with an interesting abstract artwork visible behind her. She is wearing a jacket with a Chinese collar and silk embroidery that might have looked naff on someone else but makes her look fabulous. Are there pock marks in her walls? The Zoom video isn't good enough resolution to be sure.

It is hard to see past Matthew's tattoos to focus on his surrounds because he's wearing a black tank top showing his tattoos off exceptionally well. He's lounging in a black puffy recliner with a huge television behind him on a blood-red wall and a bottle with a psychedelic logo saying Liberty Knife Party in his hand.

Barry is once again in a suit with collared shirt and a well-tied tie, seated at a desk with a can of beer in front of him. I squint to read the label – Cassels Milk Stout. Does milk stout actually have milk in it? And why do men still wear ties? When I was at high school we wore ties in winter and I thought it must surely die out because ties are so uncomfortable. Johnno and I would scramble to find our ties before school. Only one tie would be visible so we would both claim it and tell the other person to look harder because they had lost their tie. As Johnno got bigger, I stopped trying to wrestle the tie from him because he could pin me too easily.

In Greg's box I can see large posters of Teenage Mutant Ninja Turtles with ninja weapons filling the wall. A bookshelf houses a myriad of Turtle action figures. Greg disappears into his busy background in his unremarkable-coloured clothes. He's got a green Heineken bottle on his desk.

I'm feeling a bit left out. I should have made myself a cup of Kenya Bold to drink beforehand. I don't have any alcohol in the house. It's been outside my budget for a long time and Gran made it very clear to Johnno and me that alcohol was something for special occasions and drinking on your own is a slippery slope with a fall at the bottom. Mum and her parties were enough to put me off drinking, even without Gran's lectures. A bunch of drunk adults keeping you awake all night isn't something you forget in a hurry. I'm not sure that Johnno took either message to heart though; he quite often came home for a visit when at uni acting like he'd already had a few drinks.

Fran calls the meeting to order. "Welcome everyone to this first OA Zoom meeting. Please remember to turn off your microphones unless you are talking, to cut down on background noise."

While I have a new moment of panic looking for the microphone button, Fran continues. "We are living in interesting times, aren't we? That saying is supposedly an old Chinese proverb telling us to be careful what we wish for. I am sure no one would have wished for a pandemic! I hope you have all been managing okay in the nationwide lockdown and practising your resilience skills learned during the Canterbury earthquakes. One of the best things about living through a difficult time is that it sets you up for the next difficult time. Life's challenges make us the interesting people we have become, right?

"What I suggest for today is we first do our normal introductions then each share something. I would like everyone to share an experience from lockdown related to your obsession. After introductions I will give you ten minutes in which those who don't already have a drink can get one, those who do can enjoy it, and then everyone can return ready to share."

All the faces on my iPad screen look as apprehensive as I feel. Deliberately sharing something personal is a step beyond our previous activities. Fran should have warned us this was going to happen, although if she had warned us then we could have dreaded the session from when we received her email until this moment.

We go through our introduction process. Referring to my obsession with broken things barely causes me an internal quiver, despite my long-term reticence about vocalising anything bad. Who'd have thought that repeating something bad would make it feel less bad?

In the break I boil the burgundy kettle and prepare a very strong cup of Kenya Bold in the Temuka tea pot. I pour my tea into the remaining gold filigree cup. The pieces of the other cup are sitting in an old ice cream tub on the bench, waiting for me to glue them back together. It would be nice to have tea with Robbie in matching cups again. I carry the teapot and cup on the Indian tray back to the sitting room and realise I haven't put any thought into what I am going to say to the group, as Fran asks David to lead off.

"Hi everyone. This last month has been an interesting time indeed. Lucky for me that I live in a big house with a big garden so there are plenty of things to be getting on with, including working on my perennial border. What I got from COVID was time to do all the things I have been wanting to do and have never made time to get on with. It's made me realise I don't need or want to work any more so I am putting my Mitre 10 Sydenham store on the market as soon as we get to Level 2 and shopping takes off because people have been locked up for so long. I talked with a commercial property agent who reckons hardware stores are very desirable, so we are quietly building interest prior to the sale.

"You might be wondering how Mitre 10 is relevant to my obsession. What selling Mitre 10 will mean is removal of the temptation to buy power tools and other hardware items at discount to give to Diana."

David buys Diana power tools? Does Diana want power tools? Of course, women can have power tools; I would like power tools beyond my electric drill and driver set, although I have nowhere to store additional tools until my shed is clear of boxes. However, Diana doesn't look like a power tool sort of woman with her carefully presented hair and makeup and long artificial nails. Does David buy Diana power tools because David wants more power tools? That would change the nature of his obsession, wouldn't it? If the two of them are supposedly buying presents for each other but David is actually buying presents for himself? I await Diana's revelations with interest.

"Thanks David. Diana what would you like to tell us?"

"Hi everyone. I want to tell you I don't like power tools and I have never liked power tools. The last thing David bought me was an electric chainsaw and I am not a chainsaw type of person. Nor is our garden the sort that needs a chainsaw. Hasn't David noticed what I do and don't like over nearly four decades?

"When I buy presents for David, I put a huge amount of thought and energy into them. I think about what David likes doing and what might make an exciting present for him. It's got hard to find interesting presents because David has become boring since he bought the Mitre 10 store and turned it into a Mitre 10 Mega. There is always something more interesting to do at the store after hours than stay home with me. I've wondered whether he has another woman and is using the store as an excuse."

All the faces in the little boxes are watching intently. There's nothing like a potential affair to grab people's attention.

"And what about lockdown, Diana, how has that affected you?" directs Fran.

"I'd thought lockdown would be a chance for David and me to get closer, spend time reconnecting. We have been going to marriage counselling for the last year; that's why we are here because the counsellor suggested that working on our present-buying obsession might improve our relationship.

"Lockdown has been awful because we have been so worried about our son trapped in Colombia where people are dying in the streets. However, lockdown has helped fix my obsession with buying presents for David because I don't like him any more. I used to buy him presents because I loved him so much and I thought he would love me more if I gave him things. Now I am sick of the sight of him, spending all day, every day in the same house. I realise what a boon it was that he went to work all the time. I am terrified of what will happen when the store sells, and he is home constantly. You know, what I have realised is that I want a divorce."

There is dead silence on Zoom because everyone's microphones are turned off. However, if the microphones were turned on we would likely all be similarly silent.

Fran looks like she is swallowing a mouthful of food stuck in her oesophagus. She takes a deep breath. "Thank you for sharing Diana and David. We might have all reached our sharing threshold for the day. Why don't the two of you stay online and we can have a quick chat.

"Everyone else, thanks so much for participating and I will see you again a week from today on May fourteenth. By then, we will likely be in COVID Alert Level 2, isn't that exciting to think about? You will have plenty of time to reflect on what you'd like to share about lockdown and how it has or hasn't assisted you in resolving your obsession."

I don't envy David and Diana. It must feel like school days, being hauled into the principal's office after misbehaving in assembly.

Now, where is the leave meeting button? My eyes jump around the screen till I find it. Seeing people having a worse time than me puts my own life into a different perspective. I feel like my life is commencing an upward trajectory, after a long decline.

20

8–13 MAY 2020

I start investigating Robbie through social media and realise how little I know about it. I have a Facebook account I haven't used in a long time. It's a good thing I use the same password for every website so I can still log in. Ages ago I tried out Pinterest to collect ideas for 'Broken is Beautiful' repairs and still have that login. However, Robbie isn't likely to be looking up coffee foam decorations on Pinterest. I sign up to Instagram, Twitter and TikTok as sites in which Robbie might participate.

I discover investigating someone through social media is a slow process. There are innumerable rabbit holes I can go down on the way to the main burrow. An interesting post catches my eye and, the next thing I know, I am looking at a video of someone's friend's friend re-enacting an exotic South American dance routine seen on the vast world wide web. I could become obsessed with iPads and social media.

The iPad's larger screen is helping my social media exploration enormously; I should buy some glasses once we are in Level 2 to make reading my phone screen easier.

I find Robbie comes from a small village in the north of Scotland called Dingwall. On Facebook he is connected to a few of his schoolmates from there. Of the schoolmates that post significant information (as in, something beyond selfies in pubs with girlfriends), almost all have ended up in Aberdeen in work related to North Sea oil.

There are large numbers of pictures of Robbie in New Zealand, hiking the Te Araroa Trail with many other smiling faces giving the camera a V peace sign. These faces are balancing on rocks, standing on peaks, swimming in the ocean, walking through the bush and lounging around in backpacker living rooms drinking beer out of bottles. Te Araroa looks like it has more socialising and way more exercise than I am accustomed to.

There are numerous selfies with Robbie taken by a pretty, slim, brunette whose name is Sandy Walker, now that's an appropriate Te Araroa name. Sandy arrives at the south end of Ninety-Mile Beach in Northland, up the top of the North Island, and disappears somewhere in Canterbury in the South Island. She's American, from north of San Francisco. I head down a rabbit hole checking Sandy out and, before I know it, it's time to work on shed boxes.

Robbie and I have finished emptying the shed of boxes and organising them on the tarpaulins. My current job is to go through the unlabelled boxes, see if there is anything I recognise, label it, and put it in a box on the labelled tarpaulin. Items I don't recognise return to their original box which becomes labelled 'Unlabelled'. Robbie had a serious discussion with me about letting unlabelled and unrecognised items go. "These things are filling up your house lassie. Why keep them if you can't return them? You've got to let them go."

"Maybe. I will think about that once we reach Alert Level 2."

"What say we fix and sell them?"

"I don't think so. What if a neighbour turned up at a gate sale and found something they'd asked me to repair?"

Robbie's self-appointed role is to fix mundane items in the labelled boxes. I package them to put at the gate and send the owners a text saying their items are fixed, the cost, and to put the money in the tartan-covered cashbox masquerading as a doorstop. Robbie asks if that's risky, but I've never had a theft from it. I make sure all repaired items are carefully wiped with antibacterial gel while wearing gloves and a mask, following Siouxsie Wiles' instructions for vegetables. Apparently, COVID-19 virus has been found to stay alive for days on surfaces; little bomb-shaped COVIDs lurking on surfaces, waiting to leap up your nose and explode there.

The cash coming from Robbie's repairs means I can put some money aside to make a payment to Bank Aotearoa. I resolve to make a first interest payment when I have three months forward payment saved. I don't want to make one payment and then renege on the next. For the meantime I put the cash in the drawer of my bedside table. If there's one thing that's good about a house full of boxes, it's that burglars are going to be so distracted they are unlikely to make it as far as my bedroom.

After a bout of unlabelled item sorting, surreptitiously admiring Robbie's forearms as he unscrews and screws up the covers of kettles, toasters, and children's toys, I am randomly inspired to contact Mum. I haven't talked with her since the pandemic started. I call the yoga retreat and Kannika answers. She says Mum isn't living there at present but gives me another number to call in Takaka.

When I ring, I get Bruce, which throws me back in time to when Mum left for Golden Bay with him. Bruce sounds old and quavery. I remember my previous feelings of fury that Mum would prefer to leave with Bruce than stay with Johnno and me to find they have waned with time. Bruce says he will go find Mum, who is probably out communing with pumpkins. After a long wait Mum comes on the line.

"Julia, it's been ages, darling. How *are* you?"

Mum has always been like that. If you are immediately in her sight (or hearing) you are her favourite person. If you are out of sight, you are completely out of mind.

"Hi Mum. I'm fine, doing the lockdown thing. How's lockdown in Golden Bay?"

104

"I don't believe in this lockdown stuff Julia, it's all a conspiracy. Up here we are free people, we go where we want when we want. We aren't interested in Comrade Ardern telling us what to do or not to do."

"Well Mum, there is a global pandemic. The World Health Organization says it's a big deal and top New Zealand scientists are advising the Government on what's best."

"Top scientists, pfff. They're all in the Government's pocket; who do you think pays them? This is about *control*. It's a *Plandemic* not a pandemic. This Government's seen the opportunity to get its little sheeples standing in a line so they say we will die from a new disease if we don't behave. How many people do you know who have died from COVID? It's less deadly than a cold; we're being brainwashed to scare us into submission."

"True, Mum, not many people are dying of COVID in New Zealand right now. However, that's because our lockdown stopped the virus spreading."

"That's what the media would say if they're bought by government. How do you know what the *real* truth is? The pandemic was most likely planned to get Donald Trump out of office. At Davos in 2017, Bill Gates told the world there would be a pandemic shortly after Trump's inauguration. The hoax was being set up and Gates was in on it."

"Why would Bill Gates want a pandemic Mum? And why would he tell people about it if he was in on it?"

"A pandemic is great for Gates because he can sell more computers, make more money and spy on people at the same time! Everyone in the world has to stay home and use computers. The little camera on your computer is always watching you. There is no way I'd ever have a mobile phone; they are watching you and listening to you. Next thing is 5G which they say is for communication but is actually being used to spread COVID."

Mum has gone batshit crazy. How on earth do I carry on this

conversation, or retreat from it? Where has she found this information, given she doesn't have a computer or a phone?

"And big pharma is in on it. They and Bill Gates and the World Health Organization are all linked. Drug companies are rubbing their hands with glee at the thought of everyone needing vaccines. A whole world to vaccinate, eight billion people! Unbelievable amounts of money to be made. As for the USA, Fauci is pretending to advise Trump while hiding research that proves vaccines weaken people's immune systems and make people more vulnerable to COVID, not less."

"Right Mum. When I rang, Bruce answered the phone. Are you hanging out with him these days?"

"Well yes, poor Bruce," Mum whispers. "He's losing his mind. Some days he isn't sure what day of the week it is, and he can't find his way to the supermarket that's been in the same place in Takaka for decades. Because we go way back, I thought I could give him a helping hand. His house is close to everything in town and has a garden I have planted veges in. When Bruce gets too annoying I talk with the pumpkins to calm down."

"Bruce mentioned you were out with the pumpkins. How are you managing with supermarket shopping given older people are supposed to be staying home?"

"Julia, weren't you listening? And are you calling me old? We don't care about silly government regulations and nor do lots of people in Takaka. If I need to go to the supermarket I go. Nor am I listening to rules about not talking with neighbours. Shirleen and Ray have been such a support to Bruce since he became unwell last year. I can hardly ignore them when Ray is out mowing the lawn or Shirleen is pruning her roses. We have a regular glass of punch together on Friday afternoons to usher in the weekend. Shirleen and Ray know what's what, we have good discussions about how to get more people to vote for common sense in this year's elections. I might be ageing, but that doesn't mean I have to stay quiet."

Mum sounds militant in her older age. As far as I remember, she did more wafting around and partying than campaigning when we were young. However, Mum sounding militant won't necessarily translate into her doing anything.

"Mum, someone's come to the door, so I had better go. Lovely talking with you, we should call more often."

"Well, Julia, you know where I am, you can always call me."

This isn't strictly true, but I don't argue the point. "Bye Mum, love you."

It might be a while before I can talk with Mum again if she is spouting rubbish. Spying on someone through the internet is much easier than talking with people on the phone, so I return to my iPad investigations.

21

MY online investigation skills are blossoming, although I remain easily distracted by interesting things I find. I am also having trouble with advertisements. Exciting, colourful dancing windows pop up and make me want to click on them. The effort of will to avoid clicking makes me pause and then forget what I am doing. I find a fun game to play called 'Candy Crush'. I can while away hours on the internet; now I understand why Robbie always looks at his phone.

I have discovered three previous girlfriends of Robbie's. Sandy Walker was the most recent; she returned to California two days before New Zealand went into lockdown, as everyone scrambled to find flights out of the country. However, she and Robbie had already broken up because he completed the southern part of Te Araroa with no further pictures of Sandy. It looks like she stopped doing the trail after they split up; she flew up to Northland to spend time on beaches then met another guy called Andrew, from New York State. You can discover so much about people online. Should I google myself? Might I be surprised by what I find?

I could google Johnno too. He had a Facebook page but he never posted on it when I used to look at Facebook. It might be nice to be in touch with him more frequently again. The hurt I felt over him not returning at the time of Gran's death has waned and if I found out something more about his life I could send a meaningful text that he might engage with.

Considering googling myself and Johnno reminds me I haven't googled Robbie. I enter 'Robbie Sutherland' and a whole raft of hits pop up. I feel excited by my new searching prowess, then realise that most of the hits are Robbie Sutherlands other than mine. There's an ice hockey pro in the east of Canada, a comedian in London, a veteran of the US Air Force, a ranger in the outback of Australia and a Mormon spreading the good word in Southern Chile. Some Robbies are called 'Suds', which isn't an appealing nickname.

I refine my search, combining 'Robbie Sutherland' with 'Scotland', then with 'Dingwall'. A number of media articles appear, and I click on the first to find this time I have hit the jackpot. Robbie Sutherland is a well-known name in Dingwall because Robbie Sutherland ran over a toddler and killed her.

My breath catches in my throat. How could this Robbie, my Robbie, have done something so awful and appear to be such a nice person? The child he killed was nearly three years old with all her future in front of her. There is a double picture at the top of this article. One shows a woman pushing a child in a playground with brightly coloured frames and seats. You can imagine the delight on the child's face as she goes up, up, up in the swing and then down, down, down. The child's name was Krystal Campbell.

The second picture is of Marian and Dougal Campbell, with grim faces, taken on a grey day outside a brick-fronted row house. An empty pram sits in front of the house. This seems unrealistic given that, if your child is dead, you wouldn't keep their pram in your garden as a memento. Dougal is quoted, 'I would like the book thrown at the guy who ran Krystal over. How could he have killed our precious only daughter because he couldn't pay attention to the road?'

As I read this article and then more articles, I am glued to my iPad screen, discovering what happened nearly twenty years ago in Dingwall. Krystal's dad was at work. Krystal was down for a nap at home when

Marian's neighbour Jenny knocked on the door. Jenny asked Marian about making a cake for her son's third birthday; they had met at antenatal class. The two women walked towards Jenny's house and then Marian popped in to look at Jenny's newly redecorated kitchen, as Krystal was asleep at home.

Marian was sure she had closed her door, although a neighbour said it was swinging wide open after the accident. Marian was sure she was only out for five minutes at most, but another neighbour told a reporter she saw the two women chatting in the street at least fifteen minutes prior to the accident.

Marian and Jenny both said they heard a screech of brakes outside as they entered Jenny's kitchen and then a gathering commotion in the street. When they ran out the door, Jenny with little Tristan in her arms, they saw Robbie's curly red head bent over Krystal's still body and Robbie's car stopped askew in the road. Krystal was breathing but never regained consciousness, her head having been struck fatally hard in the collision.

Robbie's case didn't go to court because he was seventeen. Scotland doesn't have juvenile courts and deals with youth offenders in a children's panel, trying to prevent reoffending. Marian and Dougal were extremely angry, and their lawyer argued the case should be treated as homicide. However, there was no evidence Robbie was inappropriately distracted in any way. He wasn't speeding and there was no alcohol in his blood. He was simply seventeen and a moment's inattention resulted in a fatal mistake.

Robbie apologised formally to Marian and Dougal in a restorative justice meeting, where Dougal had to be restrained because he said he wanted to bash Robbie's skull in – Dougal was forthcoming with the media about his view on what happened, and the media had lapped up the information given its potential to grab attention.

Robbie's Mum supported him through the restorative justice process;

his dad was long gone. Robbie's Mum worked in Inverness to support Robbie and his brothers. Robbie was driving his brother's car to get to a weekend labouring job and bring some additional money into the household.

The children's panel decided Robbie should do one hundred hours of community service on the garden and play equipment at a local kindergarten. He also had to pay Marian and Dougal five thousand pounds reparation in instalments over two years.

Unfortunately, the stories didn't end there. Two years later, more articles were written about Robbie Sutherland who killed a child, when Robbie and Dougal Campbell came to blows at the local pub. Dougal claimed Robbie hit him first; Dougal was defending himself from a vicious attack. The police were called as the two scrapped on the pub floor, rolling around tables and stools. Robbie was charged with assault and this time it went to court. Robbie was given a deferred sentence, together with more community service and a restraining order preventing him coming within twenty metres of Dougal. The judge made it clear further infractions would incur harsher penalties.

Now I know why Robbie never talks about his hometown or mentions his youth. He has something really bad he is storing in a box and he's trying to leave that box behind.

I vacillate between being angry with Robbie and sorry for him. The thought of a small child being run over is distressing. However, thoughts of Amanda leak into my brain; Robbie's situation is not so very different from mine. I didn't directly contribute to Amanda's death, but I have never been able to eradicate the thought I could have prevented it. That thought mostly stays packaged away in the back of my skull, coming to the fore when I think of Amanda, steamrolling through my memories of her.

I imagine young Robbie found living in Dingwall too claustrophobic, given everyone knows everyone in a town of only five thousand inhabitants. Having to stay twenty metres away from Dougal could be difficult. Young people migrate out of Dingwall for work so leaving isn't unexpected. Did Robbie leave for an indeterminate length of time, waving goodbye to his Mum and siblings, then never return? He kept iterating further and further across the planet until he reached the far side where no one knew what he had done.

Could this be the opportunity I have been looking for to get to know Robbie better? We could talk about what happened to Krystal then I could tell him about Amanda? My chest tightens at this thought; it is years since I talked about Amanda. I don't talk about her with Mum, and I certainly don't talk about her with anyone else. But it could be nice to talk about Amanda to someone, someone who would understand because the same type of unfortunate accident happened to them.

How can I raise the topic? I can hardly ask, "Have you ever felt responsible for the death of a child?" If I raise anything specific with Robbie, it will be obvious I have been investigating him. Could I slide sideways into the topic by talking about a hypothetical situation of a child dying? Or mention something in the news at present? That seems like a good idea until I remember few children will be run over in the streets during a lockdown.

I need to be crafty about this conversation. However, I can't leave it too long or I will lose my nerve. I give myself the deadline of talking with Robbie before next weekend, which gives me four days to do something.

22

14 MAY 2020

IT'S Thursday, OA meeting day. More significantly, it's the first day of COVID Alert Level 2. Three days ago, Jacinda and Ashley's one o'clock national briefing discussed when and how New Zealand will shift down alert levels. Who ever thought we would listen regularly and avidly to pronouncements from the Government on a daily basis which included details of the numbers of people diagnosed that day with a specific illness. The good news was that COVID case numbers have remained under ten per day for the last three weeks. Our team of five million, as Jacinda continues to call us, has done great things and suppressed the virus.

Some days I definitively like Jacinda. I like her kind tone and approach. She sounds genuinely concerned about people and is impressive answering media questions calmly. She never puts people down or cuts them off and calls on the media personnel to speak by name. She defers to Ashley Bloomfield as Director General of Health on medical matters and never sounds pompous or grandstanding. When she has to announce bad news, she sounds genuinely upset.

On these good days it annoys me when I read social media posts denigrating 'Cindy'. I don't remember anyone calling our previous Prime Minister, John Key, 'Johnnie' when they didn't like how he was behaving. I think it's a misogynist thing, demeaning a woman by using a diminutive of her name. I can hear Gran telling people on social media not to be so unpleasant. It's a good thing Gran didn't live to see how badly people can behave online.

Other days I feel irritated by Jacinda. Her tone sounds condescending, as if she is treating the population like a bunch of schoolchildren hoping for gold stars. "Keep it up, you're all doing *so* well," she says. These messages sound like the times I participated in compulsory school running races and people clapped when I crossed the line dead last because I tripped over my shoelace at the start.

Social media doesn't make me feel like there is a team of five million. It makes me feel like there are a lot of nasty people out there with plenty of nasty things to say and a kind Prime Minister isn't doing much to keep them in line.

Does kindness from a leader rub off? I hope so, but I'm not sure. Traditionally people seek for strong leaders in hard times to make them feel secure. Lots of people say they would prefer a leader like Donald Trump rather than Jacinda. I can understand the rationale. We want COVID rule breakers put in stocks in Cathedral Square (with masks on) to be pelted with rotten eggs and tomatoes. We don't want rule breakers to have a nice chat with a pleasant policeman who suggests they could do better next time and asks them to behave better. However, international news articles say Jacinda is great and countries wish they could trade in their leaders for Jacinda with prime swap candidates being Donald Trump in the USA, Boris Johnson in the UK, and Jair Bolsonaro of Brazil.

On the eleventh of May, Jacinda happily announces today's move to COVID Alert Level 2. "This shift will give us back some of the freedoms which we New Zealanders value so highly. I want to acknowledge the sacrifices the team of five million have made over the last six and a half weeks. Now, together, we can unite to rebuild our economy."

To the average New Zealander, Alert Level 2 means people go back to work, children go back to school, we all go shopping and people can meet, but in groups of no more than ten. Our OA group can meet again. I felt myself responding to the message from the Prime Minister with excitement. I'm looking forward to seeing the OA group in person. Learning to Zoom was satisfying but I would rather see everyone face to face again.

Following the Level 2 announcement, Fran sent out an email.

Dear Barry, Greg, Julia, Matthew, and Monique,

I am happy our OA group can, once again, meet in person as we comprise fewer than 10 people. I look forward to seeing you at our next meeting on May 14th at the Sumner Surf Club.

In accordance with Government advice, everyone must sign in using the QR code I will supply. We will not have to wear masks during our meeting, but we will need to sit 1 metre apart. I also ask that you use socially distanced greetings when you arrive and depart, such as elbow bumps. To manage the closeness of interactions we will not have a refreshment break during the meeting.

As a reminder, the meeting activity will be each of you sharing a lockdown experience relevant to your obsession. I look forward to us talking together about our recent, challenging experiences and considering them as part of the path we are moving along towards resolving what troubles us.

Regards

Fran

Excellent, no snacks. It would have been my turn, but I am spared for the time being.

When I head along the Esplanade to the Surf Club, there are lots of people out enjoying the evening. They spill onto beachside tables outside cafés. People are already forgetting masks as they walk beside the sea and in the streets. Everyone is smiling and children on bikes or on foot are weaving between walkers. They sprint ahead of their parents without immediately being called to return. The sea sends small, calm waves onto the sand

By the time I reach the Surf Club, the sun has disappeared behind Clifton Hill and there is an autumn chill in the air, but there's warmth in the atmosphere.

I walk towards the Surf Club building with excitement in my steps. Then I slow down again. We are supposed to be sharing something about our lockdown experience relevant to our obsession. I haven't put any thought into what I will say. Initially I was too wrapped up in my investigations of Robbie. Then I became infected with Level 2 euphoria and forgot Fran's instructions.

I realise that Coffee Culture will be reopening for sit-down business so Robbie might already be back there. He didn't mention them offering him work, but he could have forgotten to tell me. I feel disappointed. Robbie won't be home as often and our routine of morning teas, box sorting and repair will be broken. I have become accustomed to a lodger who climbs in and out of his window using a stepladder, cooks me a birthday cake and makes good tea. To tell the truth, I have become more than accustomed. I am growing fond of Robbie, and I am starting to hope he is growing as fond of me.

I must focus and come up with something to say this evening. I need something personal, but not too personal. I am not going to talk about Amanda because I want to share Amanda with Robbie first. I can talk about the sense of calm and routine and forward progress Robbie and I have achieved in our box sorting. I can talk about the increased income and how I am putting it aside to soon start making repayments to Bank Aotearoa.

I enter the Surf Club after scanning the QR code on the door with my phone. Everyone else is already seated one metre apart on the colourful seats, talking rapidly. This meeting feels like reunions after the Canterbury earthquakes, when everyone told stories of what happened to them 'on the day'. Earthquake reunions could easily take an hour or more, with each party sequentially telling their story and the other parties concentratedly listening. The earthquake experience meant multiple iterations of reunions, after each major earthquake and with each different person.

Could this be the same for COVID? Is this the first of multiple reunions, each one after a lockdown caused by another outbreak of virus? Multiple lockdowns are not a happy thought. I feel a twinge of foreknowledge that Level 2 euphoria may be fleeting and the future is not a straightforward step down the COVID alert level tiers to a permanent state of Level 1.

Monique and Matthew are deep in conversation, having shuffled their chairs to be less than one metre apart. I catch fragments of their conversation.

"I had my kids home from Otago University for lockdown. It was lovely to have them both home; they don't usually come back for holidays together.

"I was seeing patients remotely from home most of the time, but I was rostered on at the medical centre two days a week. I was worried about infecting the kids with COVID after seeing patients, so I would first go into the house via the laundry, put all my clothes in the wash and then have a shower before I saw them. They weren't worried, but that's young people for you."

I imagined stylish Monique as an interior design consultant, not a medical professional. Is she a nurse? Or a doctor? Did having her children home deter Monique from chewing her walls?

"I got through the whole *Homeland* series on Netflix, and then I went onto *Tiger King*," says Matthew. "Have you watched those yet? That Joe

Exotic guy who bred tigers is quite the dude and has some nice tats. But I didn't spend the whole time sitting on my rear end, I repainted the inside of my house; did you see my red feature wall on the Zoom call? Good thing I already had the paint from last year's Resene sale. The hardest part was rehanging my big TV by myself. I love watching sports on my big screen."

Matthew doesn't mention a job, is he unemployed? I feel a slight sense of superiority over someone who spent a lot of lockdown watching TV.

On my other side I can hear Barry and Greg. "I lost my coaching job," Barry says. His demeanour is deflated, although his body doesn't appear to have reduced in size. "I coach salespeople and I love seeing them up their game. But I specialised in travel and COVID's killed the travel industry. All the people I coached are out of jobs and I am too. I don't see much of a future, when will travel happen again? I've applied for several jobs but people don't want older workers. At fifty-eight I've got lots of experience but I haven't heard back from a single application. Before travel I worked in alcohol sales, so I rang some places I used to sell to. I got a not-so-subtle brushoff – they told me sales are a youth and energy market.

"I earn the money in our house; I don't know what to do. The missus does a great job with our kids, running them to all their activities. Our oldest has her licence but she is still on a restricted so she can't take the other two or drive at night. I don't want the missus working. Children need their Mum at home when they get back from school. And she only ever did low-paid admin. I don't know how we'll manage our mortgage once the payment holiday is over. We borrowed for a big extension when the earthquake repairs were done and put in a pool and a spa so we could relax together as a family. Ha, don't know what I was thinking there. The kids would rather be round at their mates' houses than hanging out with us oldies."

"Shit mate, that sounds tough. My wife's an essential worker, at the supermarket, so I stayed home with Ruby. She's six. Normally I don't see much of her because she's in an after-school programme.

"I design stainless steel dairy equipment for an engineering company. They were great about me caring for Ruby during the day and working in the evenings. This working from home thing turned out alright. Our design team did heaps of work during lockdown."

Fran is sitting opposite me in the chair circle, too far away for me to easily start a conversation. As I turn towards her she gets everyone's attention and suggests we start the meeting. She's not very open while she wants us all to share personal things. I get that it's her role, but I would prefer she acted more like one of us than some sort of superior being. But that's hardly the case, she has an obsession too.

23

WE do our round of introductions, and, without explanation, Fran says that David and Diana won't be returning. My imagination has to fill the gaps and it supplies images of David and Diana dividing up their possessions in a divorce. Diana is piling power tools she never wanted on David's side of the line. What did she buy him? I conjure up platinum cufflinks, a wood-fired BBQ and fifty-year-old whisky, which David is happy to keep. Diana feels freer as David's piles grow and her side of the house becomes more spartan. Am I envious?

During the first part of the meeting, we all look surreptitiously at everyone else's hair. It's day one of Level 2 – who made it a priority to get a haircut? Social media has been full of memes regarding the impact of lockdowns on hair. My hair is normally tidy, given I am practiced at cutting it.

Monique looks like her perfectly attired self with no sign of grey roots or split ends in the loose bun on top of her head.

Matthew's head is shaved, showing off his skull tattoos. There is a large 'Tesla' emblazoned on the back of his head with a car driving around the maze created by the letters.

Barry's hair is a mess of wild greying curls sticking out in a halo. For someone in his fifties, Barry has a lot of hair. Pride in his thick locks may be why he hasn't resorted to a number two comb.

Greg's hair could also be tidier. It is touching his collar and has grown down over his ears, where it would normally be shaped above them.

Fran's curls remain at chin length. Either Fran has a partner who is good at hairdressing, or she booked an appointment this morning.

Fran asks Barry to start off. Barry sighs. "I could be better. I lost my job, and it was hard spending a lot of time in the house with the missus and teenagers. The missus is great with the kids but they act like I annoy them, and they sure annoy me. My daughter lolls around on the couch watching videos on her phone. The boys don't even come out of their rooms. If I open the door they ignore me and keep playing games with headphones. When I suggest they do their schoolwork or help their Mum with the dishes they just laugh at me.

"The missus suggested I could help cook meals but I don't know anything about cooking. Then she got cross and told me, seeing as I was so much more interested in cats, maybe I should live outside with them. She's the reason I'm here, you see. She wants me to get over my cat thing. She says I spend too much time thinking about cats and not enough time with my kids or with her.

"So, lockdown wasn't great because the easiest thing to do was get out of the house and feed the cats. At least they looked happy to see me. I feed the cats at our house with auto feeders that make it hard for me to get at the cat food. However, my main focus in Red Zone Cats is fund-raising. I had lots of clients who like cats and donated. Liz, the other half of Red Zone Cats, did the cat feeding in the city. But Liz has emphysema; she's a smoker. She's scared of getting sick with COVID-19 because her lungs are compromised. So she's staying home and I have to do all the feeding.

"I borrowed my daughter's bicycle and carried the food in a pack. God, my butt hurt. The worst thing was finding toilets – public toilets are all locked because of COVID. I know cat food is hard on my guts, but how can I resist it when I am always putting it on plates?"

"Why are you feeding homeless cats so long after the earthquakes? Haven't they mostly died by now?" asks Matthew.

"Some are abandoned pets, but many are the kittens of those cats." Barry sounds more comfortable talking about cats than himself. "'Red Zone Cats' feeds cats in places no one is living any more. We try to catch kittens and get them adopted out so there aren't more cats out there. For some reason, people love to adopt the Christchurch Cathedral kittens, born in the heap of stone rubble that remains. They are not nearly so keen on Bromley cats from near the sewage works."

Fran thanks Barry for sharing his experiences with us. She doesn't make suggestions about how he can improve his situation and none of the rest of us proffer anything helpful either. Barry slumps back in his chair.

Greg is the next person round the circle.

"What would you like to tell us about Greg?"

There's a pause. Greg must be thinking about something else entirely.

"Sorry, sorry guys. Away with the fairies there. Like I was saying to Barry, I was happy to stay home in lockdown with my daughter Ruby because my wife had to work. I don't know how much use I was with her schoolwork, but it was fun playing together. I got to see her school Zooms. Small children in Zoom classes are crazy. They spend most of their time pulling silly faces. Barry might have some handy suggestions for the teachers seeing as he practises herding cats!

"I dunno how great I am at looking after a child though. When I needed to have a meeting I kept her quiet with the iPad. My wife isn't impressed that now Ruby wants to go on the iPad every day and says I should have been stricter. I did get Ruby riding her bike though. I bribed her with babyccinos at the café. My wife's not so happy about her café habit either."

"It's nice to hear about Ruby, Greg, but what about the obsession you are here to resolve?" Fran prompts, as Greg evades the issue.

"My obsession, yes, sorry about that, forgot. Teenage Mutant Ninja

Turtles. I have been thinking about Turtles a lot, because Ruby is close to James' age when he died. James was my brother. He was twelve years younger than me and sometimes I felt like I was as much his parent as his brother. I remember being so excited when James was born, and Mum and Dad let me hold him for the first time. I helped feed him with a bottle and, when he cried in the night, I was often the first to hear him. I'd pick him up and walk back and forth with him close to my chest till he dropped off to sleep.

"James wasn't quick to talk but I always understood what he said. We developed a common language no one else knew. He would ask for a drink of 'wit' which was 'white' and meant 'milk'. James would run out to see me when I came home from school and bring me his toy of the day for us to play with.

"I found James his first Teenage Mutant Ninja Turtle. Donatello was lying on the side of the road. He was missing an arm but the Turtles are supposed to be mutant and James didn't know how many arms Donatello started off with. He called the Turtle 'Dello' and demanded to sleep with him. We acquired cast-off Turtle stuff as other children got bored with Turtles. James never got sick of Turtles. He would only wear his Turtle clothes, which included Turtle gumboots. When people knocked on the door, he would rush up to them yelling, "Urtle donner!" which meant "Turtles fight with honour!"

Everyone is watching Greg intently. This is the most he has said in any meeting, and no one is going to interrupt the flow.

"We covered James' bedroom walls with Turtle posters, and he got a Turtle bedspread for his fourth Christmas. James said I must be a Turtle because I was a teenager. I was Raphael and he was Donatello, and we would practise conquering the world.

"James got sick on a Friday. Mum and Dad were out at a movie. He didn't eat dinner and said his head hurt but he didn't seem particularly ill. I put him to bed under his Turtle bedspread. The next morning he didn't want to get up or eat. Mum took him to the emergency doctor, and I went along to keep James company. We waited hours and hours because Saturday is sports day and kids kept coming in with broken bones to be fixed.

"By the time we saw the doctor James had vomited up everything in his stomach. We thought maybe he'd eaten something that didn't agree with him, and the doctor said that was likely. He gave us rehydration solution and said if James got worse we should bring him back, but hopefully he'd be on the mend soon.

"When we got home, I went to get James up out of his car seat but he was floppy and wouldn't wake up. Mum drove back to the hospital like a crazy person, I thought we would all die on the way.

"A different doctor came and examined James then rushed him away. He never woke up again and I never got to say goodbye. I held onto Donatello all the time we were at the hospital, believing James would come back to grab him from me. I was going to put Donatello in James' coffin but at the last minute I couldn't bear to. Donatello felt like the final part of James I could keep hold of.

"When I left home, Mum and Dad let me take all James' Turtle things and, since then, I have bought more. Buying Turtles temporarily papers over the hole in my heart that even Ruby hasn't filled. I put a shed on our property to be a Turtle home because Claire complained Turtles were taking over the house. Ruby wants to go into the Turtle home, but I explain to her it's Daddy's place where he goes to be quiet and remember his brother.

"Sorry, sorry. I have rambled on. That's enough from me."

Fran says hesitantly, "And your obsession?"

"Yes, sorry, forgot that too. How has the pandemic affected my obsession? I wish it had done something, better or worse. All I feel is stuck in the same old place."

"Thank you for telling us about James, Greg," says Fran. "Our session should end soon, but I would like everyone to have a chance to speak tonight. How do you all feel about keeping going? We could have a quick stretch of our legs outside and return to hear from Julia, Monique, and Matthew. I have checked no one else has booked this room."

We all nod assent and put our masks on to go outside, at which point we speedily remove them. However, there is a subdued air and lack of conversation. Fran rounds us up after five minutes and we head back inside to continue.

24

FRAN turns to me, "Julia, we are looking forward to hearing about your lockdown experiences."

I provide the group with a potted account of how Robbie and I have been sorting boxes and he has helped with repairs. I speak neutrally about Robbie; I don't want the group to imagine something that is not yet happening. I see Monique looking interested at my mention of Robbie. No doubt she met him at Coffee Culture and may hope to add him to her retinue of useful and attractive men.

Matthew starts off by recounting his painting efforts, detailing the colours he used in different rooms. Fran looks meaningfully at him until he remembers that he is supposed to be telling us about lockdown and his tattooing obsession.

Matthew looks edgy, then admits, "I slipped during lockdown. I did a small tattoo on myself." We all look expectant until Matthew feels bound to tell us more. "It's 'Resene'. There was a space on the side of my foot."

We look interestedly at his foot until he pulls his Allbirds shoe off to show us. We visibly wince in unison at the idea of not only getting a tattoo on the side of your foot but doing it yourself.

The group still looks like they are waiting for more of Matthew's revelations. He steels himself. "I can see what you are all thinking. Why did I tattoo 'Resene' on my foot? Correct?" he blurts aggressively. "Why did I get 'Tesla' tattooed on my head and 'Breville' on my bicep?"

"I grew up in a foster family where money was always tight. I had to wear the same shoes to school three years in a row till I cut the ends off to stop my toes curling up. We'd have instant noodles or a packet of biscuits for dinner because that was all the food in the house.

"There were six of us kids, two foster children and four birth children. I don't know why my foster parents wanted more children when they couldn't look after their own kids properly. And I don't know why the Government thought it was okay to leave us three to a bedroom in a house with a leaking roof in winter and mould creeping up the windows and splotching out over the walls. Food, toys, the seat closest to the fire, the six of us fought over everything. We became excellent scrappers. I was in the middle, so I learned to fight hard and dirty.

"I got my first tat on a dare when I was nine. We were all bored and hungry on a rainy Saturday afternoon. Mark, the oldest, had seen other kids tattooing themselves. We stuck a needle in the pencil eraser from our school stationery so we could hold it. We got ink out of a ballpoint pen. Mark dared me to do the first tattoo. All I managed was a set of dots in an approximate circle. But I did it and the others wimped out. The tattoo was on my hand, but you can't see it any more." Matthew holds out his hand where the Nike swoosh in black on red across the back covers skin and any other ink.

We all wince again, thinking of how much sticking a needle in the back of your hand might hurt.

"I got the Nike tattoo after I bought my first pair of Nike sneakers with money I earned at the car mechanic's down the road. My foster parents wanted the money, but I hid some in a hole in a tree. Once I'd saved up for the Nikes, I wanted to record that I wore fashion items, not just Postie Plus t-shirts and scuffed shoes from the two dollar second-hand clothing store. The pain of the tattoo was so satisfying. It was like I bottled up the pain of not owning shoes, or anything I wanted, and then experienced it all at once like a bolt of lightning searing the image into my skin. Then I wanted more tattoos."

Our circle quietly observes Matthew with his armour of tattoos in which we can read the sequence of his acquisitions. There's nothing like wearing your pain on the outside.

"Thanks Matthew," Fran says after a suitable pause. "Now, Monique, what would you like to tell us."

"I was busy during lockdown," says Monique. "My children came home and I'm a GP. Our practice encouraged people to get telehealth consultations, but we had to take turns going into the surgery. Some days I spent hours wearing masks and gloves and other days I spent hours on Zoom. Thankfully, I didn't get a COVID-positive patient, or I would've had to self-isolate at home for two weeks. That would have been difficult with the kids there as it's a compact place.

"The worst thing was everyone's stress levels. So many people with mental health issues. At least there's been no flu and few colds. When everyone stays home they don't get nearly so sick! But people don't keep so mentally healthy on their own for days on end or in their family groups."

"And how about your health?" quizzed Fran. Monique, like Matthew and Greg, is not being forthcoming about her obsession.

"My issues with plasterboard weren't helped by being home. We relined the clinic with ply after the earthquakes, so I don't have any temptations there, but more time at home is hard. Home is where my problem started, years ago when I was pregnant with my son. I found myself looking at my daughter's chalk set, and the chalks looked so good, particularly the red one. I tried sucking on the end of it. It tasted great; I couldn't stop. When I was stressed I would suck on a chalk and feel much calmer; I couldn't see it was doing me harm, so I kept using chalk when I needed it.

"My problem got a lot worse after the Canterbury earthquakes. All the walls in my house were cracked, bits were falling on the floor, and I wasn't sleeping through the night. The kids were stressed, and I was a solo parent. When I was woken up by one of those thumping earthquakes, I would grab a fragment of plasterboard off the floor and suck on it. It became the only way I calmed down."

"It was a tough time, wasn't it," says Fran. "So stressful and tiring for everyone in the city."

"Yes, the lack of sleep was terrible, and I needed my plasterboard more and more. I thought about lining the house with ply during my earthquake repairs to make life easier. Fleecer had already suggested extra painting, inside and out, so the whole place would look tidy. When the costing came back it was sixty thousand dollars. Crazy amount. So I forgot the ply. I thought I could stop eating the plasterboard if I just focused but stopping hasn't turned out to be easy. Every time I try to quit eating plasterboard something stressful happens and I go back. I know I have a problem, that's why I referred myself here."

"And the pandemic?" Fran prompts again.

"The pandemic has brought back all those bad earthquake memories and now I can't cope with all my patients wanting to see me because we are back at work in Level 2. I no longer care about the holes I've made in the walls. I'm just exhausted. And the worst thing is my kids don't want to come home again. I had been good at hiding my problem from them up till now. They are too embarrassed to bring their friends round and say they would rather stay with their dad. That upsets me so much; the kids were my life when they were little. Their dad had major issues so they mostly lived with me. I can't bear the thought they don't want to come home."

Monique is another victim of Fleecers' upselling. I could feel some kinship with her if I wasn't unreasonably irritated by how she and Matthew have been thick as thieves from the start of OA. How can a doctor have a weird eating disorder and not do anything about it? Can

129

doctors be blind to their own problems, like accountants who can't manage their own budgets?

"Thanks Monique, it sounds like you are having a tough time." says Fran. "Now, let's say our karakia to close."

I surprise myself by blurting out, "Hang on, Fran, *you* haven't told us how you have been coping with lockdown and how it relates to your obsession."

The rest of the room chimes in swiftly. "Yes, your turn, we would like to hear from you."

Fran draws a deep breath. Has she not thought she ought to disclose too? This reminds me of my early misgivings as to whether someone with an obsession for helping others is running OA groups to satisfy their needs, rather than resolve them. In the face of the whole room's request, she can hardly say no.

"Okay," Fran says. "Best I tell you about me then."

25

"I'VE always enjoyed living life through my interactions with others. I like hearing people's stories. I left school early and trained as a hairdresser as a profession there's always a need for and one in which you get to talk to lots of different people. I wanted to be a different type of hairdresser, not a woman who blathers away while cutting your hair and you are looking in the mirror trying to read her lips because she is talking at machine-gun pace about people you don't know. I thought there could be a niche for a hairdresser who listens to people properly, hears what they have to say, and gives a little boost to their day through the perfect haircut together with feeling someone understands them.

"It turned out I was right. I always had more clients than I could fit into the working week. My clients would always want to stop for a chat if I saw them in the street. It was so easy to get clients that I left the salon I worked at and set up as an independent roving hairdresser providing a great service in people's homes, charging less than the salon, and making more money. My business was on a roll until it was interrupted by needing to care for my niece."

Fran looks around the circle and we look back encouragingly. It's great to start to hear something of her story.

"Holly was three when I took her on, she's fifteen now. Holly has foetal alcohol syndrome, so life is always going to be a challenge for her. My sister Ali never wanted a child. When she discovered she was pregnant she kept on drinking and smoking and partying like there was no tomorrow and she wasn't pregnant.

"After Holly was born, Ali didn't change, moving from one abusive boyfriend to another in a sequence of squalid flats and drug-fuelled nights. By the time Holly should have been learning to talk and walk, it was clear something wasn't right, and Ali wasn't coping with her.

"Shortly before Holly's third birthday, I found sufficient strength to apply for information regarding my own birth and adoption circumstances. I always knew I was adopted at eighteen months into a family that desperately wanted children. I asked Mum about my birth mother. Mum said my birth mother was a sad young person she met at work. She needed to go back to her family, but without a baby. Mum never told me anything more, no matter how much I asked over the years.

"Then Dad died suddenly of a heart attack and Mum changed her mind. I wonder if, for all that time, Mum wanted to tell me, but Dad told her not to. Dad was a private person and maybe he believed everyone else wanted things kept private too. Anyhow, Mum gave me my birth mother's name and I started looking for her. Mum also told me I was a ward of the state before she and Dad finally adopted me; I could apply to the government for information as well."

Fran's story sounds so sad. We are all hunched on the edge of our seats focusing on her face.

"I applied to the Ministry for Social Development for my records, then forgot about it for the year it took till my papers turned up in the mail. There was no phone call, no support. I got a large envelope in the mail full of photocopied pages with chunks of blacked-out text.

"I started reading one evening and kept on going till I had finished. My phone buzzed to remind me that I was due to cut someone's hair in the far west of the city in half an hour. I realised it was mid-morning and I'd read through the entire night. I could barely keep my eyes open to drive to Halswell. I have no idea what I said to the woman whose hair I was cutting, nor what state her hair was in by the time I finished. Afterwards, I parked a couple of blocks away and fell fast asleep in the car.

"It turned out my birth mother was much worse than a sad person. She didn't want me and she didn't care for me. My records show I was in state care multiple times. I was hospitalised with cigarette burns and head injuries. I struggled to deal with that reality when I found out about it and I struggle to deal with it today, many counselling sessions later. How could my mother hate me so much that she abused me or allowed someone else to abuse me? In my head, I want my adoptive mother to grab me and run away with me before it happens. Did Mum know what was going on if she knew my birth mother?

"When I learned about my early years, I knew I had to change Holly's future for the better. I couldn't sit by and watch my sister destroy her child's life. I would like to rescue all the young children out there who are being harmed, but I can't have them all in my house, so I started with Holly. Holly will always have challenges because her brain doesn't work like it should and her bones haven't grown properly. But I'm making sure she has the best life she possibly can. I have taught Holly how to cut hair – she cuts my hair beautifully – and she goes to a special school for children with disabilities, which she loves.

"In the school holidays Holly occasionally sees Ali when Ali isn't on a bender or swallowed up in her newest relationship. Mostly it's day visits because when Holly goes overnight, she returns aggressive and unhappy. I keep trying, hoping one day Ali will grow up, take some responsibility, and even want to know the person Holly is becoming.

"Looking after one person doesn't sound like an obsession but that's because one person is where I started. When I saw how much better Holly was getting, I thought I could do more. I tried fostering children, but when a ten-year-old boy punched Holly in the head, I realised I couldn't have people in the house who were a risk to her, so I looked for other ways to help. The need to feel I am helping was expanding and taking me over.

"I decided to train as a schoolteacher so I could help more children. It was tough, going to university after not having completed the last year of high school. I studied part-time because I still had to earn money and care for Holly. Those years felt never ending, there was always something more urgent to do than the thing I was doing, as I rushed between clients and classes and Holly. I would study after Holly went to bed and again early in the morning. But I got there. I finished my degree and was employed by Ferndale School as a teacher in their Linwood High School satellite programme. I love my work with the children; it is so satisfying to see them grow and thrive when education is tailored to their needs."

We are starting to shift on our seats. Fran is as bad as everyone else. She's immersed in telling her story, but she isn't telling us about lockdown, like she asked.

"I know, I need to talk about lockdown. Since I started working with children, I've kept expanding my training to help them better. Part of my job has been running peer support groups for older children, helping the children learn to help each other, as well as get help from adults. I identified this need and no one at the school had any experience. I found an online diploma course in peer support training which I am partway through.

"I have been struggling with meeting my bills because I'm still paying back my student loans. My diploma course includes news about work opportunities, and I saw the contract for providing this OA course. I didn't think I'd get it, seeing I haven't completed my diploma. But I did. I'm doing my best to provide the support you all need, but I have to admit I'm still learning about running support groups."

This explains why Fran sometimes appears out of her depth, as if she is making things up as she goes along. She *is* making things up. Finding out Fran is not a complete professional is more heartening than disturbing. We are all muddling along, and Fran now seems like one of us.

"As for lockdown, it has been close to heartbreaking. I want to do my best for my students and you but Zoom just isn't good enough when people are in trouble or find it hard to communicate. Some students don't even have access to the internet. Many of my students have been locked down in homes that are difficult, unsupportive and, at worst, dangerous. For them, school is an escape from their home lives in which they can expand their horizons.

"Holly didn't like lockdown because she likes school and her friends there. She got as sick of me as I became of her. There were days when I wondered how I could possibly juggle another eight hours of calls with students while entertaining and educating Holly. My students have gone backwards in their behaviour so the next few weeks will be just as hard, getting them used to the classroom again. All I can do is continue to support them and hope there won't be any more lockdowns.

"If anything, I feel more compelled to help other people because lockdowns have shown how many people are struggling. Parents have lost jobs. Older kids are quitting school to stack supermarket shelves. People are desperate and some take their desperation out on their kids."

Fran stops and gathers herself. "Let's say I was a happy obsessive until COVID came along, but now I see a hole opening up in society no one can fill. However, that's enough about me for the time being. We should say our karakia and head out to enjoy the rest of this first evening of freedom."

We join in the karakia which we now know by heart. Then we put our masks on to soberly file out the door, some of the Level 2 zing gone from our steps under the weight of the shared revelations. Even Monique and Matthew are keeping a degree of separation, but I'm sure that won't last.

26

THAT was a tough session. We all have such sad stories. Are there people out there with simple, happy stories? Quite possibly, but they don't need to go to a support group.

I wander home, getting my head in order. I am preparing myself to tell Robbie about Amanda. I feel strengthened by the past weeks and my sensation of coping well at OA. I can contribute something about myself and am interested in hearing the stories of others. I feel like a different person from the woman who got a letter from Bank Aotearoa requiring her to attend a support group to help manage her mortgage. I feel different from the woman who entered the COVID-19 lockdowns at risk of becoming a mad cat lady if she had been offered a few cats to look after. It's a good thing I didn't encounter Barry or the Red Zone Catters in prior years – I might have been tempted. Could I get a cat? If Robbie were around a cat could be a shared responsibility and shared pleasure.

I deviate from my Esplanade route and pass Coffee Culture, in case Robbie has been asked to take a shift there. The mood in Sumner remains joyous with people still talking to each other in the street. I consider buying a bottle of wine to take home; we could have a celebration of the first day out of lockdown. I even have enough money in my pinafore pocket from the repairs Robbie has been doing. But what wine would I buy? How much would an okay wine cost? I have absolutely no idea which wine might be good, it's been so long since I bought any. I prefer white to red, but that's about my limit. My dilemma is sorted by the Supervalue being closed.

I ponder on whether singledom can be inherited. I have never had a long-term partner as I didn't want anyone living in Gran's house. Mum never had anyone long term I remember, nor did Gran. Gran was in her early thirties when Mum was born in 1948. Mum was born shortly after Gran got married to Donald, who was a bartender in Sumner.

Gran kept a single wedding photo of her and Donald. Donald is wearing a dark suit with a tie and Gran a white wedding dress with a wide skirt. I wonder where the photo is now. Gran always referred to 'Donald', not 'my husband'. He died when Mum was three and she remembers nothing about him. He collapsed while at work and never regained consciousness. He had severe bruising from a beer keg rolling over his leg that week so he might have had a fatal blood clot, although he also hit his head on the bar on the way down which was listed as the cause of death. As far as we could tell from Gran's terse statements, Donald was well known to partake of more than a few drops while serving bar patrons, to the point where he was starting brawls in the tavern rather than preventing them. No one in Sumner would have been sorry about his death. His drinking might be part of the reason Gran thought alcohol was best avoided.

It's dark by the time I reach home and there are no lights on. That's a shame, I was looking forward to talking with Robbie. I thought I could tell him about the OA meeting revelations as a segue into revealing more about myself. If I told him about Amanda, Robbie might take my hand and say, "How sad for you, tell me more". I could tell Robbie about Amanda's brief life, bringing it back to the forefront of my brain.

Once I've told him about Amanda, Robbie might open up and tell me about what happened in Dingwall. We could compare our feelings about how a moment of inattention can change the course of many people's lives.

I head to the kitchen to make a cup of tea in the Temuka teapot. I will use the gold filigree teacup because Robbie isn't here. I put my teacup and teapot on the inlaid Indian tray. Will I have it inside or take it outside? It is dark but there is no wind, and the garden is peaceful at night. I don't bother switching any lights on. Negotiating the house is much easier since Robbie started to move inside boxes to the outside box sorting station, so the stacks are much reduced in size. The day for unlocking Amanda's door is getting closer.

I open the sitting room door and step out into the garden. That's when I see them. Robbie and Rosemary of the iPad. They are seated on my mosaic sofa; two sets of bright red curls close together. They aren't just sitting; they are kissing on my sofa.

Fury boils through my veins. How dare Robbie bring someone else into my space? Someone he is interested in who he never mentioned to me. Did he already know Rosemary when he suggested repairing the iPad? Did they have a laugh about it?

I didn't care about that iPad, says the Rosemary in my mind. I thought I could help Julia by giving her something to repair I didn't need. She did do a lovely job on my cup, but iPads are not the same as cups.

You know what, I did the same, the Robbie in my mind replies. I gave her my pack and three cables to repair. I don't have much stuff so it was hard to find anything that could credibly need a repair. Lucky I didn't need my things because she hasn't even started repairing them. I will fix my own cables and take the pack. Isn't it funny, she wanted to use your iPad so badly she pretended to forget who owned it.

She's pathetic, isn't she? Gosh, I hope I'm not like that when I'm – how old is Julia? Fifty?

No way, you will never be like that. Julia's drifted through life without getting a qualification and now she's drifting without direction. She's not focused enough to even do things she is capable of. She must thank her lucky stars her Gran gave her a house to live in or she'd be destitute on the street. Though the house isn't up to much, is it? Badly needs a paint on the outside and full of boxes on the inside. You know I can't get in the door of my room? I have to climb in through the window using a step ladder. Every time I worry a neighbour will see me and think I am a burglar.

The conversation in my head infuriates me. How dare they talk about me this way? I'm not fifty, I am only forty-nine. Have I drifted directionless through life? I thought I was doing well to be earning a living and caring for my grandmother in my early twenties when people I went to school with were mostly holidaying overseas or having fun at university. How dare they feel pity for me and call me pathetic?

I carefully put down the tray. I am not sacrificing another teacup at the altar of Robbie. I stride forward, tripping over a box I can't see in the dark and almost landing on top of the pair. "How dare you? This is my garden and my sofa. Who invited you in?"

Rosemary looks startled and starts to apologise but I talk right over her.

"You're a doctor, right? You care about people? You know what this guy you're kissing did? He ran over a little girl called Krystal who was only three years old. He wasn't paying attention and ran her over in the street. Then he only had to do some community service for it. Can you believe that, if you kill a little girl, all you have to do is clean murals off walls? And that wasn't all. He beat up the child's father when he met him at a pub. Is that why you ran to the other side of the world, Robbie? To get away from the terrible thing you did?"

Rosemary looks upset and Robbie furious.

"You've been spying on me behind my back? Why didn't you ask me about my side of the story? You're one to talk about hiding things.

You've a bedroom full of children's clothes and toys but you have never mentioned them! So, what's going on there? Huh? What about your fetish with stuff in boxes and under all your furniture? I'm not going to stay in this hovel one minute longer. Rosemary, you grab my bike and I'll get my surfboard."

I watch mutely as Robbie and Rosemary exit the garden with his toys in tow. Then I hear thumping sounds as Robbie climbs in the window of his room to retrieve the rest of his gear. Finally, I hear their footsteps and voices fade away down the street.

27

JUNE 2020–25 FEBRUARY 2021

MONTHS pass in which I care about so little that time passes both painfully slowly and so unremarkably I can barely remember that the months have happened. If I allow myself to surface from my fog of not caring, I revisit the knowledge that I deliberately destroyed the only good thing that had happened to me in more than eight years. I don't want to know this, so I sink back into not caring.

There is the odd punctuation in my not-caring oblivion. In August, toilet paper, hand sanitiser and pasta sauce disappear off supermarket shelves, so I check the headlines to find Auckland is in Alert Level 3 again and the rest of the country in Level 2, ratcheting up from the Level 1 we achieved in June.

In September, when everyone stops wearing masks, I deduce we are back in Level 1 in time for the New Zealand parliamentary elections.

In the October election Jacinda Ardern and her Labour Government return to power in a landslide win. I don't vote because I am in a particularly not-caring mood on the day of the election. A single vote doesn't make a difference, so why bother? I hear Gran telling me voting is an essential duty for every adult citizen to be part of a functioning democracy, but I ignore her.

The only other occurrence of note is Bank Aotearoa offering to extend my loan repayment holiday until the end of March 2021. Another six months in which I have to care about very little indeed. Sounds good to me.

The money I had saved to start making my repayments is turning out to be handy, but not for the bank. I only go shopping when I absolutely must, but, when necessary, I open my bedside drawer and take a note out of my reserves.

I summon up the effort to email Bank Aotearoa to request a further repayment holiday extension, which is granted. A letter attached to the offer reiterates I must keep attending my support group.

OA is indeed all I keep doing, beyond the basics required to survive. Most OA days the same sort of refrain plays in my head … I have to get out of bed and go to the OA meeting … I don't have to get out of bed and go to the OA meeting … I don't want to get out of bed and go to the OA meeting … I have to attend all but two meetings of the OA group to meet Bank Aotearoa's conditions … I could not attend this particular OA meeting … I don't want to have to explain at the next meeting why I didn't attend today's meeting. Going to OA always falls out of the mix as the lesser of a variety of evils so I attend the meetings.

On Thursdays therefore, I reluctantly shed my brown check flannel pyjamas which also form my daywear. When it's cold I wear a red synthetic dressing gown over my pyjamas at home. Why get out of my nightwear if I am not going to leave the house before having to put it back on again? If I have to get out of my PJs, my not-caring self puts on a dull blue pinafore with olive green crocs. It's one of the worst coloured pinafores I ever sewed and wearing crocs out of the house is another mark of not caring. If it's cold I put on a heavy black duffel coat bought at the 'Time and Time Again' second-hand clothes shop in Sumner. It is several sizes too big, and I like the way I disappear inside it. I might be disappearing more every week; it feels like the coat is getting bigger. Perhaps I can disappear entirely.

If Alan-next-door calls out as I go past, I ignore him. He likely wants to spout conspiracy theories at me and, even if he doesn't, there isn't anything I want to say to him. He corners me on one occasion when I am unobservant. "Where's that red-haired guy who broke lockdown rules? Did you hear Bill Gates secretly met our traitor of a Prime Minister? Gates was here organising trials of an unproven COVID vaccine on innocentful New Zealanders to microchip and track us."

Would a microchip fit in a vaccine needle, and would it hurt when it went in? If someone tracked me they would get pretty bored given my most exciting trips are to the supermarket. I nod vaguely in Alan's direction and proceed down Head Street as his expletives about Cindy fade into the distance.

Every so often when I'm out I think there's someone with red curls pedalling past and my heart pounds. I snap my head in an automatic reflex but the person cycling has never been Robbie. Every time this happens, I castigate myself for being more pathetic than before. Why would I want Robbie to come back? Why would I imagine Robbie might return? He isn't interested in me, only in Rosemary and using me and my house during lockdown.

In contrast to the blue skies and the still, warm weather of lockdown, the remainder of the year is typified by grey skies and cold north-easterly winds. Spring bulbs breaking the ground do not excite me. I just feel annoyed because chickweed, dock and grass are overtaking the garden and I can't be bothered doing anything about them.

Christmas and New Year are signalled by red and green decorations in the shops and sickly songs on the radio. The removal of the decorations tells me we have moved from 2020 into 2021. If you don't have family or friends to get together with, neither festivity is of much import. I have no sense this New Year signals anything better than the last year.

Pumpkins, potatoes, and beans grow unattended in Gran's garden, trailing over the tarpaulins covering piles of sorted boxes. I wonder if the boxes are getting wet, but I don't wonder very much. I got as far as taking a priority set of boxes into the hallway to queue for repair of which I have emptied a small number, fixing their contents to pay for essentials.

However, not everyone is collecting their goods, which isn't surprising given the time gap between when they dropped their items off and when I repaired them. The lack of income is starting to weigh on my mind as my bedside drawer is emptying and eating isn't optional. I consider the benefit again and reject it just as firmly as before. I wouldn't know how to do someone else's job; all I know how to do is my own work.

I also know what Gran would tell me. "None of my family have *ever* relied on the government for handouts until *you*," she spat at my mother when Mum came around to collect us and complained about how difficult her life was. "I don't know how you live with yourself, sponging off the state and never trying to get a job."

"I have two children to look after, I don't have time to get a job."

"No time, my arse. You barely look after these children, they are at my house half the week or more, not that I don't want you to be with me, my loves. Caroline, you need to take a good hard look at yourself and at your wastrel boyfriends."

I never forgot Gran's disgust and internally vowed I would never ask the government for help. I wish Gran had influenced me as strongly about taking out a loan. How could I have been so stupid as to take a mortgage out on her house? March and the end of my loan holiday are getting closer, however much I try to forget that time is moving on.

The OA group continues to meet weekly with full attendance; are we all feeling like it is actually offering some support in these difficult times? We are comfortable with one another, which means it is a surprise to go to a meeting in late February and see a new face. It's awkward to know where to sit, we have become so accustomed to sitting in the same chairs in the same order.

I am sure Matthew and Monique are a couple now. They sit down and stand up at the same time, finish each other's sentences and sit on Fran's left. Barry and Greg appear to be getting on well, as if they are getting to know each other outside of OA meetings. They sit on Fran's right. I sit in the middle of the two pairs, feeling the odd one out. Fran tries to engage with me but mostly I drop my eyes and pretend not to hear her. She keeps asking me if I am eating enough. I'm not, but I don't want to talk about that with her.

The new woman sits down next to me, in the extra chair Fran has introduced to our circle. Fran is on a purple chair, Barry and Greg on orange chairs, Matthew and Monique green chairs and the new woman and I are on yellow chairs.

"We have a new member joining our group today, let's all welcome Lynda," says Fran.

"Hello Lynda."

We go around our introductions and Lynda says, "Hi, I'm Lynda and I am obsessed with dolls."

Fran asks Lynda if she can tell us something about how she is coping with the vicissitudes of COVID and how that is related to her obsession.

"This is throwing you in the deep end Lynda, because everyone else attended several sessions before providing an in-depth introduction. However, I hope you were primed by your introductory emails

"This is our one-year anniversary, which means two things. First, I have brought extra snacks. Second, I want us to take an active step up in our approach to dealing with our obsessions. I've some new ideas from my course. Nothing to worry about and I will explain more at the next meeting.

"Lynda, to give you a few minutes to think, we will have our food and drink break first and then come back in ten minutes."

That's worrying. Are we going to have to do something more meaningful in the coming year than turn up regularly and drink tea and provide relatively superficial commentary on our mental states? The best thing about OA is our sense of camaraderie, having weathered the COVID year together, without any requirement for deeper connections.

Fran has gradually encouraged us to become more verbally

introspective about how we have got to our current state of obsession and how we might back away from the state we have reached, without requiring us to expose too much to the group. Thank goodness we haven't had to explain too much because I feel like a miserable failure given my brief period of progress when sorting boxes with Robbie ended with his departure.

I head over to get my tea and snack. The snacks are good because they relieve me from thinking about dinner on Thursdays, except the Thursdays when it's my turn to bring snacks. I haven't been interested in cooking or eating and skipping meals reduces my budgetary strain. This week it's Matthew's turn and he has brought vegan, gluten-free brownies with faces drawn on each segment in white icing. The brownie shapes range from normal smiley round faces to demonic grins with large incisors. First I choose a demonic brownie then, while no one is looking, I slip two more brownies into my pocket for later.

Fran has brought a special treat – vegan chocolate mousse in flowered cup-cake holders. I eat one with the almost-good lime tea because it won't survive my pocket.

Fran corners me when I'm not looking. I would have sidestepped to the toilet if I had seen her coming. "How have you been Julia? I'm glad to see you eating something. You've been looking a bit drawn. What do you think of the chocolate mousse? It's made with cashews and dairy-free chocolate."

I am not sure whether I would rather have cashews in mousse, or on their own. Nuts are a treat far beyond anything my budget might stretch to. "I'm fine, nothing out of the ordinary going on."

"I'm hoping you and Lynda will find you have something in common to talk about. It's going to be challenging for her, coming into an already formed group."

"Yes, maybe we will." Or maybe we won't, and I have no intention of making any particular effort to find out.

28

WE return from our snacks and drinks to our circle.

"Lynda, we are looking forward to learning something more about you." Fran says. "Please tell us whatever you are comfortable sharing."

"Hi everyone." Lynda is a ball of energy. Her brunette hair is cut pixie style around her pointed face which radiates intensity. She's wearing skin-tight jeggings, baseball boots and a cropped top showing off her toned midriff. Lynda could be a challenge for the attention of the men that Monique will feel the obligation to take up. Lynda's feet tap on the floor while she is talking to us, as if they want to get up and run away.

"Like I already said, I collect too many dolls." Fran dips her head and Lynda rephrases. "I am obsessed with collecting dolls. My house is full of dolls, full to the point of bursting. I only collect second-hand dolls. When I see a doll that no one loves I feel sad. I need to take it home to join my doll family. I don't need to buy new dolls. New dolls all end up going to homes like SPCA kittens. Everyone wants a kitten and no one wants a used cat.

"What has the last year been like? Frustrating and boring! I go overseas on holiday a lot. That's not happening. I like to go to challenging places. I like not being able to speak the language or recognise the food. I want to visit a country starting with every letter of the alphabet. I was so close to finishing, only Qatar and Yemen to go.

"Yemen is a dangerous country. But I was working on it. I refuse to go on tours. Who wants to see what everyone else sees? Who wants to travel with people you might not like? My friend was doing UNICEF humanitarian work in Yemen and said he could get me in. But now he's back, because of COVID, so that chance is gone. Who knows when travel will be possible again."

"Your travel sounds interesting," says Fran. "But what about your life here? How has COVID affected you?"

"I'm a textile conservator at Canterbury Museum. During lockdown I wrote stories about garments as the basis for future displays. It was interesting, calling up the original owners to talk about their ancestors, and researching Canterbury history. But what I really love are the clothes themselves. I keep our huge collection of old clothing safe in special rooms, away from light and fabric-eating bugs.

"With shipping disruptions, I can't get the supplies I need to store textiles. I ordered garment boxes in May, and they didn't turn up. When I spoke to the supplier in June they apologised and ordered a new set. When those didn't turn up by October I rang again. They re-ordered them. The week before Christmas, all three lots of boxes turned up. It's lucky the Museum is a rabbit warren of seven different buildings jammed together with funny little connector tunnels into which you can shove boxes.

"The worst thing about lockdowns were the rules to stay near home. I run marathons and running is how I destress. When we went into lockdown my running was going great. I was building up to a mountain marathon near Queenstown called Mt Difficulty. Good name, huh? I tried to keep training because I thought COVID couldn't last long; how could my running hurt anyone? If I hurt myself, I was determined I'd drag myself home without help if I had to sit on my bottom the whole way."

"Some of the Government rules haven't made a lot of sense, have they," Fran says.

"The rules made running stressful if I saw people. I had a couple of people shove me with their walking poles. I was tempted to see what they'd do if I stuck my pole out in a fencing stance. Of course, I never actually did that. I just ran off the trail into the tussocks.

"It's been bad, people being frightened and cross with other people. I don't like how people are telling each other off. I don't like the Government telling us what to do. Are all our COVID rules necessary? Did we need lockdown or was it an overreaction? Could we have acted like Sweden where the Government encouraged people to socially distance but kept schools, cafés, and workplaces open? Swedes can travel overseas, and people can visit Sweden. This has all got to end sometime. We can't stay isolated in New Zealand forever."

Fran starts to look edgy, COVID-19 discussions are not something the group engages in collectively during sessions, we keep them for conversations in little groups. She brings Lynda to a close. "Thank you, Lynda, it has been great hearing about your interesting and varied life. Thanks everyone, for attending, and let's say our karakia before leaving. Lynda, the words are in the email I sent you yesterday."

Session concluded I slide out of the room. Lynda has opened a small window in my not-caring state. Her pre-COVID life sounds a lot more interesting than mine. Where does all her energy come from? And why is she expending energy on dolls? Collecting dolls is a strange obsession for an adult. I was always proud of not being a doll girl. Dolls were something girls were supposed to like but sitting around pretending an inanimate object was real didn't seem interesting to me. I preferred constructing and repairing things and roaming around Sumner with Johnno.

Lynda's doll obsession takes away from her general air of competence, but she might be interesting to talk to. Should I have stayed longer after the session to engage? It doesn't matter, there's always next week.

29

4 MARCH 2021

ANOTHER week rolls around which feels both long and short in my life of little action. It isn't only my lack of action that makes time distort. The procession of COVID with lockdowns, slowdowns and multiple disruptions has turned time into a strange rubber band that stretches and contracts at will. It's hard to remember when things happened and whether they were last year, or this year. The only hard edge to hold onto is the big lockdown of 2020.

It's Thursday morning – is it my turn for OA snacks tonight? I have followed on from Matthew for the last year, in our reverse alphabetical order. Fran didn't say anything to Lynda in the meeting about snacks. However, when I look in my cupboard, I don't see much that I can turn into delicious vegan snacks. I don't want to fail in any way at OA because my loan holiday is about to end, making my ownership of Gran's house feel tenuous.

I go out to the garden to seek inspiration. I still flinch slightly when I look at the mosaic bench and remember Robbie and Rosemary. I prefer to sit on my log rather than the bench. I spot a bright orange pumpkin hanging off the fence. Hurray for garden inspiration, I can make pumpkin pie. Gran used to make pumpkin pie, which was odd because it's an American tradition. No one else I knew ate pumpkin pie. Probably Gran was looking for ways to use her produce and her pumpkins were always prolific. I pull out my – Rosemary's – iPad to find a recipe and check whether I have pumpkin pie ingredients.

Vegan, gluten-free pumpkin pie is going to be trickier than I thought but I now have a goal in mind, and I am going to achieve it. I have thirty dollars in my wallet from a recently completed toaster, kettle, and extension cord repair. I will see how far I can stretch my funds.

The baking process turns out to take the entire day. I walk to Sumner Supervalue, but they don't stock vegan butter, essential for vegan pie crust. I walk back home and get on my bike to cycle seven kilometres to Ferrymead Countdown. When I return I make pie crust and go to bake it but find my gas bottle has run out. Then I hitch my trailer to my bike and cycle back to Ferrymead Mitre 10 to swap the empty bottle for a full one.

After my second trip to Ferrymead I feel like a rest. However, I have acquired more determination in the process of shopping than I have felt in some time, so I persevere. I make two muffin trays of mini pumpkin pies and decorate them with little pumpkins cut out of vegan pastry; Gran would have been proud of me. I haven't been feeling she would be proud of me for a while because Gran loved her house and her garden. She would not be proud of me running out of energy and letting it slide to rack and ruin.

I put my feelings and memories of Gran back in a box before I lose momentum. I head to OA group with my mini pumpkin pies carefully nestled in a box in my arms. We have returned to beautiful autumn weather like lockdown last year and the sun reflects on the blue sea with surfers carving graceful turns in the waves.

I am early to OA, having been more concerned with getting the pumpkin pies there safely than my normal practice of minimising exposure to other people by arriving with thirty seconds to spare. Matthew and Monique are deep in conversation. Barry, Fran, and Lynda are still to arrive, so I go and chat with Greg after putting my pies on a plate.

Chatting with Greg turns out to be easy because Greg launches into a monologue. Greg must have been building up a head of steam on this matter which he is keen to release. He's normally retiring and apologetic but today it's a different Greg who would get on well with Alan-next-door.

"I can't believe the behaviour of the sheeples. Everyone believing the government exists for the good of the people. Ha. Politicians are in it for the limelight and the salaries. You should read what the Plan B academics from University of Auckland have to say – they don't think the Government is right. Too many people believe that pink-haired Wiles woman and the Baker guy with round glasses from the University of Otago. Why aren't the Plan B people getting more media attention? Because they aren't toeing the Government line?"

Greg's vehemence is frightening. "What do you think is going on?"

"I don't think, I *know* the New Zealand medical system appears confident when it doesn't have a clue. Look at what happened to James. That doctor pretended he knew what he was on about and James died. All that supposed knowledge, but he couldn't save a child. Now doctors are telling us to get excited about new vaccines that are coming. What do they know about the vaccines? Did you know the vaccine we will get is a new type never trialled on humans?"

"Not trialled in humans? Why would they give it to us?" I don't like the sound of this.

"The vaccine will tell your cells to make chemicals *in your body*. Programme cells to do things they wouldn't normally. That's like cancer with cells going rogue and doing their own thing until the rogue cells kill you. Testing of vaccines has been rushed – normally it takes years. This vaccine has been developed in a few months and now we are supposed to be a bunch of placid human guinea pigs."

I don't know much about medicine. I have been lucky enough to rarely get sick. My main exposure to the New Zealand health system was when

I was pregnant with Amanda and when she was a baby. That was a long time ago now and all those memories live in closed boxes in my brain.

I haven't thought much about COVID vaccination either. Vaccines sound fine if they end the pandemic and return life to something like it used to be. However, my life hasn't been so different from normal during the pandemic therefore I haven't been very concerned. Maybe I should be more concerned, but once there was no COVID in New Zealand after lockdown, why would I worry about it? Anyhow, it's mostly old people who die of COVID. I will be fifty in April and that's hardly old.

Gran told us she had made sure we got our vaccinations because Mum wasn't responsible about such things. Gran believed in vaccines because she lived through the New Zealand polio epidemics. She told the polio vaccine story in a way that made Johnno and me listen. She was nine years old during the 1924 polio epidemic. Most of the people who got sick were children and Gran remembered being scared she would catch polio. Adults had whispered conversations in which they wished sick children would die, rather than surviving as cripples who couldn't fend for themselves. Very sick children were put in iron lungs which breathed for them. Living in a metal tube didn't sound comfortable. How did they go to the toilet?

If anyone in a family got sick, the whole family were shut in their house, so they didn't spread disease. In 1936, when Gran was a young woman, Dunedin was isolated from the rest of New Zealand because they had a polio outbreak. Then there was a three-year epidemic in the late 1940s while Mum was a baby. If Mum had got polio, Gran and Donald would have had to isolate at home for weeks and wouldn't have been able to earn any income.

Gran said there were all sorts of theories as to why people got polio. She was told to stay off the beach, wear a sunhat and not run around a lot because people thought the virus could be lurking in the sand or you might get sick from too much sun or too much activity.

In 1956 New Zealand started administering polio vaccines and Gran wanted Mum to get one. When Sumner Primary School sent a consent card home, Gran signed Mum up right away. By the time we were born, a set of vaccines was available for babies which Gran took us to get. I have always assumed vaccines are good things and you should get vaccinated, like you should drink milk because it is good for your bones. Is it possible vaccines can also be bad for you?

"Greg, are there times vaccines have been harmful?"

"Absolutely, vaccines have hurt huge numbers of people. Early polio vaccines were bad. Hundreds of thousands of children in the United States were given live polio vaccine and tens of thousands of them got sick. The measles-mumps-rubella vaccine caused autism. A doctor in Britain found the link after noticing autism was becoming more common. That vaccine was supposedly well tested. If a tested vaccine can give you autism, would you risk putting something into your body that has barely been tested?"

I don't like the idea of trying out a vaccine that hasn't been well tested and where we don't know the long-term effects. I don't want to get COVID, but I also don't want a vaccine that will make me ill.

At this point Fran and Lynda come into the Surf Club. Lynda is wearing a colourful mask with a tūī embroidered on the side. How the world has changed that I see a mask as pretty. She is also carrying a platter of snacks. The snacks are little pies with pumpkin decorations on top.

I feel stupid. Why didn't I ask Fran who was supposed to be bringing snacks today? What a loser. I can't even get snack making right. Now not only have I brought snacks on the same day as Lynda, but I have brought the same snacks as Lynda. As I think this, Lynda heads over to the bench and exclaims loudly, "Who else thought it was a great idea to make pumpkin pies?"

"Me," I say in barely more than a whisper.

Lynda comes over to where I'm sitting with Greg. "I knew we were going to be friends from last meeting. This proves it. Great minds think alike, right?"

"Looks like you two have something in common," says Fran from behind us. "That's excellent, because I want everyone to pair up for homework between our upcoming sessions and I thought you could join forces."

I look at the evening sun reflecting off the sea and feel a glimmer of a new kind of hope. Perhaps I could get on well with a doll-obsessed bundle of hyperactivity who also likes making pumpkin pies.

30

"YOUR homework for the week will be to talk in pairs and each identify at least one concrete step you can take towards being in control of your obsession. The pairings will be Julia and Lynda, Greg and Barry, and Matthew and Monique." As Fran is explaining this, Barry comes in late and apologises. Fran smiles briefly at him. "No problem, Barry. You can all communicate electronically or in person, whatever suits you best. What I would like for next week is for you each to identify a step you are comfortable sharing and on which you can continue to report.

"Because we are going to do more between sessions, I am going to reduce the frequency of our meetings to fortnightly. I hope you are all okay with that?" Everyone nods in general agreement. I feel a slight, surprising, pang. As the only constant activity in my life, I could miss OA.

After the karakia, Lynda and I go outside, sit on a bench along from the Surf Club, and discuss what we will do. We see Matthew and Monique wandering down the beach holding hands. That's one sort of success for Fran – the OA sessions have created a couple who would not likely have met otherwise.

Greg and Barry have a brief chat outside the Surf Club door then drive off. Greg has a practical white Toyota station wagon that looks appropriate for taking a family on trips. Barry has a stylish and impractical black Audi two-door coupe. He lost his job, didn't he? Why is he still driving such an expensive car? Does Barry's missus drive a family car which fits his teenage children?

As Barry pulls out of the parking lot I catch a glimpse of someone in the passenger seat of his coupe. At this distance the person looks like Fran. Would Barry be giving her a ride home? But if Barry was giving Fran a ride, why didn't they arrive together?

I watch the coupe depart round the corner, bracketed on one side by fifty-metre cliffs and on the other by the sea leading towards the estuary mouth. A memory flits through my brain of when that corner was barricaded with piles of containers. Following the February 2011 earthquake there was a van abandoned for days in the road with a large rock sitting in the passenger seat. The driver must have got the fright of his life when the rock smashed through the windscreen and landed on the seat.

During the aftershocks, the cliffs remained unstable with rocks rolling down intermittently. After the June earthquake, a container wall was built to protect cars and walkers. The containers were a mix of unattractive blues, reds, and greys with company logos – Maersk, P&O, Royal Wolf. At the time, people were too scared to come out to Sumner because of possible rock fall and the cafés were struggling. A local art gallery owner and a graphic designer got together to inspire artworks on canvases stretched over the containers. They paired artists with sponsors to turn an eyesore into an asset that people came specifically to view.

My favourite artwork was a huge blanket of knitted and crocheted squares in every colour of the rainbow. People from all over the globe sent squares in and a local woman sewed them into 'Container Love'. Today the art is gone, replaced by a huge wall of protective rocks covered with ngaio trees bursting out in all directions.

Lynda is talking to me, and I have been wrapped up in earthquake memories in an impolite way. "Sorry, what were you were saying? I was in a complete daydream about Sumner after the earthquakes. Were you in Christchurch then?"

It turns out Lynda was in Christchurch, and we have one of the earthquake conversations that will typify the 'getting to know you' phase of Christchurch people's relationships, until we are all doddering on walking sticks in nursing homes and yelling into one another's faces because we forgot to put our hearing aids in. Unless we are all locked in our rooms because of a pandemic.

"Yes, I was in Christchurch and a conservator at the Museum. In September nothing much happened to my house. A few cracks. February was a different story. I was on a run in my lunch break in the Botanical Gardens behind the Museum. Trees swayed, the ground shook and I fell over. I could hear car sirens going off and see clouds of dust opposite the Museum.

"When the shaking stopped I got up off the grass. I didn't think about going back into the Museum. Too many things to fall on you. I had my phone and bank cards in my pocket. My bike was behind the Museum in a shed. I planned to head home. Later I realised I hadn't once thought about other Museum staff. My brain can't have been working properly.

"I headed south towards the hospital. The old Arts Centre buildings on the other side of the road had dropped big pieces of stone on the footpath. Ambulance sirens started to wail. I thought I should try to help, so I turned east towards the city centre. The roads had rips in the tarmac and I fell off and bashed my knee. I didn't see the deep gouge till much later. When I reached Cashel Street Mall it looked like a disaster. Piles of bricks everywhere. Shop awnings collapsed on the pavement. People wandering around looking dazed.

"There were people lying on the ground. People were pulling at rubble, looking for survivors. Dust filled the air, pools of water from burst pipes ran between the rubble and people were screaming. I didn't know if the screaming people were on the street or under the buildings."

Lynda is pacing back and forth, like she is back in Cashel Street Mall.

"I joined a team of people pulling rubble off a pile beside Whitcoulls. An elderly woman was talking frantically. Her husband had gone into Whitcoulls to get a pen. He always lost his pens and then needed another one. Why couldn't he be more careful? She kept her pens in her handbag. She had owned the same pens for years. She was supposed to meet him in front of Whitcoulls when he finished shopping. She had gone into Ballantynes to look at dinnerware. Had he bought the pen and gone into Ballantynes looking for her? She wasn't in Ballantynes long.

"I don't know what happened to her, or him. At some stage her voice went away. I left the rubble when we uncovered an arm and half a head. It was clear the arm's owner was dead. My hands were bleeding from grasping stone. I could no longer see any point scrabbling at bricks to find dead people. I cycled home to Cashmere past streams of people walking. Women in bare feet carrying high heels. School children in uniforms. Where were their parents?

"There was no one at home to worry about me other than Freddy the cat. But cats don't worry. However, I started worrying about Freddy when I remembered him. He was a fluffy ginger cat with one eye. I got Freddy from the SPCA with my neighbour. She looked after him when I was overseas. I tried texting my neighbour to ask about Freddy. Cell phones weren't working.

"When I got home, I walked around the garden calling for Freddy. He didn't come. It took him a week to turn up. From outside I could see my floor piled with dolls and books and pictures and food. Bricks from my house cladding had fallen out.

"My neighbour was worse off. Her brick house had completely collapsed walls. She came home early evening, sat in her car looking at her misshapen home, then drove away without talking to me. I heard from other neighbours she went to stay with family in Nelson. She never returned.

"It was late evening when I finally went inside. I cleared a path to my bed by pushing everything towards the walls. I slept fitfully between whumping aftershocks.

"When I got up I gave myself a good talking to. I dug a pit toilet in the garden because the water wasn't working. At least there was no neighbour to watch me use my toilet."

"But that's enough about my earthquake experiences. I think because COVID times are so strange I keep reliving the weird earthquake times. What happened to you in the earthquakes?"

"Why don't we talk about my earthquakes another time? My house was okay enough. A mess like everyone else's but the outside wasn't too bad because it's weatherboard." There's no way I'm bringing Amanda up in a conversation with a woman I barely know, even if I think we could be friends. "What about our homework? Where shall we meet? I don't have a car, so it needs to be cycling distance from Sumner."

"No problem. Let's cycle to a mid-point. How about UpShot Café? It's by the Heathcote Valley Riding School. Meet there Sunday afternoon? I go for a long run early on Sunday mornings. By lunch I'm starving. I can support their business by eating two lunches."

"Sure," I say. Then I realise I have little money remaining because I spent my week's earnings on mini pumpkin pies, the remainder of which I have left together with the container in the Sumner Surf Club. My bedside drawer is almost empty. Can I rustle up some income between now and the weekend? I don't have much choice. "See you Sunday."

31

7 MARCH 2021

IN anticipation of Sunday, I feel more energetic than at any time since Robbie left. In two days, I complete ten jobs from the top of my recent queue. A trickle of repair work has been arriving in response to my trickle of repairs performed. The repair work turns up on my doorstep, sometimes with a note, sometimes just an item in a box with a name and phone number. It is interesting how COVID times are making what would previously have seemed odd, commonplace. Social distancing is the norm so there's nothing strange about socially distanced repair work. It has been hard to get new things because of broken supply chains so people are ever more interested in getting what they own fixed.

Luckily some clients are prompt with pickups, so I have a small amount of cash in my pinafore pocket when I cycle to UpShot. Once through Sumner, I head along the rock barrier past the Clifton cliffs. I go past Shag Pile, a sea stack previously known as 'Shag Rock' because of the perching birds who make it their home. Its name was changed after the earthquakes reduced it to a sorry heap.

I cycle through Moncks Bay towards Redcliffs, where ostentatious mansions are being developed along the estuary-front sections trashed by liquefaction. How quickly human memory fades and desire overcomes common sense. Those sections are still prone to liquefaction and sea level rise, as the land is only a metre above the high tide. I can already hear residents howling for compensation when floods start to enter their houses.

I pass the closed New World supermarket in Redcliffs which was another casualty of the earthquakes and is now a white elephant monstrosity in the centre of the village. The New World was a bustling supermarket prior to the earthquakes, with densely packed shelves containing everything I needed in a compact footprint easy to get around. However, the earthquakes destroyed the building and the insurance and rebuild took four years. By the time it was reconstructed, much larger and grander than before, everyone was used to shopping elsewhere and didn't return. I tried it out but didn't go back either, as it didn't stock Kenya Bold and the prices were high. The store limped on for six more years, raising prices and driving away customers, before finally shutting its doors. Now it is an ugly, multicoloured reminder of how your world can change in ways you can't predict.

As I cross the estuary causeway the tide is going out and the current is strong, with smelly sea lettuce swirling in the water. On the far side of the estuary, the sand dunes of Southshore Spit define the estuary mouth. Southshore was even worse off than Redcliffs after the earthquakes when liquefaction and land subsidence took broken houses below sea level. No doubt there are a few of Barry's Red Zone cats there.

On I go, to the wide Heathcote Bridge where I turn left to skirt round the base of the Port Hills on Bridle Path Road. The bridge leapt in the air during the February earthquake and was left so damaged it was only accessible to cyclists and walkers. The road was pitted with liquefaction holes; for several weeks there was a two-metre-deep hole with a car and a tour bus on their noses with their ends standing proud.

Bridle Path Road feels like a mini oasis because it has farmland on the river side and leafy sections rising up the hill opposite.

I reach UpShot and see Lynda already there, sitting outside. Most of UpShot's seating is outside. The café shifted to the riding school after their city location collapsed in the earthquakes; they thought it was a temporary move. However, temporary has now lasted a decade and the outdoor setting is entirely suitable to COVID times, when we don't want to be exposed to germs spread by people.

Lynda and I are dressed very differently. I have my dull blue pinafore on, which I am now regretting. Couldn't I have made more of an effort rather than picking the same old dress up off the floor? At least I checked it didn't have food stains on it.

Lynda is clad head to toe in Lycra and looks as fit and strong as her marathon running would indicate. She is wearing wrap-around sunglasses with an iridescent lens reminiscent of a beetle carapace and the strange shoes worn by road cyclists which clack when they walk and look extremely uncomfortable.

"Can I get you a coffee?" asks Lynda. I struggle between pride and poverty.

"That would be lovely. I'll buy next time." I am already hoping there will be a next time, despite the ensuing drain on my underpopulated dress pocket.

"What'd you like?"

"A latte with oat milk, thanks."

"Oat milk, isn't it the best? The flavour goes perfectly with the coffee taste. I don't know about veganism though, it seems contrived. I think it's nuts, ha, to have Christmas nut roast instead of turkey roast. If we are going to have food it should stand on its own two feet, or own two stalks. Food shouldn't pretend to be something else. Would you like anything to eat with your coffee?"

I consider my pocket contents and the cost of buying three lunches next time around, given Lynda said she normally ate double lunch after her long run. "A piece of quiche? Whatever looks good to you."

Lynda heads to the café counter to order our drinks and food and I feel warm from the sun and conversation. Have I missed talking with other people? I have almost forgotten how it's done; I don't count my prickly discussions with Alan-next-door as conversations. When was the last time I had coffee with someone who could be a friend? It must have been with Robbie at Coffee Culture a year ago.

Lynda returns with a number in a wire stand. I consider the possibilities of making attractive number holders and selling them to cafés as a point of interest. I could do themed holders; would there be sufficient china horses in second-hand shops to supply UpShot with a set of holders? I feel my creative brain returning from its long holiday.

"Right, Julia, we need to talk. We need to know each other better. Then we can figure what to do about our obsessions."

I shrink back into my protective carapace. I am not accustomed to people being so direct.

"I live in Sumner, in a house Gran left to me. It has a beautiful red front door, although the rest of the outside could do with a paint."

"C'mon Julia, you can do better than that." Lynda smiles encouragingly. "I told you all about my dolls at the meeting, so you can tell me how you ended up at OA."

A dam starts to crumble inside my head. Not all the way, there's a lot of dam structure still to go, but my story starts to seep out. I tell Lynda about my repair business and my house and how my repair business resulted in my having a lot of broken things and then how the earthquake upset me so that broken things started taking over my house, and taking over my life, to the point where I am now submerged beneath the broken things and would like to find a route to the surface.

What I don't tell Lynda – not yet – is anything about Robbie or Amanda. Amanda is still mine. There is a glimmering possibility of talking about her in the future. Robbie … the Robbie story is too embarrassing to tell anyone. I would like to construct a version of the Robbie story in which he betrays my trust by moving out without bothering to tell me he is leaving. "What ingratitude!" I can say energetically. "I found him on a bench on the Esplanade, invited him home, let him stay in my house without paying rent and then he repays me by moving out without a thank you." However, my internal Gran sternly says, "Don't kid yourself my darling. You know the truth."

Our coffees and food come and Lynda eats an unbelievable amount of lunch for someone so petite, enjoying her eggs benedict and blueberry pancakes. I eat my quiche and side salad slowly, drawing out the experience, as my mouth waters at the thought of pancakes with maple syrup. Why didn't I order that? Lynda offers me a taste, but I decline, thinking one mouthful might make me want more. Next time perhaps I could order an extra breakfast too. I haven't been eating enough for a long time, but I am remembering I like food.

A couple of hours have passed, and we have discussed many things about houses becoming full of belongings and how the belongings squeeze you out of your own space without you knowing it is happening. We circle around the topic of our forward steps. Then Lynda says, "Isn't it obvious? We need to be each other's clutter buddy!"

"What's a clutter buddy?"

"It's someone who helps you declutter. For sure neither of us need help increasing clutter! We take turns. You come to my house and help me with decluttering, then I come to your house. We figure out together how to control our things, rather than our things controlling us."

"That sounds like a good approach." It could be nice to have someone visit my house. I could even repair the broken gold filigree teacup so we could share a cup of Kenya Bold in matching cups. I need some time to prepare. "Shall I come to your place first?"

"It's a date. Oh, but what date?"

"Two weeks? Let's not rush things."

"The twenty-first then. See you at OA week after next."

"Looking forward to it."

32

18 MARCH 2021

TEN days later, I am eagerly anticipating our OA meeting. I feel like Lynda and I are becoming a team, warding off my ongoing irritation about the Matthew and Monique team. I am looking forward to the next OA meeting so much I think more broadly about what I should be doing and decide to call my mother. Is it the better part of a year since I talked with her, yet again? I fear it is. Not that Mum has called me, but the blue moon hasn't risen, nor a pig flown by.

I call the last number I had for Mum, and she answers immediately.

"Hi, Mum, thought it was time I gave you a call."

"Julia, darling, how are you? I can't remember when we last talked."

"I'm okay, not much new in my life. Still mending things to earn money, still enjoying living in Sumner. What have you been up to?"

"I stay home mostly because Bruce isn't doing so well. He's having problems eating, forgets his food and stares at the wall. I found a lovely plate with Noah's ark animals on it at the Hospice Shop. The nurse said a bright plate would help catch his attention. I don't know how much difference it's made but he does like the animals, particularly the elephants. He will eat some food to uncover the elephants.

"Cooking was never my strong point when you were kids but I am getting much better so I can feed Bruce well. I prefer to feed him produce straight from the garden because that's the healthiest way to eat. We've been eating lots of pumpkins and courgettes."

I feel for Bruce. Mum was indeed not much of a cook, and I can imagine her deciding fresh food is best then cooking meal after meal with just pumpkin and courgette. Does she mix the vegetables together or cook them separately? I remember dreadful meals with multiple vegetables boiled in a single pot until their flavours combined and their colours departed with the water.

"How's your health been Mum?"

"Well, to tell the truth, I had a little trip to the hospital. Shirleen and Ray were so helpful. They came in to see Bruce every day and made sure he got his supplements and his meals. They all watched TV together in the evenings. They weren't great on toileting and cleaning; he was a bit messy when I got back. But mustn't complain, it's lovely to have such willing neighbours."

Mum is not only cooking but is helping Bruce with toileting? I find this hard to picture. Caregiving wasn't Mum's forte in our youth, or even a second-string ability.

"Why'd you go to hospital, Mum?"

"Oh, the odd bout of breathlessness and the dizzies, you know. Sometimes I'm in the garden talking to the pumpkins then next thing I'm lying down with the pumpkins. I haven't felt very ill so didn't want to bother anyone. And I wouldn't have bothered anyone if Shirleen hadn't looked over the fence and wondered why I was flat on my back in the vegetables. First thing I remember, ambulance staff were leaning over me. Then they whipped me onto a stretcher and into the ambulance before I could protest. I was only in the medical centre for a night then they sent me home with a prescription. I can't be very ill."

"What did they say was the problem?"

"Just something about the heart not pumping properly. What would you expect? I'm eighty-one, all my bits aren't going to be working as well as they once were, are they? It isn't like I need to run long distances or outspring sabre tooth tigers. I'll be fine."

"Does the medicine help you feel better?"

"Pfff. I wouldn't know about that. I'm not going to take medicine from doctors. I have my supplements from Sharon at Wildflower and Shirleen makes me a nice herbal tea with liquorice when we get together, to have after our punch. Her tea puts me right to sleep. I like to keep my body natural; Brucey and I have gone vegan. No eating poor little animals for us. Bruce used to grumble about missing sausages. But as his memory's deteriorated he's forgotten about sausages. If he does ask for meat I offer him coconut ice cream and he forgets again. He can eat huge amounts of coconut ice cream. It's pricey but I like to keep old Brucey happy."

Old Brucey?! Mum is reinventing herself before my eyes, or at least my ears. Old age is having far more effect on her than she knows if it has turned her into a caregiver who cooks, cleans, and keeps someone happy by feeding them ice cream. The child in me is yelling it would have liked more ice cream and home cooking. However, I am in such a good mood that I settle the child down and keep listening to Mum.

"Julia, I do hope you won't be getting vaccinated. You know how dangerous vaccinations are, right? The Government is telling us when we should have vaccinations, but they aren't properly explaining *why* we should have vaccinations. They aren't telling us half the story. It's lucky there are other sources to draw on. Have you read the 'Real News'? Sharon printed it out for me. It is full of great articles, like one pointing out how ridiculous masks are. Do you know how tiny a virus is? So teeny tiny you need a huge microscope to see one. Why would a virus have any difficulty getting through a mask? And masks get all sorts of nasty diseases living in them. Your mask can make you sick."

"Gosh, I hadn't thought about how small viruses are. That's interesting Mum."

"You know these new vaccines, like the Pfizer one New Zealand is getting? They don't work. In Chile, people are getting vaccinated *and* infection rates are increasing. How could that happen if vaccines worked? But it's worse than vaccines not working. *The Real News* says it's likely Pfizer is *killing* people. They get blood clots, brain inflammation, heart attacks. In Germany, a quarter of the residents in a rest home died after getting Pfizer jabs."

"A quarter, really?"

"*And* it's not just about the vaccine hurting you straight away. The vaccine can get into your brain. Who knows what it might do there. Likely lots of people will start getting sick soon and our Government will pretend they have no idea why. The vaccine could be messing with unborn babies, but the Government wants pregnant women to get vaccinated. It is so, so wrong.

"It's not just New Zealand, it's everywhere. Before people started getting sick, Bill Gates got together with the World Bank, the CIA, the Chinese Government and vaccine makers to plan the stories about the COVID pandemic, what to put in social media and how to suppress the truth."

My mind is wavering. Is Mum batshit crazy like I thought last time I talked with her, or is there something real here she is tapping into? Greg was also adamant about how bad vaccines can be and he seems educated and sane. I might need to employ my investigation skills, last used on Robbie, to find out more about what is going on before I decide whether to get vaccinated. Luckily, I still have a few months to figure out what to do as the Government says vaccines will come later in the year.

"Thanks for telling me, Mum. Vaccines do sound scary. I promise I won't have one before I find out more. Lots of love to you and Bruce. Hopefully one day soon I can come up to visit and meet Shirleen and Ray."

"You are always welcome at my house … well, Brucey's house. But he would say you are very welcome if he remembered you, Julia. Come any time."

I get off the phone feeling good. This was the best phone call I have had with Mum in a long time. I feel proud of myself for listening so well and taking Mum's information and feelings into consideration. Now it is time to have a quick bowl of soup before I walk to OA.

33

WHEN I reach the Surf Club Lynda is hopping off her bike, as radiantly full of energy as ever. How does she cycle and run such long distances and still appear so bouncy? I would be exhausted. I am exhausted thinking about it.

We walk into the room together and take our middle seats, between Monique and Matthew and Greg and Barry.

Fran welcomes everyone. "How have you got on with your homework? Are you all ready to share something?"

Everyone nods enthusiastically; the last two weeks must have been as much a success for the others as for Lynda and me. Barry and Greg go first, and Barry speaks for the two of them. He might have a new job because he is behaving a lot more like the original Barry who knows everything and wants to tell everyone about it, rather than a long-haired, ageing cat-man.

"Greg and I had a great session over a beer at Cassels Brewery. That tavern is a nice venue. I like the Milk Stout and Greg stepped up from his Heinekens to try a Nectaron IPA. You thought it wasn't half bad, right Greg?"

"Yep, not bad at all."

"Alistair Cassels was laughed at when he developed a plan for a semi-derelict site near a stinky gelatine factory during the earthquakes. But look at it now – a thriving group of retail outlets and a great brewery. It just shows you can never underestimate teams and their vision. Teamwork is the way to go in business, everyone on board, strong leadership, you know the drill. Greg and I have agreed to be a team. When I get the urge to eat some ahemmm, I give Greg a call, right Greg?"

I assume 'ahemmm' is otherwise known as cat food and Barry is still finding it hard to completely own up to his obsession.

"When Greg feels the need to add to his Teenage Mutant Ninja Turtle collection, he will give me a call, right Greg?"

"Yep," says Greg.

"But we have a much bigger plan. Greg gave me new ideas. We are going to turn Red Zone Cats into a social enterprise, making money from Red Zone Cat tours. Then we could employ students to help with cat feeding. Greg will bring Claire and Ruby on a tour, and I'll bring my kids too, as a trial."

"Thanks Barry and Greg," says Fran. "I like your mutual support agreement and I love your lateral business thinking. Julia and Lynda, how did you get on?"

Lynda and I explain our clutter buddy approach. Lynda adds brightly, "Greg, you could be a clutter buddy too. We could help you with your Turtle collection." Greg shrinks, retreating into an invisible green mutant carapace at the thought of people interfering with his collection.

"That's a helpful idea Lynda, but for the meantime let's keep to our assigned pairs," says Fran.

"So who's your pair?" Lynda snaps back.

Fran looks momentarily taken aback but rallies. "Good point Lynda. Because there are an odd number of people, I thought it best if I got you six to pair up. But if I'm your peer, I should act like one. What d'you think. Would any of you take me into your teams?"

I can see all of us wondering which pair Fran could join. I don't want her butting in on Lynda and my developing friendship and I can't imagine Matthew and Monique want an extra participant either.

I wonder how Greg and Barry might feel about having Fran join them over a beer.

"Let's hear from Matthew and Monique before we have our snack, shall we?" Fran moves on before anyone voices an objection.

Matthew and Monique turn to each other. "Do you want to say, or shall I?" Monique ends up taking the lead. "It's exciting. Matthew and I are moving in together!"

A round of congratulations ensue before Monique continues. "We were talking about steps we could take to work on our obsessions and supporting each other. Moving in together seemed obvious. If we sell our houses and buy one together, we can pay off our mortgages and reduce stress.

"We have specific steps too. I'm going to ring Symbolic Tattoos in Brighton, who do Matthew's tattooing. I'm going to tell them he won't be having any more tattoos. Right Matthew?"

"Yes," Matthew says, looking embarrassed. Has Monique taken control of their plan? Is Matthew agreeing but not feeling agreeable?

"Matthew's going to come to my place and help me patch plasterboard holes. I have promised not to create new holes and he will keep me on track. I've decided we'll put ply in our new house. I have a real incentive because I want the best sale price for my house. I will help Matthew do up his house for sale; paint it more neutral colours."

"That's great progress, Matthew and Monique," says Fran. "And so exciting. Now, who brought today's snacks?"

Everyone looks at each other as we realise last week's confusion with Lynda and me has knocked the group out of snack kilter. Greg would bring snacks after Lynda, but on the original schedule he wasn't due to bring snacks until next meeting. Lynda thought her snack duty happened two weeks ago. We all look a bit disappointed and get up to have a snack-free cup of tea. I am going to have to eat a bowl of cereal when I get home, I was counting on some nice snacks to follow my soup dinner.

There's lots of chatter around the herbal teacups. "That's so great." I hear Lynda gushing to Monique and Matthew. "Are you doing lots of planning? Have you chosen a real estate agent? I know a great Harcourts agent. Where will you buy?"

"I think we'll stay in Sumner-Redcliffs, near the sea."

A stab of jealousy shoots through me. Why is Lynda talking with Monique and Matthew? Isn't she *my* friend? Aren't Monique and Matthew enough for each other? I go to talk with Fran instead. Feeling brave, I ask her, "What will you do if no one asks you to join their group?"

Fran looks taken aback then rejigs her face. "Julia, I take it you and Lynda aren't offering?"

"Uh, no, sorry. I mean, I haven't asked Lynda."

"That's okay, Julia. I'm sure one of the other pairs will be happy if I join them."

Was that a reasonable response? Or a put-down?

"Of course. It's just Lynda and I are still getting to know each other. Not that we don't like you, or anything."

Fran helps me out of the hole I am digging myself. "No problem, Julia. These are tricky times, as our esteemed Prime Minister would say when referring to the virus. We are all just trying to get through the best we can."

34

21 MARCH 2021

ON Sunday, Lynda and I have our first clutter buddy meeting. We're meeting at her house in the Cashmere Hills, a significant bike ride away for me. I leave home with two hours to spare for what should be a one-hour cycle ride. I discover I need every minute of my two hours to reach Lynda's without expiring from exhaustion. I ride out of Sumner, across the causeway, over the Heathcote Bridge and around the base of the hills, assisted by a gentle easterly tailwind. I hope it doesn't pick up to become a stiff easterly for my return journey.

My pleasant cruise takes on a different aspect as I turn up Dyers Pass Road. How long is it since I cycled up a hill? Too long to remember. I alternate sitting on the seat and standing on the pedals. Then I alternate riding and walking. Finally, I swap between riding, walking, and sitting to catch my breath.

I reach the Sign of the Takahe, another restored neo-Gothic stone building that was surrounded by rubble and cyclone fencing for many years after the earthquakes. I would like to go in and ask hopefully for a cup of Kenya Bold. However, I'm managing to build up a financial reserve again and it's feeling good. My bedside drawer contains a growing pile of notes, and I am feeling confident I can start making repayments to Bank Aotearoa, as well as buy Lynda lunch next time we get together at a café. I value that good feeling more than even a cup of tea.

I walk my bike up the last slope to Lynda's house on Victoria Park

Road. She lives in a very ugly house with an amazing view. In contrast to Gran's cute weatherboard house, Lynda's is vomit-coloured brick with a roof like a brown witch's hat. However, you can see across the city and the Canterbury Plains to the Southern Alps. There's an amazing feeling of space in a view of mountains rather than the neighbour's fence. Fences feel even more claustrophobic when you don't want to talk with your neighbour.

I walk up steps to the brown front door which bursts open with Lynda standing behind it. "Welcome to my humble abode! Tea, or coffee? I have a machine!"

"Coffee please." Getting coffee from a machine I don't have to pay for will be a treat.

"What sort? Latte, cappuccino? I have chocolate to sprinkle on top."

"Cappuccino with chocolate sounds great."

I take in my surroundings as Lynda makes coffee in the kitchen and I sit at a dining table outside of the L-shaped kitchen bench. Lynda's doll problem is staring me in the face, from every surface. On high kitchen shelves stand dolls dressed as chefs and wait staff. Her salt and pepper shakers are little people with holes in their heads. The pepper doll is bright red in the face with puffed up cheeks, and the salt doll is a snow figure with a tiny carrot nose and scarf. There's a row of Toby Jugs and mugs, both real and fictional characters.

Lynda sees me looking at the mugs. "Cappuccino in a mug? You have a favourite character?"

I happily opt for Garfield the cat.

"What happened to Freddy? From the earthquake time?"

"Freddy died just after lockdown. It was nice to have him around when I was stuck at home. He was fifteen, so it wasn't a big surprise."

"Must have been sad, though."

"Yes, sometimes I still look for him when I come home. I think about getting another cat, but surely we will be able to travel again soon and it's easier with no responsibilities."

The dining area has glass shelves around the walls with dolls on them. There's a doll performance with circus dolls at the front and spectator dolls on rows of seats. A large group of Barbie dolls are having a get-together in sparkly dresses, high heels, and handbags. An outcast Barbie on a bicycle and clad in Lycra cycles away from the socialites.

Does Lynda have a cleaner or does she dust the dolls herself, between working and running and cycling? The room is spotless and the glass shelves sparkling. The room also feels cram-packed with tiny eyes gazing at me. Does Lynda have an inquisitor doll questioning a group of incarcerated dolls somewhere?

There's a particularly intriguing display in the corner of the dining room. It's a plinth topped with an octagonal glass container, like a three-dimensional leadlight window. What is in the container is less obvious. It could be a partially burned teddy bear. I try not to stare at this object because it appears important, but also strange and disturbing.

Lynda brings our coffees with brownies that she apologises for not baking. We go to the deck running across the front of the house to sit looking at the view. The deck is populated with sporting dolls and gnomes. Rock climbing dolls scale the house and mountain biking dolls navigate vomit-coloured brick descents. Skiing dolls are ready to leap off the edge of the balcony and golfing dolls swing at little golf balls sitting on tees. I back away from the dolls on the balustrade in case I knock them off.

We drink our coffees slowly, delaying the moment when we must embark on our decluttering mission. I eat three brownies and ask where she bought them. We chat about the nice late-summer weather and how Lynda's garden hedges need trimming. We touch briefly on COVID because Lynda is keen to get back to her international travel. There's no timeline yet for the New Zealand border to open. It would have been unthinkable a year ago that almost no one, other than New Zealand nationals and permanent residents, would enter our country for a year.

However, NZ has a COVID elimination strategy which it's holding tight to in the face of continuing global waves of COVID.

Lynda is grouchy about the restrictions. "I'll get a vaccination as soon as I can. I want to travel. My medic friends are desperate to get vaccinated because COVID's going to hit our country sooner or later and they'll be on the front line. They're annoyed other countries are already vaccinating but New Zealand hasn't started. It'll be really bad if COVID gets in again before we start vaccinating."

Oh. Lynda believes in vaccinations. I could tell her what I've found out – after talking with Mum, I got hold of *The Real News*. It has convincing articles about the risks of vaccination. However, I decide now is not the time. I still have a few months to explain the dangers to her. I shift away from vaccination discussions. "Have you thought more about decluttering?"

"I've been looking for ideas on the internet," Linda responds. "One idea is to start in one part of your house then branch out to an adjacent area. Another is to choose how many items you'll get rid of each day. Like today is March fourteenth so we would get rid of fourteen items. That sounds hard but we could wait till April first. What do you think?"

Uh, oh, the ball is back in my court. I haven't thought about decluttering nor searched for ideas. Was I expecting fantastic solutions to spring organically from our conversation? Getting rid of fourteen items in one go seems way too hard, let alone thirty-one on the last day of the month. "I like the area approach. Let's each identify an area to clear and a timeframe. We'll check in with each other on progress. Today we figure out your area, next Sunday we do the same at mine. We have a week decluttering. Then we meet at each other's houses on the following two Sundays to talk about how we got on and pick the next area."

My strategy sounds logical, with a suitable degree of delaying tactic so I don't have to commence major operations yet.

Lynda screws up her face and runs her hand through her short hair. "Okay then."

"How about starting in this open living space," I suggest. "What area would be easiest, or make the most difference?" There must be somewhere Lynda would rather put things other than dolls. "How about the dining room shelves? You could put books there instead."

"Definitely not the glass shelves. That's my international Barbie collection. And the circus dolls are special, I've had them since I was a child."

"What about a coffee table?" None of Lynda's coffee tables are available to coffee mugs which might be one reason for having coffee on the deck. The tables support tea party dolls around tiny cup and saucer sets and plates with tinier pieces of cake. One coffee table hosts a Furby party around a fruit bowl full of ornamental grapes, apples, and apricots. The size of the fruit is bizarrely unrelated, so monstrous grapes weigh down little apples.

"Maybe a coffee table. How about I let you know which one next week. When we meet at your house?"

"That sounds fair." How can Lynda be so attached to a bunch of Furbies and fake fruit? Furbies were a supposedly interactive toy of the 1990s whose action consisted of blinking their eyes and making burbling sounds.

"Hey, Lynda, it's been lovely but I should be leaving, the bike ride might take me a while."

"Yes, time to be getting on and doing my garden chores. It has been lovely having you over. I can hardly wait until I see your house next week."

I can wait. I might need to do some cleaning so Lynda arrives at a house I would like her to see. If I'm lucky the weather will be fine and we can sit in the garden.

I walk down the entrance stairs and jump on my bicycle in an energetic manner to hide my fears about the length of my cycle ride home. "See you next Sunday!"

35

22–28 MARCH 2021

HAVING a date for Lynda's visit gives me momentum. I consider the broken gold filigree cup which has resided on the kitchen table for the better part of a year. I feel sad looking at the cup, remembering my forty-ninth birthday when Robbie made me a scone cake and I dropped the cup while immersed in memories of Amanda. I tell myself firmly Robbie is gone and isn't coming back, ever. I haven't seen him again; he has probably left Christchurch for good. I could check up on him through social media, but it is better I don't think about him. Is that a positive sign, that looking him up on social media hasn't occurred to me?

Considering the cup, I feel I can go beyond repairing it, I can re-create it. It would be nice to have tea with Lynda in Gran's two cups and explain my re-creations with a beautiful example.

Over the next few days, I carefully glue in one shard at a time using epoxy and being sure no glue spills over the edge to mar the look of the cup. The pieces lock together successfully, and I am satisfied by how the cup is restored. Once it regains its former shape, the repair can go to the next level of beautification.

I create clusters of tiny gold roses to attach along the cracks and glue them on sequentially. The painstaking nature of the repair means I don't get a lot of sleep during the week. This has always been a flaw in my business model. It is impossible to charge enough to cover the hours required to enact a repair that is also a work of art.

Once my cup enhancement is finished, I consider it with significant contentment and satisfaction. I achieved something. I haven't yet embarked on clutter reduction, but I have proved I can still create something beautiful.

Next Sunday rolls around and it is nearly time for Lynda to knock on my beautiful red front door. The problem is that my red front door is the only beautiful thing about my house apart from my impressively repaired cup. That isn't quite true, the mosaic seat in the garden and my Marimekko chair are also beautiful, but the mosaic seat is invisible under encroaching pumpkins and the Marimekko chair has acquired two boxes without my noticing.

I am seeing Gran's house relatively clearly for the first time since Robbie was around and more clearly than I saw it then. Gran's house is not looking attractive. I appear to be living in a rubbish tip with tarpaulin covered heaps in the garden. I have been keeping up with recent repair requests, but I have also been ignoring the sorted boxes. Something in the rear corner of my mind says this realisation is a good thing but the front of my mind is horrified because tidy Lynda is about to arrive, and parts of Gran's house may not have been dusted since EQC repairs ended six years ago.

Although Robbie had started shifting boxes and items to repair out of the house so long ago, there are still quite a few cluttering the spaces and it's been too much effort to clean around them. I settle for shifting pumpkin vines off the mosaic sofa to make it appealing with a plan of ushering Lynda rapidly through the house. I try not to disturb developing pumpkins as there is no point in wasting a good pumpkin crop.

When I hear Lynda knocking, I rush to the front door. "Come in, come in." Lynda controls her face well, but I am sure it falls slightly when she sees the chaos. Am I imagining things because I am hyper-aware of what someone else is seeing?

"How are you? Would you like a cup of tea? I am not so good on the coffee front, but I make a mean cup of Kenya Bold."

"Great, thanks. I don't know what Kenya Bold tastes like. But I'm keen to try it."

"Let's sit in the garden? I'll show you the way and come right back with the tea."

"Yes, I'd love to see your garden."

Lynda smiles appreciatively at my mosaic sofa after we wind our way through the sitting room piles. The uncovered taniwha gleams in the sunlight and wields its claws through the foam on the waves. Lynda steps carefully over the pumpkins to sit on the sofa.

"I'll be back in a tick," I say, hurrying to the kitchen where I should have preboiled the jug. At least I made scones earlier in the day.

When I return with the brown Temuka teapot and gold filigree cups on the inlaid Indian tray, together with scones piled high with jam and cream, I find Lynda deep in conversation over the fence with Alan-next-door. Oh no. I have been successful of late at keeping Alan-next-door at a cautious remove and I don't want him getting closer again.

"I'm not living here," I hear Lynda saying. "I'm visiting for a cup of tea."

"The last time someone visited he stayed for weeks. It isn't right in COVID times. You can't have unknown people turning up and staying. He was a foreigner; he should have gone back where he belonged. Bloody foreigners, sponging off us taxpayers and making us pay their airfares to go home. Time the Government got tough. Make them do some hard labour. Make them pay their airfares first before they get to fly home. There's got to be ditches needing digging.

"You know you'd better watch out with Julia. She's strange. Not salt of the earth like her Gran who gave me veges and chatted whenever we crossed paths. Julia avoids me in the street. And she likes Cindy."

Lynda breaks into the flow. "I like Cindy too."

"Oh, are you an uppity woman-loving woman too? Don't know

where your rightful place is? Imagine it could be running the country? The only place Cindy is running the country is into the ground. She closes our borders so we can't trade. She's soft on useless layabouts who won't go home. She allows the Ozzie Government to send criminants to New Zealand. It's the Ozzies who raised those criminants to be bad, they should keep them!"

"Lynda, I've made tea!" I call loudly from the sitting room door.

Lynda swivels, throws a quick, "Gotta go," in Alan's direction, and returns to the mosaic sofa. "Wow, he's talkative. I might avoid him another time."

"I generally try not to talk with him." While saying I don't want to talk with Alan, I remember Alan mentioning his concerns about vaccines. He might have found out more about vaccines since we last talked. Perhaps I should raise the topic when I next see him lurking around.

"Oh, that's amazing, absolutely amazing. Could you do something like it for me?" Lynda has spotted the repaired gold filigree teacup. It's a long time since someone said they were impressed by my work.

"Sure, do you have anything broken I could improve?"

"I accidentally knocked my Trump Toby mug off the shelf. What could you do with him?"

We spend a happy few minutes considering adornments for the erstwhile American president. I could add a greatly lengthened nose, to parallel Pinocchio. How about a syringe of bleach in his neck? A Make America Great Again cap? Lynda says she will bring broken Trump to the next OA meeting and then I can have a go at him.

We eventually get to the task of the day, identifying the area I will clear. As a distraction tactic, I remind Lynda she promised to decide on her decluttering starting point.

"I'll clear the Furby table. I am not very attached to the Furbies."

"What will you do with them?" I ask.

"Maybe take them to a second-hand store. I don't like throwing them away. I imagine their little personalities being chucked in the trash like mini humans nobody cares about." We agree that if Lynda starts to have second thoughts about disposing of Furbies, she will give me a call and I will help her to remain true to the mission.

"Where will you clear?" Lynda asks.

This time I am prepared. "I will clear my red flowered chair." The Marimekko chair only has two boxes on it. I will be happy to be able to sit in my chair again and it won't be too hard.

We agree we will check in on each other's progress at the next OA meeting, then I will go to Lynda's on the eleventh of April, to celebrate the successful clearance of the Furby side table and identify her next area to address. On April eighteenth we will convene at my house again. We can celebrate my fiftieth birthday a couple of days early.

We spontaneously hug each other on the doorstep before Lynda leaves. That's the first full-on human contact I have had in years. Have I found a new friend?

36

1 APRIL 2021

I arranged to catch up with Lynda outside the Surf Club prior to our OA meeting. I am looking forward to seeing her, so I arrive early. I sit on a bench between the car park and the building, watching small waves rolling onto the beach, and dogs with their walkers trailing behind.

Barry's Audi pulls into the far end of the car park. There are two people in the car. I try to watch without appearing obvious. This is difficult as I have to squint sideways, like a mad woman on a bench with her eyes swivelling. The person in the passenger seat is small enough to be Fran and has a similar haircut. As I watch some more, Barry and the woman start kissing, awkwardly as is necessitated in a small car if you are a large man. The woman is not likely to be Barry's wife given that people with three teenagers don't usually have kissing sessions in convertibles at dinner time.

As I attempt to conclusively identify the woman, Lynda arrives on her bicycle from the opposite direction. "Hi Lynda, nice bike ride?"

"Yes, great. Doesn't take long from the Museum to Sumner. The wind gave me a boost across the causeway. I maxed out at fifty-seven kilometres per hour. Then I drafted behind a car till someone tooted."

How can you cycle as fast as a car? I start saying, "Have a look over there in the car park …" to see Barry walking towards us with an empty car behind him. I can't say anything more to Lynda because Barry strolls up and says hello.

"Hey Barry, how're you going? How are the Red Zone Cat Tours?"

Barry plops his sizeable behind on the bench between Lynda and me. "Our trial tours are very popular. People love cats. When Greg brought Claire and Ruby, we found a new set of kittens and Ruby wanted one named after her. That gave us the idea of people naming kittens or cats if they commit to supporting them through to adoption. It's like supporting a child through UNICEF, but much more immediate.

"Ruby told her school friends and some parents asked for tours. We are trying Red Zone Cat Tours as children's birthday parties. We set up a picnic in a place where cats regularly come. Greg's working on our website to tell the cats' stories. We want them to sound appealing to donors. We need stories that sell; you can't take the sales out of the salesman!"

"How's your cat food obsession?" Lynda says daringly. I wish I could be as forthright as she is. "How does it work? Do you feel the need to eat cat food all the time? Or just some of the time? Do you eat it when you're stressed?"

"I'm not bad, thanks. It's great being able to call Greg when I feel the urge to take food out of the mouths of cats, ha ha. This support idea is more effective than I'd have ever guessed. Probably a male thing, that. You know, why would you look like you can't cope? It's great having Fran on our team too. We invited her. She and Holly are helping with the cats. Holly's a real laugh; she loves animals and has a different take on the world."

Fran joining the Barry/Greg team fans the flames of my suspicion. Fran going on Red Zone Cat Tours would give her plenty of time to hang out with Barry. What does she see in him? At this point Fran crosses through the plantings from the street, she doesn't come out of the car park. I watch carefully for tell-tale body language but can discern nothing.

"Hi Julia, Lynda, Barry," Fran says neutrally. "Nice to see everyone socialising outside of meeting time. What a lovely evening."

"So Fran," says Lynda, "what do you think of the Red Zone Cat Tours? A good outing?" Lynda isn't afraid of pushing people's buttons. She has had a try with Fran before, and here she is having another go.

Fran looks unfazed. "Holly and I enjoyed the tour. We got to see a part of Christchurch where we don't normally go. But it was sad too. All those properties with no people and abandoned cats. Holly wanted to take one home, but I don't need another dependent. Barry let Holly name a kitten after herself because she's going to offer a year of free haircuts as an incentive for someone to adopt it."

Matthew and Monique arrive on their bicycles, and we troop into the Surf Club building to start the formal part of the meeting.

Fran gets everyone to say how their support systems have been going. Matthew and Monique give us an exposé I didn't need to hear, about how well their house titivation for sale is progressing and how keen the estate agents are to put their houses on the market. "I think spring will be best," says Monique. "My garden is particularly beautiful then and it will give enough time to finish repairs, given how scarce building materials are at present.

"And, can you believe I am almost over my plasterboard obsession? It's wonderful. I haven't had the urge to eat a piece of plasterboard in several weeks. It might be thanks to Matthew." She looks adoringly at Matthew, who smiles back at her in a sickeningly dopy way.

"How about your tattooing, Matthew?" asks Fran.

"If I can be in a house with Monique, I will have everything I need. Although, there is one more tattoo I would like. My skin wouldn't be complete without a memorial to Monique."

This conversation is too nausea-inducing. Even when I was liking the look of Robbie, I wouldn't have considered getting a tattoo of his name. I could have had a red love heart with an arrow through it and curly writing saying *Robbie* on my arm. Then I would have had to pay to get the tattoo removed, after paying large sums of money to get it put there in the first place.

Lynda and I explain how we are progressing with our decluttering. Lynda tells the group about my teacup enhancement and passes round her phone with pictures of the tiny gold roses. Everyone says "Ooh" and "Aah" and asks whether I could do something for them. I look hesitant and Fran helpfully steps in.

"Let's all remember Julia is trying to deal with an excess of other people's broken possessions, she isn't wanting you all to heap more items on her.

"Julia, if and when you are ready to carry out creative repairs do feel free to tell the group. But it's important you don't feel under pressure to take on anything more till you're ready."

Fran says everyone is going so well a quick check in is all that's required.

We have our herbal tea at the end of the session after the karakia. Greg has brought snacks he made with Ruby. He apologises in advance because Ruby cut them too large. His apology is unnecessary – they are deep-fried vegan mozzarella sticks with home-made gooseberry chutney which vanish off the plate. It's lucky my increased energy has led to my cooking more because there were only two each and none left over.

On my way home I channel Lynda and walk slowly by Alan's house to see if he will call out. Alan is digging in his front garden, looking old and bent. "Hey Alan, how are things?"

"Could be better, could be worse. My arthrippled knee is playing up something wicked, doesn't help my gardening."

"That's no good, I hope it feels better soon. Alan, you were telling me about vaccines last time we talked, and I wondered if you had been thinking more about them?"

"Thinking about vaccines? I'm not going to waste my brain space on vaccines. Just like I don't spend time thinking about poison. I'm not having an injection that could kill me. No chance. My doctor said I could have a vaccine next month because I'm eighty-three. He must be in on the Government conspiration. Probably gets paid for every shot he puts in someone's arm. If I get COVID I'll just have some sheep drench, it's cheap and has a one hundred per cent cure rate. Why aren't doctors using that? Another Government cover-up."

"Thanks for the info Alan. I didn't know about sheep drench. Enjoy your digging." I might be interested in Alan's thoughts on COVID-19 and vaccines, but I don't need to talk to him for too long. My cup of Kenya Bold is beckoning, and I have remembered Bev's broken vase placed at the front of my repair queue when I was sorting boxes with Robbie. My roses have inspired me towards new repair enhancements and the vase has lots of potential. I can see how bouquets of flowers will curl out of the fractures.

I will glue the vase back together then begin modelling the roses, peonies and dahlias that will line its sides, extending the vase's bright colour scheme to be a stunning show piece Clarice Cliff would have been proud to make. How excited will Bev be to get the vase back?

37

2–10 APRIL 2021

THE next ten days go by in a pleasant autumn glow; the weather is like lockdown last year. Was it a year ago the whole country had to stay home for a month? Time feels like it is expanding and contracting at will; the 2020 lockdown feels both distant and proximal. When I try to remember the timeframe in which something happened, the best I can do is pre-COVID or during COVID. The Canterbury earthquakes had the same effect – there was before the earthquakes and after the earthquakes. That's a line I still can't bear to cross.

I work diligently on Bev's vase. How could I have forgotten how good this feels? I have been living in a twilight zone for so long. Repairing broken toasters is not a patch on truly achieving 'Broken is Beautiful'. I remember the inordinate sense of satisfaction from enhancement, the reason I started the creative side of my business.

Between stages of gluing, I work on other repair and enhancement jobs. I remove the Marimekko chair boxes and empty them. The beauty of a clutter buddy approach is you don't want to fail in the other person's eyes.

I am also diligent about cooking meals and eating them. I'm still not the most enthusiastic cook; I prefer to cook enough for three nights at one time because I don't mind the same meals multiple days in a row. However, I am a long way from the self that starved in bed after Robbie left.

I even start looking at the garden boxes under the tarpaulins. Boxes at the edges are soggy and some of the objects rusted beyond repair. I resolve to get everything rescuable to a weatherproof state in the next month.

Last week I made my first repayment on my loan. I went in person to the only Bank Aotearoa branch in Christchurch. The teller didn't seem as excited as I was and suggested I organise a direct debit. That was okay, I was excited enough for both of us and I took the direct debit form to fill in. I am definitely on the way to a life where I'm in control again.

Having completed Bev's vase, I want to take it to her house rather than leaving it for a secretive pick-up on my front doorstep. I want Bev to see it and love it and I hope it will trigger happy memories for Bill. I wrap the vase in brown paper that came from one of the boxes previously on the chair.

I walk along Head Street with the vase in my arms. A sense of trepidation slows my steps. Am I too late? Bev and Bill are both old and Bill not well. Might they have had to move into care? However, from a block away I see bright dahlias and marigolds in front of their fence and throughout the garden. Dahlias shine red, orange, yellow, pink, purple, white and green, and marigolds are yellow and orange suns. There is no grass anywhere in sight. Surely Bev must still be living in the house and keeping the garden?

I head up concrete steps to the house hiding behind the garden. I knock, noticing Bev needs a nice door knocker like my brass lion head. I hear nothing. The front door glass has a bobbly pattern obscuring the interior. I knock louder, call out, then hear someone making their way towards the door.

When Bev sees me with the paper wrapped parcel her face lights up. "Come in and have a cup of tea, Julia. I've been looking forward to you coming and Bill will be delighted to see you." Either Bev has dementia and has forgotten I was supposed to come years ago, or she is someone who makes you feel welcome, no matter when you drop in, or what you've brought, or are wearing. I feel welcomed, although I do hope her tea is Kenya Bold.

Bev and Bill's house is tidy, or is a house without boxes and other people's things tidy by definition? You can see their shared history everywhere, including pictures of Bev, Bill and their family lining the hallway. There's a picture of them smiling broadly in front of a small, white-painted church. There are black and whites of two sturdy toddlers on Sumner Beach and children in school uniform. There are colour pictures of the same children getting married and then with their own children.

Bev smiles fondly at the pictures. "They help us remember, deary. Bill and I look at them every day and talk about all the people. Bill rarely remembers people's names now, but his eyes light up when we talk about Sonia and Graham and their partners and our grandchildren. I know Bill remembers them on the inside, even if he can't get the words out.

"I wish we could see our family more often, but the grandkids are doing their own thing, as they should. Sonia's Nydia and Felix are both living in Auckland; they would have gone overseas if it hadn't been for COVID. They're waiting till the world settles down. Graham's Kirsty married a farmer near Timaru, and I imagine soon we'll have the excitement of a great-grandchild. Nic made it to London before the world tilted on its axis. She has had COVID but not badly. We talk with her on Skype more regularly than the grandkids in New Zealand. She was always a lovely child and is a lovely adult.

"Now, come through and see Bill."

Bill is in their sitting room on a pink La-Z-Boy recliner. His expression suggests he has no idea who I am, but he isn't going to admit it. "Hello!" he says. "Lovely to see you, do have a seat."

"Bill, love, Julia is returning our vase that broke in the earthquakes."

I place the Clarice Cliff vase on a side table and slowly remove the paper, drawing the moment out. The colours of the vase start to show and then the flowers emerge. The vase now has flowers sprouting from every crack, and there were a lot of cracks. The flowers are in as many colours as the flowers of Bev and Bill's garden.

"Oh my, Julia. It's amazing. I don't know how to thank you enough for creating something so beautiful. That's our vase, for sure, but a completely new version. Who would believe a vase could get a new life. I wish I could be re-created like that. Can you make flowers growing out of my wrinkles, so I look like a stunning bouquet?

"Bill, what do you think? You bought me this vase as a special present when you got a bonus from work. You went to Ballantynes because I'd told you I'd seen a vase I liked there."

Bev is very careful not to ask Bill whether he remembers. She's telling the story, with little pauses so he can join in, never setting him up to fail. Suddenly his face opens up and he does join in.

"Of course I remember, love. How could I forget bringing home your vase? When I saw it in the store with its flowers and bright colours I knew it should belong to you. But as I went out the door and looked at my bicycle I thought I must have gone mad. All the way home I was terrified I would crash. I was wobbling all over the place, trying to balance the box on my bike bar.

"When I reached Clifton Hill, I knew I couldn't hold it with one hand and steer with the other, so I took the belt out of my trousers and strapped the box to my handlebars.

"By the time I got home I was sweating buckets. You took one look at me and said, 'Bill, hand me that shirt so I can wash it. You can't go to work tomorrow with big sweat stains on your front'. Then I gave you the vase and when you got it out of the box you had the biggest smile ever on your beautiful face. You've always been beautiful to me, and you still are."

Bev's nearly crying and so am I. She hugs Bill as well as she can, given he's sitting in a La-Z-Boy. "Now I'll make the cup of tea I promised Julia and we will have a shortbread biscuit with it."

The tea isn't Kenya Bold but I don't mind too much, and the shortbread biscuit is home baked and delicious, so I have a second. I'm no longer starving, but I can't resist a good biscuit.

I look at my vase and out the sitting room window at the dahlias. I have done the right thing, for once, and I vow to continue doing the right thing.

Bev sends me home with more shortbread biscuits wrapped in a serviette. She asks how much she owes me for the vase, and I find it difficult to ask for money. "Of course I must pay you Julia. You have given us so much joy today. I want to say thank you and I want to pay you because people need to buy food as well as get thanks."

I suggest twenty dollars, but Bev says that's ridiculous and gives me eighty dollars. I put the money in my pinafore pocket; I can afford to invite Lynda to have lunch at a café *and* put some of it aside towards my loan repayments.

We do a quick tour of Bev's vegetable garden; she picks tomatoes off the vines and hands them to me. I need to remember to remove them from my pinafore pocket at home before I squash them.

"Don't be a stranger," Bev says. "You're only a few blocks away. I will pop in and see you when I am coming back from the beach."

"That would be lovely," I say, and mean it.

38

11 APRIL 2021

WHEN I cycle to Lynda's house, Cashmere Hill feels no easier and I feel dishevelled on arrival. Lynda is looking as bright and bouncy as ever and welcomes me in. The promised clearing of the side table of Furbies and ornamental fruit has taken place.

"What did you do with them?"

"I discovered Furbies are collectors' items, so I sold them on TradeMe. I got over two hundred dollars for each one! I'm sure they'll be cared for if people pay that much money."

"How about the fruit?"

"A second-hand store in Sydenham took it. Fruit doesn't have stories or feelings, so it was easy to get rid of. I only had the fruit as Furby food."

"Do Furbies eat fruit?"

"Absolutely. When you play 'Feed My Furby' it tells you which food Furbies like. They like sweet fruit. They don't like garlic or cactus."

"Are Furbies vampires if they don't like garlic? That would be scary, vampiric Furbies flying round at night. Good thing you got rid of them."

"Ha, ha, maybe." I am not sure if Lynda liked my joke. "Coffee?"

"Cappuccino with chocolate like last time in Garfield would be great."

"No problem. I'll give you the Trump mug while I remember. I forgot to bring him to the meeting. Could you fix him for me by next week?" I too had forgotten the Trump mug repair, but a Trump redesign will be fun. Lynda hands Trump over, and I put him by the door to take out to my bike.

While Lynda is making coffee, I wander around her dining area considering which display she might choose to get rid of next. The burned item in the octagonal container looks like it would be simple to get rid of and would save a lot of space. Its plinth takes up an excessive amount of room in the small space. However, as I get close to the plinth Lynda reacts.

"Don't touch that."

"Sorry, what is it?"

"Nothing important. I just don't want the glass broken."

The octagonal display clearly houses something particularly important. However, Lynda's tone makes it clear I'm not going to find out anything more, so I sit at the dining table and wait for my coffee. We have them on the deck again with a repeat of the brownies. I was quite enthusiastic about them last time; Lynda remembered and bought more.

Lynda brings up COVID almost immediately, which is a shame because it's a beautiful day and talking about COVID always feels like it brings a cloud over the sun. She is up in arms about New Zealand stopping people coming in from India because of a significant upsurge in COVID cases there. "Imagine if you were overseas and you weren't allowed to come home."

Not being able to return to New Zealand is hard for me to imagine because I have never left the country. "We wouldn't want lots of infected people coming in, would we? Not while we don't have any virus and do have a lot of freedom compared to the rest of the world."

"But they are New Zealand citizens and residents! If they don't have the right to come home, where can they go? Isn't it a basic right to enter your own country?" Lynda has a point. I wonder if she is thinking about herself wanting to go overseas. Both our views have merit, but they are in complete opposition. I duck away from expanding the argument.

"We should talk about your next area to clear."

"Yes I suppose we should."

"What about this gnome collection?" Not only are there the biking and skiing dolls on the walls and balustrade, there are groups of garden gnomes on the deck. The gnomes are doing recreational activities including fishing, weeding, peeing, and investigating mushrooms.

"Absolutely not. That was Dad's garden gnome collection."

"Could the gnomes live in the garden? Then you would have more space in your house without having to get rid of them?"

Lynda looks thoughtful and then agrees to relocation. Relocation may not be within the letter of the decluttering law, because Lynda will still have the gnomes. However, they will be out of the house. Also, if she sees them less often, they might be easier to dispose of at some point in the future.

We continue to chat on the deck about gardens and houses until the sun starts to lose its heat. Lynda has never grown vegetables but is interested in trying some easy ones. I suggest a few lettuces, because it might be warm enough on the hill for them to grow in April. Lynda says I can help her out with planting next spring.

I remember to put the Toby Jug in my pannier before I freewheel down the hill on my bike, feeling like life is continuing to look up.

39

12–18 APRIL 2021

OVER the following week I focus on the Toby Jug and start exhuming the garden boxes. I am happy to be sitting in my red flower-covered chair once again on cold days. I will also be glad when I get paid two hundred dollars for the repairs I have done this week. Maybe this month I can make a larger payment to Bank Aotearoa, including a proportion of capital.

The Toby Jug is easy to glue back together and Trump sure needs improving. I make a MAGA cap out of red, white, and blue fabric for Trump's head. I paint an American flag on card and attach it to a toothpick which I glue to Trump's hand. I give Trump American-flag-decorated glasses and a three-dimensional speech bubble saying 'Vote Me' which issues from his mouth.

I think about Sunday when Lynda and I will celebrate my birthday. I told Lynda it was my birthday soon, though I didn't mention it will be my fiftieth. Lynda said she would bring a cake, then asked how many candles it would need. I laughed and said, "How about ten? That's a nice round number which will fit well on a cake."

What I didn't say is ten would have been the number of candles on Amanda's birthday cake this year. Ten candles, ten little girls coming round for a sleepover and cramming in together on the sitting room floor. Unlike 2020, this year Amanda could have had a sleepover because there is no COVID lockdown. She would be starting her senior year in the primary section at Sumner school. Would she have liked maths? Or writing stories? Or both? Would she have waited to find out what her birthday present was? Or would she have hunted throughout the house until she found the wrapped present and carefully felt the parcel until she figured out the contents?

Will I tell Lynda about Amanda? Is it time to try to open Amanda's room? But what story will I tell? Will Lynda still like me if she finds out I was so unobservant that I let a mirror detach from the wall and crush my baby daughter to death?

On Sunday I take some interest in my clothes because Lynda always looks great, even in her cycling gear. I find I don't have anything attractive to wear because I haven't bought clothes in a long time. My home-made pinafores are comfortable and convenient for many activities, including repairs. However, far too many repairs have left their mark on the pinafore fronts.

I rummage through my drawers in despair, to discover one of Mum's brightly coloured caftans at the bottom. She must have left it when she departed precipitately after Amanda's death. I don't remember putting it in my drawer and doubt it has seen the light of day for over nine years. It's rather loose but I tie a scarf round the waist and feel I look okay.

Lynda brings a carrot cake with cream cheese icing, ten candles, a big box of Lindt chocolates and a bottle of Lindauer sparkling wine. "For the woman who has too many things!" she announces. "We are both trying to declutter, so the best gift is one you can eat and drink with maximum enjoyment."

"Oh, thanks. That's so nice. Maybe we save the sparkling wine for another day? It's an awful lot to drink, just the two of us."

"No problem, Julia. Whatever makes you happy. It's *your* birthday."

I show Lynda the reappearance of the Marimekko chair and give her the Toby mug. She laughs out loud at the sight of the new and improved

Trump. Then I load up the inlaid Indian tray with Kenya Bold, plates and forks and we take everything outside to eat in the garden.

We savour large pieces of cake with tea, sitting on the mosaic sofa. We talk about how one might make vegan carrot cake. It would be pretty easy; all you'd have to do is replace the butter in the icing. Then we start on the chocolates, trying one of every flavour to find out whether our favourites are the same. We both settle on the dark chocolate as best.

We congratulate ourselves on our progress and chat about our OA compatriots.

Lynda is in awe of Monique's style, not surprising given Lynda's interest in textiles and clothing. I grudgingly admit that Monique's style sense is impressive.

We consider how successful the Monique-Matthew combination might be. Given neither of us have long-term partners, we might not be the right people to be make judgements about other people's relationships, but they are always a good topic of conversation. We agree that they seem a reasonably unlikely twosome, but they appear to be absolutely doting on each other. Is Monique overcome by Matthew's good looks? He must be ten years her junior at the very least. What does Matthew see in Monique? Did he have a controlling mother and is living out his childhood relationship again?

We touch on the potential Fran-Barry liaison. Lynda is sceptical because she thinks the pairing is so unlikely. Fran is tidy and reserved and Barry is fat and overbearing. What could the attraction possibly be? I can't get past what I have seen – the woman in Barry's car looked like Fran. We discuss how a relationship between the group co-ordinator and a group member could be catastrophic if it falls apart and hope that, if it is a thing, Fran will break it off quietly and soon. OA is going better than we could have imagined and we don't want the group to dissolve.

My courage to tell Lynda about Amanda wanes as we talk because I can't cope with the thought of Lynda rejecting me for my horrific mistake.

If a time machine appeared that allowed me to step inside and then be squashed by the mirror in Amanda's stead, I would leap in without hesitation. But how can I convince someone else of that?

Lynda asks me about my next decluttering goal. For once, I am actually ahead of the game. I tell her how I have already started on the soggy garden boxes. I almost tell her about Robbie as I remember that it's because of him the piles are there. I discover the thought of Robbie is no longer particularly painful. When did that happen?

"So, what's your goal, Julia? When can you have the garden clear of boxes?"

That's a big step but I'm up for it. "By the end of May my garden will be clear of boxes, and I won't have just shifted the boxes to somewhere else. If things are too broken to repair, I will throw them away and if they are repairable, I will fix them." The number of rusty and damp objects will speed up the repair side of the job.

As well as not finding the thought of Robbie painful, I realise that I can also contemplate taking a load of broken things to the transfer station and waving happily goodbye to them.

It's a cool autumn afternoon. When we finish our tea and cake, it's too cold to sit in the garden any longer so Lynda heads home. I still haven't told her anything about Amanda but that's okay, there's always next time.

40

27 MAY 2021

IT'S late May, the light is fading, and I am waiting for Lynda on a bench outside the Surf Club. I'm wearing a puffer jacket the colour of my front door which I bought at 'Time and Time Again'. Puffer jackets were not previously my sort of clothing, but I have learned a lot from Lynda and her outdoor wear. Puffers are warm and light and, when I saw the colour, I couldn't resist this one. It's a lot more comfortable than the heavy woollen coats I used to wear. I sold my two coats at 'Time and Time Again' and was pleasantly surprised to get forty dollars with which I also bought a bright blue Icebreaker merino. People sell amazingly good second-hand clothes.

Lynda and I are both progressing well with decluttering and our friendship is increasingly strong. I haven't had someone with whom to celebrate successes since Gran got dementia.

My decade of lonely life now looks strange. Not only do I have Lynda as a friend, I also regularly visit Bev and Bill. Bill has never been as lucid as the day I took the enhanced Clarice Cliff vase around, but his sporadic moments of clarity make Bev happy. Bill's easy to be with because he is mostly content, watching TV in his recliner.

I usually go to Bev and Bill's on Tuesday for the morning so Bev can go out without worrying Bill might hurt himself in her absence. I do repairs while Bill watches whatever is on the screen. Sometimes he watches *Teenage Mutant Ninja Turtles* repeats. Does Greg watch the programme in his sleepout to remember his brother? I understand Turtles much better than *The Office*, which Bill also watches. Why would anyone want to go to the same place they don't particularly like, at the same time every day, to work with the same set of people, who they don't like either? As difficult as it has been making a solo living from my own work, my life looks much better than theirs.

When Bev returns from surfing, shopping, or meeting a friend in Sumner, we have a shared cup of tea. I have introduced Bev and Bill to Kenya Bold, and they like it much better than the Bell tea they previously drank. Bev reminds me of Gran with her practicality and interest in others. Seeing Bev helps me remember Gran from before dementia, the person Gran actually was rather than the shrunken person she became before she died. Do memories of before sustain Bev in caring for the Bill of now? I bet she misses the old Bill.

I arrive early at the Surf Club because I remain dead curious about whether Barry and Fran are having an affair. Part of me is disapproving. Another part of me feels a twinge of jealousy, as when I see Matthew and Monique together. I wouldn't mind that sort of excitement and interest in my life.

Barry's Audi pulls up at the far end of the car park. He hasn't arrived early for the last few meetings so there has been nothing to discover.

There are definitely two people in the car, and one is a woman. I see little cigarette glows light up in the car. This doesn't fit. I can't imagine health-conscious Fran smoking and her clothes never smell of smoke. I see nothing more because the woman gets out on the far side of the Audi and walks away through the vegetation towards Sumner.

Lynda arrives with bike lights blazing. We hug hello and I tell her about Barry smoking with someone in the car. We agree Fran smoking is highly unlikely.

Fran walks across the car park towards the building and I attempt to follow her swiftly but inconspicuously to find out whether her clothing smells of smoke. I can't smell anything but that isn't conclusive.

After our introductions, Fran says she would like to discuss something that is concerning her. This isn't normal routine for OA, nor normal for Fran. "I want to talk with you about COVID vaccinations. My daughter Holly has compromised immunity because of her foetal alcohol syndrome, so she is eligible to get vaccinated now but it will be six weeks till she gets both shots and develops full immunity. The earliest she will be protected against COVID is the beginning of August, which feels a long time away when the person you love could get seriously ill from a highly infectious disease. I know there's no COVID in the community at present, but you never know when there will be a slip-up at the border."

There's silence. Greg sits with his arms crossed and a scowl on his face.

"Basically, I can't afford to get COVID. So, I'm hoping you are all considering getting vaccinated as soon as you can, because my attendance at this group is one of my potential areas of exposure. Obviously, I could get it at school, but the school community is especially careful because so many of the children have other illnesses. We are already discussing whether everyone should mutually agree to be vaccinated if they work at the school. I'm getting vaccinated the same time as Holly because we are in the same household."

"People are getting vaccinated already?" asks Barry, looking surprised.

Monique fields that question. "Sure, I'm already vaccinated, as a doctor."

Fran says, "Yes, I imagine most of you are in Group 4, the last group to be eligible for vaccination. But did you know vaccination centres often have shots available at the end of the day for people who aren't yet eligible? You can sign up with your local doctor's surgery to call you if they have vaccine left over. Right, Monique?"

Monique nods while the rest of us are silent. I keep my head down because I don't want to say anything. Funny that Barry isn't leaping in.

It's Monique who continues. "Obviously not a problem for me Fran, or for Matthew. I got signed up at our surgery. You might have heard about a few doctors who don't believe in vaccines, but I am not one of them."

"What might their concerns be?" asks Fran.

"I wonder – if doctors don't believe in vaccines, what parts of modern medicine do they believe in?" Monique says. "COVID vaccines have been tested exactly the same way as all other modern medicine."

"Really?" asks Greg.

"Definitely. But there's a lot of misinformation out there. People say things like, 'The vaccines were rushed through trials in a hurry so it wasn't done properly', and 'Pfizer is a new type of vaccine, so it can't be trusted'. It's true we haven't had an mRNA vaccine—"

"What's mRNA?" asks Fran.

"It's the type of vaccine that Pfizer is using, and others. The method has been in development for thirty years, so it isn't that new. Scientists have hoped to use it to develop a vaccine for Ebola. Nearly everyone who gets Ebola dies." Monique pauses to let that sink in.

"But the biggest difference between Ebola and COVID is that there's lots of money to be made in vaccinating a rich world, rather than small parts of poor Africa. And governments know they can't save people through lockdowns forever. So suddenly there was lots of investment in trials."

Greg follows up. "You still didn't say what an mRNA vaccine actually is."

Monique smiles, comfortable in her explanations. "It very clever. Old-style vaccines, like for flu, inject you with either a whole dead virus or a part of a virus so your body learns how to fight it without being under attack. Like self-defence classes. Practise twisting the little finger of a friendly guy, so the next drunk guy that approaches you gets his finger ripped off. Without practise, your body has to learn to fight while it's under attack.

"The problem with this method is you have to produce lots of dead virus in expensive and slow biological factories. What the mRNA vaccine does is turn your own body into a temporary factory for a tiny, safe, part of the virus. In the case of COVID, your body manufactures the little spikes you see in the COVID cartoons; the spikes are—"

Greg interrupts. "Our bodies are turned into biological factories?"

Monique hesitates as most of us look concerned.

"Yes, but only for a short time. mRNA is very fragile, that's why it's stored in very cold freezers and must be treated carefully. It falls apart after a small number of weeks, once your body is ready to defend itself. Researchers think mRNA will be useful for lots of other medical treatment in future, like teaching your body to attack cancer cells growing in it. It's amazing how good things can come out of a pandemic."

Monique sounds convinced, I'm not so sure. Vaccines teaching your body to manufacture bits of COVID doesn't sound good to me, it sounds downright scary. Could the vaccine be teaching your body to manufacture other things we don't know about and thus make you sick? There are articles saying rates of cancer are rising in countries where COVID vaccines are being administered.

Monique continues, "If you are still worried about the trials or the risks, one of the best things about New Zealand keeping COVID out is that other countries have already vaccinated hundreds of millions of people. If there are issues with vaccines, we will hear about them long before they happen here. Pfizer is currently thought to be one of the best vaccines preventing you getting seriously ill with COVID."

Greg doesn't look happy, and I don't feel happy. I feel like there are still a lot of unanswered questions.

"Thanks for all your interesting information, Monique," says Fran, after no one asks any more questions. "I should learn more about the vaccine I am going to choose to have injected into Holly, and into me. I've been so concerned about the risk to Holly if she catches COVID, that I haven't thought to question whether there could be any risk from vaccination.

"Now, shall we all have our cup of tea with the beautiful vegan eclairs Monique has brought? After tea we can have a further discussion about vaccines if people want to, but we also need to fit in an update on team progress."

41

THERE is less chatter than normal at tea break. It feels like everyone is listening to everyone else's conversations, watching how people are positioning themselves on COVID vaccinations.

Monique and Matthew take their tea and eclairs to the far corner of the room and have an intense discussion, which could be about vaccinations or about their wall colours. But surely they have their vaccination positions sorted and aligned, given they have been a couple for a while and Monique's position is clear?

My mind is doing whirling rainbow circles like a stalled computer. I don't want to say I don't like vaccines in front of the group. I know Lynda is pro-vaccine like Fran. I know Greg is anti-vaccine. That leaves Barry's position to be discovered. The best-case scenario is three people who don't want to get vaccinated against four people who do. I am so distracted I don't properly enjoy my eclair, which is a pity, because despite being vegan eclairs, they are very good.

Fran calls us back to our circle of coloured chairs.

Matthew is eager to speak as soon as we are seated. "I totally support Monique. Vaccines are essential in the fight against COVID-19, and we don't want lots of New Zealanders dying like in Europe and America.

"Needles are hardly a big deal; one little prick and your vaccination is all over. Of course, needles aren't something a tattoo-lover is concerned about. Goodness knows why doctors say 'This is going to hurt' when you get a vaccine. It's like they are priming you for pain. Why do they say that, Monique? Anyhow, both Monique and I are vaccinated, and we didn't have any bad effects. I know a few of Monique's colleagues felt a bit tired. Right Monique?"

"Yes, some people feel a little off-colour, but only for two or three days."

Matthew continues, "I haven't grown two heads and my tattoos haven't faded. If I was going to worry about something, it would be damage to my tattoos!"

Lynda chimes in. "I'm happy to get vaccinated. Sooner is fine with me. Enough people overseas have been vaccinated for serious problems to have shown up. I want life to get back to something close to normal. I don't like the Government telling us what we should do but I also don't see there is any choice if we want to avoid getting sick."

There's Barry and Greg left to speak. Barry looks like good things are happening in his life. His demeanour is upbeat and he's losing weight. Is that because he is having an affair? I expect Barry will back Fran, as would be the case if the two of them are getting together.

"I haven't thought too much about vaccines because that's what the missus does. She reminds me to go to the doctor to get the flu vaccine or whatever. She knows what's up with all the kid's medical stuff and with mine and her own. I rely on her to tell me what to do and book my appointments. I tend to think about things when they need to be thought about and, according to what I've heard, my turn to be vaccinated won't be till sometime in July or August.

"But Fran, if you are saying it is important to you we get vaccinated, I'll do it. I don't want you to be upset. Keeping a happy family or a happy group, that's what the world's all about, isn't it? That's why I went into travel sales because travel makes people happy and excited. When I get home, I will ask the missus to ring our doctor's clinic and get me put on the list for spare vaccines."

Greg looks like he is trying to keep from speaking out and failing. When Fran turns towards him, the cork ejects from Greg's bottle. "I'm sorry but this is horrendous. Fran, I can't believe you are putting pressure on people this way. It's totally inappropriate. Medical decisions should be everyone's personal choice. No one should be forced to discuss them in a room full of random people."

Fran looks taken aback. Did she imagine we would all be happy to go along with her vaccination suggestions? Did she not contemplate people might have differing views?

"But Greg, the group is hardly random—"

Greg continues over her, "I'm sorry, but I am amazed how you're all buying the Government line that we should get vaccinated without properly checking out the data. This is a disease of old people, not young people. We need to protect old people and let the disease sweep through the country to create herd immunity. We need to reopen our borders not become an isolated little island everyone forgets about.

"Sweden nearly got it sorted. They kept their borders open so workers and trade could keep going. They didn't use lockdowns, just asked people to be sensible. They admit they didn't protect retirement villages well enough, but now everyone knows how to do it better. We can live nearly normally without having to stick dubious medicines into our bodies."

No one else is trying to say anything because Greg has become an unstoppable force. "And what about the paper from the United Kingdom showing more vaccinated people than unvaccinated people are dying from COVID? Hard evidence – vaccines are killing some people!"

Monique tries to break in, with her doctor's hat on. "Greg, is there anything that would change your mind about vaccines? Evidence about their safety or efficacy? The evidence that the UK study data is biased?"

"Monique, I'm sorry but nothing will change my mind. I have friends who were vaccinated as part of Group 2 and are now so ill they can't work. After vaccination, young, healthy men are getting inflammation of their heart muscle and dying. Men who are very unlikely to die from COVID. Men like me! I take care of my body and I eat well, and I believe that will give me good protection against COVID; nothing will protect me from a dodgy vaccine.

"In the end, why would I trust the medical profession? I couldn't trust them with James' life. If doctors did their jobs properly James wouldn't have died of meningitis. Why would I trust doctors to tell me a good or right thing if they can't save the life of a small child with a diagnosable illness?"

That's a good point. You might believe doctors know what they are doing and talking about, but Greg has the ultimate evidence. Doctors don't necessarily know what they are doing, and their stuff-ups can ruin, or lose, your life. There isn't much difference between not giving someone the medicine they need and giving someone medicine they don't need.

Monique says carefully, "Greg, it was an unbearably sad event that happened to your brother, and I am so sorry for you and for him. I don't know what reasons or explanations the coroner's report found but failing to diagnose meningitis is not good. I hope that, at some point, you can see the failure of one doctor in one circumstance doesn't mean our entire profession is fundamentally flawed."

Fran looks around the circle to see if anyone else has more to say. In her eagerness to shift the conversation she forgets I haven't expressed my views on vaccination as I sit with a deliberately neutral expression on my face. "Apologies, I didn't realise how difficult this discussion might get. That was naive of me. I don't want to give the impression I am requiring you to do anything to be part of the group and I don't want to put pressure on anyone. Can we please put my raising vaccinations down to my concerns for Holly's wellbeing?

"Let's move on to OA business. Does anyone have anything they would like to share about how they are progressing?"

Monique and Matthew don't have anything new to tell us. They talk about the colours they are painting their houses, again, and Monique reiterates how the intact walls are putting nails in the coffin of her plasterboard obsession.

Barry and Greg are looking uncomfortably at each other. Presumably they hadn't talked about COVID or vaccines much, so had little idea of their respective positions and now, how to relate to one another.

"We've been getting increasing interest in Red Zone Cat Tours," says Barry. "Even better, I've been cat-food-free for two whole months. I have an iPhone app counting the days. It rings a short bell every evening after I complete a whole day without cat food and a longer bell when I finish a cat-food-free week. I've also got the cats I used to feed at home adopted out by people who have done tours. The missus is pretty happy about that."

Greg isn't keen to contribute further. "I haven't bought new Turtle stuff recently," is all he's prepared to add.

Lynda waxes loquacious about my repair of her Toby Jug and shows pictures again. "Julia is just so talented. I'm hoping she will move away from repairs to more enhancements. So much more potential for added value and income."

Really? She didn't say that to me.

"We are going so well. I have cleared most of my living and dining area of dolls and got a lot of money for some of them. Not only are Furbies popular, old Barbies turn out to be valuable. Julia's going great on her box sorting too. Aren't you Julia?"

"Yes, I have cleared all the boxes from the garden and emptied part of my shed as well. I can get to my garden tools. It's good."

I am too worried about the growing vaccination issue to be very focused on what I am saying. I thought I had lots of time to persuade Lynda she is misguided in her vaccination position, but it no longer looks like time is on my side.

42

28 MAY–5 JUNE 2021

I need to talk to Lynda about vaccines and I don't want to talk with Lynda about vaccines. I need to put her right, but I am confused. I heard what Monique said, but I am not sure she answered all Greg's questions. I am not certain that vaccines are effective or safe. There is plenty of evidence in *The Real News* that they are neither.

It's time for me to go back online to do more than look at funny cat pictures. I got out of the habit of looking at the internet much after Robbie left, when nothing seemed interesting. When I search, I find a whole lot of information showing that COVID vaccines are not safe and why big interest groups, who likely don't have your best interests at heart, want you vaccinated.

Governments are using COVID to pacify and control people because it's easy to control people when they are scared. I read articles about how small a proportion of people are dying from COVID but how big a deal our Government makes it sound. So far, twenty-five people have died from COVID while five hundred a year typically die from flu and four hundred people a year in road crashes. The government doesn't enforce flu vaccinations or stop people driving.

Big pharma will sell billions of vaccines every year over however many years COVID is around, maybe forever. In Israel they are already using a third 'booster' shot because they say immunity is waning after about six months. Big pharma would want to say you need a new shot every six months, or for every new COVID variant, to keep their revenue streams flowing.

Numerous eminent doctors are against COVID vaccinations. They speak movingly and convincingly on YouTube videos. French virologist and Nobel Prize winner Luc Montagnier says vaccination is creating and helping spread new COVID variants as does Sir John Bell of Oxford University. Montagnier has discovered COVID is genetically modified and has been spliced to include DNA from the AIDS virus.

Why would high-flying doctors tell you it is dangerous to get vaccinated unless it was true? But why would other doctors *want* you to get vaccinated if it was dangerous and didn't work? What would the doctors get out of it? In New Zealand, the Government is paying for vaccines and for people to do the vaccinations, so doctors won't be making money out of COVID. Could big pharma be paying them? This is difficult.

I feel there is a strong case that vaccination may not be necessary and, at worst, could be harmful. It is a frightening proposition to choose to have an injection that could make you sick now, or maybe later. What if people's future children have their DNA altered by COVID and have deformed babies, or no babies? Thalidomide was trialled on rabbits, and it was fine, then a whole lot of women had children with arms and legs that never developed beyond little flippers.

I do need to talk with Lynda; it should be at her house because everyone feels safer in their own home. We are due to meet at her house in early June so I will do it then.

However, something unexpected happens before my get-together with Lynda. Fran calls me. "Hi Julia, how are you doing?"

I mightn't have answered my mobile if I had known it was Fran calling but I don't have her number stored in my phone.

"I'm fine thanks, how are you, Fran?"

"Could I meet with you and Lynda when you next get together? I have something I need assistance with, and I thought you two could help me think it through."

This is a turn up, Fran wants assistance. Isn't she paid to be the OA facilitator? Why should we help her out? And she's in a three-way buddy group with Greg and Barry. Why would she need Lynda and me?

"Aren't you in a team with Greg and Barry?"

"Well, yes. However, this isn't something I can discuss with them."

I doubt Fran is going to raise the vaccine question again soon, so it won't be vaccines. Perhaps Fran is wanting to break up with Barry? She has come to her senses and wants to back out of the complicated situation. I can understand why she doesn't want to discuss that with Greg and Barry.

"It's okay with me. But you need to discuss it with Lynda too."

"Of course, Julia. I already had a chat with Lynda after our last meeting." Fran had a chat with Lynda, and Lynda hasn't told me about it? I feel hurt. Why isn't Lynda telling me things?

"I specifically asked Lynda not to say anything until I talked with you as well." Fran added. "After our last meeting I realise I need to be careful about pressuring people, so I want to assure you this is entirely up to you."

"Fine, there's no problem then. We normally meet on Sunday, late morning, but Lynda will have told you that. Our next meeting will be at hers on Cashmere Hill on Sunday."

"I would appreciate it a lot if I can join you then," Fran says. "Would you like me to arrive later, so you can have time on your own first?"

"That's a good idea. Why don't you come around eleven thirty in the morning?"

"Thanks Julia. I don't have many people I can call on for help, so it is nice to know you two are there for me."

After she hangs up, I feel more sanguine about Fran coming on Sunday, when I consider we might be able to help her. I remember the warm feeling from knowing I had done the right thing for Bev and Bill, and how nice it has been helping Lynda. I can do that for Fran too. It is sad someone who is running a support group and assists children for a living, doesn't have people she can call on when she needs support. Support doesn't necessarily come as a reciprocal package.

Later I remember I am planning on discussing vaccines with Lynda on Sunday. I don't want Fran there, given her view on vaccination. I can't take on two pro-vaccine people at once. I text Lynda to see if we can start earlier so I have enough time with her alone.

> J: Earlier start Sun cos Fran cming?

L: Sure. When?

> J: 10.30am?

L: OK. Will run early. U mite have 2 watch me eat 2nd bkfst. Or join?!

> J: Mite need 2nd bkfst after ur hill. Still HARD.

L: Stick at it. C u Sun. Xox

> J: C u Sun. xox

I have been learning text jargon from Lynda. I didn't have anyone to text before, apart from repair clients, who don't normally text hugs and kisses. Being able to text competently is another part of the confidence I am getting from Lynda, together with improving my wardrobe and decluttering my house. I can't lose her as my friend. I will explain about vaccines on Sunday, clearly and non-judgmentally. She will see I am right – she doesn't need a vaccine and I don't either.

43

6 JUNE 2021

THERE'S a strong north-westerly wind blowing as I cycle across the causeway, headed to Lynda's house. The 'nor'wester' is a hot wind that blows across the Canterbury Plains, drawing heat from the earth as it goes, until it scorches the city and makes everyone feel cross. I feel cross because cycling into a headwind is tough. A nor'wester in June is unusual but it has been a mild winter so far with no sign of the usual frosts.

I am wearing clothing Lynda thinks is more fit for purpose for cycling than a pinafore. I'm wearing my blue merino and Lycra leggings. My bike remains the same, a granny bike with a basket; I can't afford a better one yet. My finances are improving and my pace of repairs and creations picking up, but I don't yet feel financially secure. I still have most of my loan to pay back, even if I have now made two monthly payments that included capital.

I cut my rest stops by one on my ascent to Lynda's house. Am I getting fitter? I wish it would happen more quickly. When cyclists pass me, I look hopefully to see if they are on an e-bike, which makes me feel less incompetent. In my rest stops I compile my thoughts on vaccines, but I haven't come up with a way to raise the topic, let alone a structured approach to discussing it.

Lynda welcomes me and makes my cappuccino with chocolate. We sit on the deck, now empty of gnomes.

"Is your doll clearing still progressing well, Lynda? Your living space is looking great."

"It's okay, but I'm hitting roadblocks now. I have so many dolls whose stories I know, and I can't just let those stories end."

"Maybe we need to talk about how many dolls are enough? You don't have to empty your entire house of dolls. Once you can use all your furniture and rooms that could be enough."

It's so much easier encouraging someone else rather than trying to fix my own issues. Right now what I don't want to tackle are vaccines, but I must. I suddenly blurt out, "I would like to talk with you about vaccines. I am not sure they are a good idea."

"Not a good idea? What do you mean?"

"There's a lot we aren't being told about vaccines and we are also not being told about other important things to do with the pandemic. Remember how Greg said that more people who have been vaccinated are dying of COVID than people who haven't been vaccinated?"

"Yes, I do, but I asked Monique about it afterwards. Turns out, the vaccinated people who are dying are elderly. They were the first to get vaccinated and their vaccinations are wearing off, they need a booster shot."

"Don't you think something strange is happening? If that's true, we are being given vaccines that don't even last six months. Couldn't scientists develop better vaccines? Have the pharmaceutical companies calculated they can make more money by vaccinating people regularly? It's like shampoo – manufacturers encourage people to wash their hair twice. We are being given shampoo that doesn't work well the first time, so you have to apply it again. It seems like a money-making venture for big pharma if there ever was one."

"I see your argument," Lynda replies. "However, because companies make money out of vaccines doesn't make them bad, does it?"

"Not necessarily, but vaccines are not working properly *and* are making people sick. There are reports of lots of people getting sick after being vaccinated. Pharmaceutical companies and governments are trying to suppress the information but organisations like *The Real News* are finding it out and telling us."

"Oh, come on, Julia. You don't believe everything you read in *The Real News*, do you? It's a weird mishmash of real information combined with complete rubbish. You can't tell what's true and what's false. It is a classic trick, mixing truth with falsehoods to confuse people."

"What do you mean by 'complete rubbish'? Can you prove what they are saying is wrong?"

"Did you see the article on magnetisation after vaccination? Pictures of people with magnets and spoons stuck to their skin. It's easy to stick a magnet to your skin if you are sweaty enough. I can do it any time after cycling. The article also says non-magnetic items will stick to people who have been vaccinated. That's confused, isn't it? They are saying people have been magnetised *and* things stick to them which are not magnetic."

"Okay, maybe that article isn't well argued, but there's enough information about vaccination risks to make me not want one.

"My mother told me about the herbal supplements she's taking to fight off COVID naturally. *The Real News* has plenty of information on how to stay healthy without vaccines." This is a stretch. I know Mum talked about taking herbal supplements, but I don't remember her taking them to prevent getting COVID.

"My next-door neighbour says he's not getting vaccinated because of all the risks. Greg isn't either. Do you think they're all out to lunch?"

"I wasn't saying they're out to lunch, Julia. Just that there's a lot of evidence vaccines help the fight against COVID-19. It's exceptionally infectious and kills one to two per cent of people who catch it. I'm confident vaccines are much safer than catching COVID."

I am not listening to Lynda properly now because she isn't listening to me. She hasn't believed anything I've said and keeps countering everything I say.

"I think your mind's made up so you're ignoring the evidence against

COVID vaccines. You want vaccines to be safe so that's all you listen to. You need to investigate more broadly to find out the truth."

"I would say the same about you Julia. You believe your relatives and neighbours and dodgy internet sources. You ignore the Director General of Health's messages. You ignore information from Medsafe and the Government. You ignore doctors saying they are scared about COVID sweeping through old people and sick people. Your relatives and neighbours know better than doctors and the Government?"

"Don't start dissing my relatives and neighbours, you don't even know them, you haven't met them."

"I did meet one neighbour. The guy with strong views about Cindy."

"Okay, you met Alan with a fence between you. I still think you're as closed-minded as you suggest my friends and neighbours are. And you're implying I'm like them."

"What do you mean Julia? I wasn't saying anything about you."

"You don't need to say anything, I can interpret what you aren't saying from what you have said. I don't know how you can say anything about me because you hardly know me at all!"

"Fine, Julia. I could say the same. You barely know me. You haven't tried to find out about me either. You could look at yourself harder. You think your life is difficult. You have no idea how difficult other people's lives are. You don't seem interested in other people."

At this moment Fran knocks on the front door. Our conversation has reached a level of intensity and pitch such that we didn't notice her parking outside or walking up the front steps.

"Hi, anybody home?" she calls.

"Lynda is home, and I am leaving. The two of you can have a nice confab without me about how wonderful vaccines are and how my relatives and neighbours are crazy, and I am too!"

I storm out the door, down the steps, get onto my bike and discover I left my puffer jacket on the deck. Too bad, there's no way I am going back. I let my brakes off and fly down the hill. Who cares if I have an accident? Who cares about anything? COVID has spoiled the world.

44

44

I cycle home furiously. The rising nor'wester speeds me around the base of the hills to Sumner.

I drop my bike in the garden and storm up to my front door, kicking it in frustration when my key sticks in the lock. I kick the few remaining boxes in the entrance, enjoy seeing their contents spill over the floor, then stamp on fallen objects on my way to the kitchen.

How dare Lynda put me down? I thought she was my friend, but she can't be trusted. I imagine her and Fran laughing about my behaviour, querying each other on why I am so weird about vaccines. I feel even more rage.

Before I know it, I am calling Mum, because I need someone to back me up. The only proximal person is Alan-next-door and I'm not having a chat with him about my friend ditching me. Alan would probably tell me she was a weird sort of woman, liking Cindy. While I am angry with Lynda, I am not ready to have someone else tell me I'm a fool for being friends with her.

It's very rare I call Mum when in need. Mostly I call her when I am feeling strong enough to deal with her. The lizard parts of my brain must be remembering Mum grew me in her body and that was a sort of caring. Gran is no use to me as she would say vaccines are life savers and people mean well and do their best. I want someone to say, "How could she? How awful for you, Julia."

"Hi Mum. Thought I'd give you a call. I know I should call you more often."

"Julia darling, always lovely to hear from you. Bruce and I have just returned from an outing to the doctor."

"The doctor? Are you still not feeling well Mum?"

"Visits to the doctor are part of our weekly routine. Today the incontinence nurse was coming through Takaka and my doctor, Wendy, booked me in to talk about Brucey. He isn't in control of things down there any more and I was having to do so much washing. The trouble is, I can't hold my arms above my head for long enough to hang up the washing, so we constantly run out of his underwear and trousers. Adult diapers are the solution, but you wouldn't believe how expensive they are."

This is more information about Bruce than I ever wanted to know although I have diaper experience from Gran.

"Right Mum, that must be difficult for you."

"You know, I thought it would be, but in the end we all pee and poo, don't we. As long as it stays contained it isn't so hard to deal with. The incontinence nurse was lovely, and she gets us free diapers that the government pays for."

"Did you talk with the doctor about your dizzies? How are you feeling now?"

"I talked with Wendy about my dizzies, it's not a big deal, Julia. Wendy's keeping a close eye on me, she's such a nice person. She has given me something to spray under my tongue when I get chest pains and told me not to climb ladders or stand on chairs. I have to ask Ray to come over when a light bulb needs changing, but he's such a nice neighbour there's no problem."

"I wish I had enough money to come visit you. I'm making more money than I have for years, so hopefully it will be soon."

"That would be lovely Julia, you could help me with Brucey. It does get tiring sometimes because he doesn't have much to add to the conversation and there is a lot to do around the house, even though social welfare's giving us two hours of paid cleaning a week."

An invitation to help with Brucey does not fill me with excitement so I make a non-committal, "Mmm."

"Now Julia, before I forget, you don't need to worry about me and Bruce getting COVID, we have both been vaccinated."

"You have been vaccinated against COVID? What do you mean? The last time we talked, you told me there was no way you'd get vaccinated because vaccinations were killing people! You told me about *The Real News* and I found out there are all sorts of things the Government and doctors aren't telling us. And I told my friend, and she didn't believe me. And …"

I am so mad I am hyperventilating. My flip-flop mother has done it again. One day she's telling me vaccinations are terrible and the next day she has one. She was never to be trusted. I am close to hanging up because I don't want to hear anything more she has to say.

"Julia, Julia, darling, you shouldn't take everything I say so literally. You know what I have always been like. I say whatever's going through my head today but what's going through my head tomorrow could be different. I thought you knew that from when you were a little girl. You liked being with your Gran so much more than with me because she was a person like you. Gran figured things out in her head and, when she was sure about them, she talked about them. I talk about things to figure them out, always have, always will.

"I have talked about vaccines a lot with Wendy because she's helped Brucey and me so much. I told her about my herbal supplements, and she said they are all good. There's no problem supporting my health with different approaches. She explained clearly why a vaccine would be unlikely to make me sick, while COVID could make me extremely sick. Because of my heart. Brucey could get even sicker because there are lots of bits of him not working well. For old people like us with parts breaking down it's important to be as protected as possible. I'd feel terrible if I got Brucey sick. I don't want to give Shirleen and Ray COVID either. They're younger than us but not exactly young.

"So yes, we got our first vaccination in May and our second dose today. A little prick and it was over. I never felt sick at all. I don't know what I was so worried about."

"What about vaccines being able to change your DNA and then you get sick years down the track?"

"Julia, sweet, realistically I am not going to be around for many years, so it doesn't matter. But Wendy reassured me on that too. Vaccines aren't messing with your DNA; they are just helping your body prepare to fight COVID."

"Weren't your friends upset when you changed your mind about vaccinations?"

"Cushla and Danny were annoyed because they are totally against vaccinations, so we're having a friend break. I hope they will get over it sooner rather than later. But, funny, it turned out lots of our friends weren't so sure whether they were pro or anti. When Brucey and I got vaccinated I told them they could talk with Wendy. She wouldn't try to convince them of anything they didn't want to do. Then quite a few of them decided to get vaccinated too.

"Not everyone jumped in right away, of course. Some of our friends are still waiting to see if vaccinated people get sick. Some are waiting till COVID gets into New Zealand again, because there's no problem right now. Why get a vaccine when there isn't a problem? Some of our friends are young so can't get vaccinated yet anyhow."

I feel the rug has been pulled out from under me with Mum's change of heart. I no longer know what to think about vaccination, nor how to think about what I should be thinking about vaccination. This is all messed up. There's no point telling Mum about my conversation with Lynda because I'm going to look stupid. Mum has had another of her regular goes at wrecking my life, by telling me things that now she says aren't true.

"Mum, I don't want to continue this conversation. We'll talk another time, okay?"

"That's fine darling. I hope I'll see you up here soon. Don't bother coming if it's only for my funeral though, alright?"

Mum, she might not be consistent, but she knows how to have the last word.

45

STUFF all those people who like the idea of vaccination. They can go hang in their vaccination club and I will keep doing my repairs and pay off my loan so I can stop going to OA and it won't matter. I am not going to wallow in the pit of depression and lethargy I now see I was submerged in for years. It is onwards and upwards for me.

I spend Monday repairing items, putting them on the doorstep and texting people to come and pick them up. I have enough space in the shed to take in new items. My house is close to cleared of queued jobs.

I have set a maximum two-week timeline in which to do each repair and I'm giving it to clients to keep myself on track. I'm also bringing up my re-creation work with anyone I talk to, and I have a few commissions lined up. I can see there's much more potential to make money from re-creation than repair, like Lynda suggested. Even if I don't want her to be right.

While I'm working my phone rings numerous times. When I see the calls are coming from Fran and Lynda, I turn the sound off.

Tuesday is my day to see Bev and Bill. I haven't talked about COVID with Bev. We have plenty of other things to discuss. When I get to their house, Bev is headed out the door with her surfboard. She says she already rode to the Esplanade and the surf is looking just the right size. Bev is wearing a blue and black wetsuit.

"How come you are wearing a shortie wetsuit in the middle of winter?"

"A journalist wanted to make a film about me and gave me the wetsuit because I'd have to be in the water for a long time to get the right shots. I didn't want to use it. I've spent my life surfing in my swimsuit and didn't want to look soft in a film. I have to admit it's actually quite nice to be warmer. Isn't it annoying when you disagree and then people turn out to be right. She's such a nice person though that I don't mind."

I wonder why the journalist didn't get Bev a long-sleeved wetsuit. Bev must be super tough.

"Have a lovely surf. Bill and I will have a nice morning hanging out."

Bill is already watching television, it's *Teenage Mutant Ninja Turtles* again. I try to have a conversation with Bill about which Turtle he likes best but my interrupting the TV irritates him, so I keep quiet and let him watch in peace. He sits happily in his recliner, waving his fist when an evil protagonist attacks a Turtle.

The Turtles remind me of Greg and James and Greg's concerns about vaccination. I start telling Bill about my vaccination worries in a quiet voice, so I don't disturb his TV watching.

I tell Bill how Alan-next-door and Mum and Greg got me worried about vaccinations. How Mum told me about *The Real News* and how scary many of the articles were. How I looked up other articles, searching from the information in *The Real News*, and found lots of links backing up the articles I'd already read. There is so much information out there explaining the dangers of vaccination and the real objectives of the powerful people. I am amazed so many people are uninformed.

I don't stop at telling Bill about vaccinations, I explain how I learned to do research on the internet to find out about Robbie. I tell him what I found, how Robbie had killed a little girl by accident, her family wouldn't forgive him, and his best escape was to come to the other side of the world.

I tell Bill how I dreamed Robbie might be starting to love me and about feeling stupid when I found Robbie with Rosemary and realised

Robbie was just being nice to me. Or was Robbie being nice to me because he liked me as a friend, and it was my mistake for imagining Robbie could be something more? I lost our whole friendship by expecting something Robbie had never suggested was a possibility, it was all in my mind.

Talking to Bill is so easy I keep right on going. I tell him about the boxes and broken objects in my house that I am starting to overcome. How could I have lost the plot so badly as to turn Gran's house into an ugly rubbish dump I don't like? I haven't properly cared for the house or the garden in years and it badly needs painting. I have existed around its periphery, enjoying specific items like my front door, Marimekko chair and mosaic seat while ignoring the rest of the chaos taking over my life since …

I pause to see what Bill is doing. He's happily cheering for Donatello, so I continue, given I'm on a roll.

"This chaos has been taking over my life since not long after my daughter, Amanda, died. She didn't get to have her first Christmas, or her first birthday, or first many, many other things. I couldn't keep the most precious thing in my life safe, so I stopped caring about the myriad other less precious things. It crept up on me, the not caring, and then it took me over, so I submerged under the tidal wave of broken things that everyone's lives are made up of. It's what I felt I deserved, broken things, because I couldn't keep things whole.

"My business was a good idea when I started, when I was making broken things better and more beautiful. But once I lost the ability to beautify, when the cracks in everything made me remember the cracks in everything else, when little could be beautiful, my business felt as much a failure as the rest of me."

Tears are running down my face so hard I can't see properly. What I do see is Bill looking up happily and expectantly, as he does when Bev comes home and it's time for a cup of tea and a biscuit.

I turn my head to see Bev shivering by the door, listening. I have no idea how long she has been there until she comes and gives me a big, cold, wet hug and says, "Julia, it sounds like you have a lot to tell us, if you want to. First, I need a shower before I freeze to death. Why don't you make us a nice cup of Kenya Bold to chat over while I'm in the shower?"

"A cup of tea would be perfect, and I will go make it," I gurgle through my snot and tears. I am grateful Bev has already disappeared back into the hallway, giving me time to put myself back together. Bill, upon hearing a cup of tea is in the imminent offing, has happily gone back to watching TV.

I clatter around Bev and Bill's kitchen finding mugs; their mugs are all different shapes and colours. There is something soothing about the lack of a set of mugs. If you drop a mug it doesn't matter because you can go to the second-hand store and pick out another interesting mug whose colour and shape you like. A friend can give you a special mug that becomes part of your collection. Your mugs can have a set of stories behind them, far more interesting than the story of going to a store to buy a single set. When you have a set they break, one by one, until your set of mugs is no longer a set, but some lonely mugs that are insufficient. In comparison, your mismatched mugs are always enough.

Bev has an excellent teapot in the form of a large egg with a tiny chicken sitting on it as a lid. I find a tray to put the pot on. The base is covered with a map of New Zealand created from pictures of old New Zealand postage stamps. I select a mug with a happy face, a mug with a child's drawing of their family, house, street and city, and a rainbow unicorn mug. A Portmeirion flower and insect milk jug and a sugar bowl in the shape of a ladybird complete the tea offering. I put shortbread biscuits on a plate with a smiling cat in the centre and take everything to the living room.

Bev switches the TV off because they have their cup of tea and biscuit without background disturbance.

"Julia, I would love to hear more about what you were telling Bill. Is there some of your story you'd like to share?"

230

I spill out the story I told Bill, and more, with some things straight and some jumbled up. This is the first time I have told anyone about Amanda, her death, her locked room and how terrified I am of opening the door and what might happen if I do. I tell them about OA, the different people, and their different obsessions. I tell them about Fran wanting us to get vaccinated and how scared I am of vaccinations. I tell them about Mum and about Johnno and Gran and how I don't know who ever really cared about me other than Gran.

Bev sips her tea and listens. Bill sips his tea and eats all the shortbread biscuits without Bev noticing or telling him he needs to watch what he eats because he has high blood sugar.

By the time I finish talking it's time for lunch. Bev and I make sandwiches in the kitchen. Bill likes white bread sandwiches with the crust cut off and the insides to be only ham and cheese. Bev wants him to eat more greens but is happy if he eats anything willingly, so she gives him what he wants with a trio of cherry tomatoes on the side. Bev and I have thick sandwiches of sourdough from the Sumner bakery with cheese and home-made chutney and lashings of bean sprouts Bev grows in jars. We have another cup of Kenya Bold with the sandwiches.

"Well," Bev says, "your story tells of big challenges you are overcoming, Julia. I am so sorry about Amanda. As well as our children, I enjoyed so many other children in my life through teaching them music at school. I still see some of my pupils around Sumner and they introduce me to their own children. It makes me feel connected through the generations, particularly when we don't see much of our grandchildren.

"All those shining little faces I taught, with so much potential. How sad it was every time children couldn't reach their potential, for many different reasons. There's no joy without loss, is there? You just hope the joy will be longer and the loss will be less.

Bev looks over at Bill. "So many lucky, happy years together, that's what I remind myself of every day when I feel infuriated he can't get up off his

231

rear end to make a cup of tea. He will always be the man who cycled home balancing a Clarice Cliff vase on his handlebars as a special present for me.

"Vaccination's such a tricky issue at the moment, isn't it. I need to tell you that both Bill and I are vaccinated against COVID."

"Oh," I say, shrinking a little.

"I thought about vaccinations and decided they make sense for us. Like your Mum, if bad things happen down the track because we're vaccinated, we haven't got a long track left. I don't want to give Bill COVID and he wouldn't want to give it to me. As far as I can understand, vaccination won't completely stop us getting COVID and it won't completely prevent us from getting sick. However, it will make us less likely to get very ill or go to hospital, and that's the best we can do. I made the considered choice to get us both vaccinated, because Bill is finding it hard to make his own decisions now.

"We all need to take charge of our own lives as far as we can and tell our own stories, figuring out how we want our plots to go. Don't let circumstance or other people tell your story for you. How you tell your story changes how your life works out and your story needs to be the best for you it can be. The difficult part is when best for you and best for other people collide."

I am sitting with Gran in her house. I am small, on a stool in the kitchen, kicking my heels against its wooden legs while Gran talks to me. I am cross because Mum has forgotten Johnno's and my birthday, again, and the presents and cakes Gran has made for us don't feel like enough. "She doesn't love us!"

"Of course she loves you, Julia sweet." says Gran. "She isn't good at doing practical things to show her love. I promise you she is doing her best, even if you would like her best to be better. Your Mum is figuring out her story as she goes, and she still isn't good at writing a happy plot with other people in it. She never was good at that when she was little and getting bigger doesn't always mean knowing better. But I'm here to make sure the two of you write excellent stories for your lives."

I didn't get what Gran meant at the time. How was my life a story? Stories were what you read in books with witches and goblins and orcs and all sorts of other scary things in them. Later, I wrote my own storyline without remembering what Gran had told me, creating 'Broken is Beautiful' and running my life the way I wanted it. But after the earthquakes and Amanda's death, I truly lost the plot to the point I didn't remember I should be writing one. Now I remember what I should do, even if I have not fully gained the ability to write my own contented storyline.

In Bev and Bill's living room, where my legs reach the floor when seated in a royal-blue, velour-covered easy chair, I say, "Yes, I get it. I have to take charge of my story, and I am starting to remember how."

"That's the one," says Bev. "Telling your story, as you were to Bill, is a great way to improve on your storyline. All stories have ups and downs, but we have the power to make our lives better, or worse. Your best with our vase was absolutely amazing, so I'm sure you will figure out how to write your own best story."

46

I feel hugely relieved after telling Bev and Bill about Amanda. A weight is lifting, although Amanda's death is as real as it ever was. I finally see a path to remembering her and the joy of her brief existence, rather than relegating her to a closed box in my mind.

Since my day with Bev and Bill, my thoughts about vaccinations are also becoming clearer, though I haven't reached any conclusion. How was I so cavalier when I got Amanda vaccinated, starting when she was six weeks old? I was influenced by everyone around me saying vaccinations were good, and Gran as a loud pro-vaccine voice in my head. I didn't have any reason to question vaccination, so I didn't, although the imperative to question should have been as relevant then as it is for COVID vaccines today. The tricky part remains, how do I find the right answers to my questions?

Monique and Lynda's surety about vaccines finally leads me to look for the information they are claiming. It is unlikely they are making statements with no backing, so what has convinced them they are right, and I am wrong?

I search the internet for counter-arguments to *The Real News* articles and discover as many arguments for vaccination as I previously found against it. The internet leads you to find what you search for, and I have now found there is more than one story told. But which to believe?

I anticipate the next OA meeting with trepidation and resolve. It will be embarrassing and difficult to see Lynda and Fran again, however, I need to see them because I want my story to include them.

I am determined I will manage things well. Should I ask to meet them before OA to get the initial difficult conversation out of the way? I would like to share some more of my story. They might understand me better once they hear where I am coming from. But what if they say they don't want to meet? I vacillate back and forth and almost get to the point of contacting them, when a very disappointing email arrives from Fran.

Dear Thursday Group Members

I am sorry to have to postpone our next OA meeting, scheduled for June 10th. Three of our group members are otherwise engaged and I have a significant conflict myself on that date. Please do send me an email or give me a call if you need to talk about this. I hope we will be able to get back together on June 24th but will contact you when a next meeting is feasible, giving you at least 5 days' notice.

Matthew, I believe it will be your turn to bring tea break snacks when we reconvene.

For anyone requiring proof of attendance, just ask me for an email and tell me who it should be addressed to.

Regards

Fran

This is odd. We've never had an OA session cancelled and I didn't think it was possible for us to say we are 'otherwise engaged'. What sort of conflict could Fran have with the meeting? She has to be available because she is the organiser. The more I look at it, the more the email looks phoney. There is a reason Fran doesn't want the meeting to happen, but she isn't telling us. Does it have anything to do with Barry and ending their relationship? I will just wait until June twenty-fourth to see Fran and Lynda, given Fran is clearly stressed.

I continue working on my repairs, enhancements, and recreations with my new resolve to move forward in life. I build a devil mask for a vacuum cleaner head to make vacuuming exciting. I am making a chandelier with broken glass from a house destroyed in the earthquakes. The owners had a significant blown glass collection in a range of vivid colours. We have devised a plan to use the chandelier in their spectacular new build above Redcliffs, which is finally taking place. It 'only' took them a decade of fighting with their insurance company.

Fran and Lynda text me sporadically but I not only ignore the messages, I delete them. It takes a significant effort of will and concentration to delete texts before reading them, but I do not want to risk getting into an electronic shouting match. I need to resolve our situation in person.

On Sunday I am having a break with a cup of Kenya Bold in the garden, happily surveying the lack of boxes and considering winter pruning. I spot a grey pumpkin that has been revealed in the autumn die-back. That's a bonus, I can cook myself up a batch of Thai pumpkin soup. Unexpectedly, the front door lion emits several thumps.

I don't hurry, thinking it must be someone whose item I have repaired and who can't identify it. The person hasn't bothered to read the large names written on the enclosing paper bags. Or perhaps they can't see the names and forgot to put their reading glasses in their pocket when they came out to collect their goods.

However, it is not someone picking up a repair, it is Fran and Lynda on my doorstep. Lynda is carrying my poppy-red puffer jacket. This shouldn't be entirely surprising, since it is the Sunday Lynda and I would have met at my house. But after last week's fiasco, I didn't for a moment contemplate we would stick to our schedule. Should I have read those texts?

"Lynda, Fran. Were you passing by?"

"Not at all Julia, we came specifically to see you," Lynda replies.

"I'm not sure I want to see *you*," I say. "Do we have anything to talk about?"

"C'mon Julia, we're your friends and we care about you. We aren't here to convince you to get a vaccine. Or for you to convince us we don't need a vaccine. We came to see you."

I frustrate myself by bursting into tears. Once I thought I could cope on my own, but it doesn't look like I can. I no longer even want to cope on my own. I want friends, which means I am going to have to do the hard work friendship requires.

Fran and Lynda spontaneously step forward and hug me and I cry some more. Then I become more gracious and offer to make them tea.

"Kenya Bold would be perfect," Lynda says. "Fran, Julia's introduced me to the best black tea you can buy in the supermarket. She can introduce you to Kenya Bold if you haven't yet tried it."

"I don't believe I've had the pleasure of Kenya Bold," says Fran.

We take the tea to the garden on the Indian inlaid tray. Lynda points out to Fran how beautiful the mosaic sofa is before they sit on it, and I pull my log over. Then our conversation becomes more serious.

"Right," says Fran. "It's more than time we all put our cards on the table. Each of us has been holding some cards closely in our hands. Right?"

Lynda and I look at each other and slowly nod our heads.

"Yes, it's time I told parts of my story I have been holding onto," I say.

"Me too." Lynda agrees.

Fran says, "How about I go first, given I am supposed to be the OA group facilitator, although the longer time goes on, the less capable I think I am of facilitating this type of group. I should stick to my children.

"You will remember me telling you about where my obsessive desire to help others came from. My birth mother didn't want me, to the point she physically injured me. I don't want other people to suffer like that. I want to be there for people, so they know someone cares about them. Part of me is still the sad little girl whose birth mother beat her up and I use helping other people so that little girl feels better. Everywhere I turn there are more people who need help. I know I can't help them all, but I'm still figuring out where to draw the line, because no amount of helping feels like enough.

"As a result of not setting boundaries and needing a relief valve, I have created a new problem that affects me and the OA group. I have reluctantly concluded I need help to solve this problem because I'm not getting anywhere on my own. That's why I wanted to meet with the two of you; I am struggling to know what to do, and I need help from people who know what it is like to struggle to find a solution."

"Got it." Lynda says. "So, when are you going to spill the beans? You scooted off pretty fast from my house the other day without saying anything."

Lynda's words sound harsh. Fran's finding it hard to tell us about her problem and needs more encouragement than attack.

"Sure Fran, I'm happy to listen," I say.

"So, my problem is – well the problem I have created is – it's actually – Matthew and I have been seeing each other."

Fran is going to need to pick Lynda and my jaws up off the floor, our mouths are so wide open. This is a possibility that hadn't crossed the most remote part of my mind. Fran is having an affair with Matthew? Matthew of the Matthew and Monique couple who appear so deeply immersed in coupledom as to be obscenely drowning in it? Matthew who has helped Monique overcome her plasterboard addiction? Matthew who is proposing to get a final tattoo on his arm that says 'Monique'? Matthew and Monique who are going to buy a house together?

My mouth spits out, "But Fran, I thought you were having an affair with Barry. I saw the two of you sitting in his Audi before OA."

Fran bursts into gales of laughter, relieved by my inappropriate reaction. "An affair with boring Barry? You've got to be kidding. Anyhow, Barry is already in an extramarital relationship with his Red Zone Cat assistant, Liz. I could tell from all their little glances and touches when Holly and I did our Red Zone Cat tour. It's usually easy to see what people are doing, which is why Matthew and I have been scrupulously careful about staying separate from each other at OA. Not that being careful has done me much good in the end.

"My problem is not about whether people have guessed what we are doing, but about how to persuade Matthew we need to stop doing it. Matthew wants us to be a couple, in the open, and to move in with Holly and me, but that isn't a starter. Holly doesn't need someone else in her life, she needs stability. She never meets any of the guys I get together with.

"Mostly I've used Tinder to for the odd hook-up – no expectations, no guilt. I should never have taken the risk of getting together with someone in the group. It started when Matthew confided in me that Monique was treating him more like a collectable than a lover, he wasn't sure she cared for him the way he cared for her. We went out for a drink, had a few too many, and the rest is unfortunate history.

"So, here I am, coming to the people I'm paid to help and asking them to help me."

This is a problem without an obvious solution. While I am thinking what to say, Fran continues, "Now my story is on the table, how about you two?"

47

LYNDA and I look at each other. Lynda takes the plunge. "You both know my obsession is dolls, but you don't know why.

"For much of my young life I was a happy only child with wonderful parents. My parents and I had so much fun together. My early memories are of outdoor adventures. Mum and Dad were teachers so we would pack up the car at the end of term then drive to Totaranui, or Pelorus Bridge, or Manapouri. We'd live in a tent for weeks. We'd cook outside, except when the sandflies got too bad. I didn't have to wash my hair or go to bed before dark. I'd play for hours with kids at the campground till Mum would yell, 'This is the fifth time I've said come for dinner,' and I'd scurry back.

"As I got older, we went overseas. On one memorable trip we backpacked in the Himalayas, walking between tea houses in the Everest mountains. The Sherpas loved children and would give me treats. I'd hang out with their kids while Mum and Dad drank endless cups of lemon and ginger tea.

"We bought dolls in every country we visited to hold memories. We named them after people we met. There was Erminda, the Chilean woman in Parinacota on the border of Bolivia and Chile. She lived by a volcano near a lake with flamingos. Erminda had a snorkelling mask, snorkel, and a stuffed hairy armadillo on her dresser. 'My son gave me the mask and snorkel,' she said. 'They are for use in dust storms.' I can see Erminda with her two dark braids, bowler hat, and layers of skirts, walking through a dust storm in a mask and snorkel."

Fran and I stay silent. Neither of us has travelled like Lynda. She is lucky she went to such exciting places as a child.

"I'm sure our lives had ups and downs. But all I remember were ups until Dad committed suicide when I was twelve years old. One day I went to school and by the time I came home he was dead, and Mum was a shadow of herself, who grew more transparent every day.

"No one explained what happened, why he did it. Mum told me he was very sad but that didn't sound like enough. Now I wonder if he had a mental illness no one wanted to talk about.

"Mum needed help. Both her parents and Dad's parents were already dead. She had a much older sister who we didn't see much of. Angeline was fifteen years older than Mum. They didn't know each other well because Angeline left home when Mum was young. However, family ties prevailed, and Angeline came to stay with us.

"Mum and Angeline didn't get on, so our house felt continuously cheerless and tense. Then, six months after Dad died, Mum committed suicide."

"Oh Lynda, that's so sad for you," Fran says. "So terribly sad to lose both your parents."

"I can't remember how bad it was because the next year is blank in my head. I must have gone to school. Angeline and I lived in Mum and Dad's house. However, it's like I stopped making memories because there were no memories I wanted to keep. Angeline explained that Mum had appointed her as my guardian. She must have agreed but it clearly wasn't what she wanted. Angeline resented giving up her own life to move to Christchurch. Mum must have made staying in our house a condition of the guardianship, otherwise, I'm sure Angeline would have tried to sell the house and return to Timaru.

"Angeline cared for me, but I never felt she loved me. I don't know if she loved anyone. She worked hard at discharging her duty, but I knew I was a burden.

"Angeline liked a tidy house and children aren't tidy. She was also obsessive about cleanliness. She constantly reminded me to wash my hands and required I keep my room perfect. Mum and Dad were not tidy people, so the first major thing Angeline did was tidy up, everywhere.

"Tidying quickly turned into throwing away. Then Angeline and I had our first big fight. I found her throwing my Erminda into the bin. Erminda sat in the home I'd made her in my diving goggles, on the living room dresser. Angeline couldn't make sense of a doll sitting in diving goggles, so into the bin she went.

"I screamed and yelled and tried to punch Angeline. When she threatened to call the police, I grabbed Erminda and stormed into my room. I slammed the door and piled furniture against it. It took a day before Angeline understood I was serious and got worried. I was getting worried too – I had a bowl in my room for pee but knew I couldn't hold poo in forever.

"Eventually Angeline coaxed me out with food, and I agreed to talk. All dolls would live in my room and Angeline would buy me shelves for them. I would dust the shelves once a week and never leave dolls in the rest of the house or Angeline would throw them away."

"That must have been tough, for a child," says Fran. "Having your most precious possessions constantly under threat."

"It made me very careful to keep my end of the bargain. Life with Angeline became a manageable routine; we intersected minimally. I counted down the days till I'd be eighteen and she'd leave.

"Angeline showed me how to do my washing. I made my own lunches, cooked dinner every second night. I got an after-school job to supplement my allowance from my parents' estate.

"Angeline and I only had one more big bust-up before she left. I had a koala we bought in Brisbane. I have a picture of a tiny me with a terrified expression on my face, holding a koala nearly half my size at a koala sanctuary. Our memorial doll had to be a koala and 'Mi-Ko' became my favourite soft toy. She went on every trip because I refused to sleep without her. Mi-Ko's presence was checked at every step. She lived in Mum's backpack during the day.

"Mi-Ko became grubby, and her fur deteriorated. She looked like she had patches of mange. I didn't notice, she was my most precious possession. Mum and Dad tried to persuade me to wash Mi-Ko because she smelt. For me the smell was a sleeping pill. I hadn't grown out of Mi-Ko when Mum and Dad died. She still slept in my bed. After they died, there was no chance she'd sleep anywhere but with me.

"However, by the time I was fifteen, even I started to realise Mi-Ko didn't smell good. I thought I'd give her a wash. One Saturday when Angeline was out, I took Mi-Ko to the laundry. I was suddenly overcome by hunger because I'd been for a long beach run. I went to the kitchen, made myself two huge sandwiches and wolfed them down. I forgot Mi-Ko waiting in the laundry."

Fran and I sit quietly. There can't be a good end to this story.

"It was a cold August day with a stiff easterly wind blowing off the sea. Angeline came home and lit the log burner. I went to my bedroom to start maths homework, then I thought it would be nicer to do my homework by the fire. When I went into the living room, Angeline was putting Mi-Ko in the log burner. I screamed and launched myself at Angeline, who dropped Mi-Ko and fell sideways. I tried to rescue Mi-Ko from the flames. I burnt myself, you can still see the scars on my arm. I got Mi-Ko out of the log burner and threw a rug over her. But she was already half burned.

"I never forgave Angeline. We had another three painful years together. They must have been as miserable for her as they were for me. When I turned eighteen, she gladly returned to Timaru and we have barely been in touch since. Sometimes I think I should contact her. It must have been a thankless task, taking on a surly teenager. If only she had shown a little more compassion, we could have got on better.

"Julia, now you'll understand why I didn't want you investigating my display case. That's where Mi-Ko lives. At first she lived on my bedroom shelf. But the fire had burned her beyond reconstruction, so she constantly shed fur and stuffing. When I became a conservator, I learned the best thing for Mi-Ko was to keep her in a climate-controlled case. So now she's centre stage and reminds me of Mum and Dad every day. I didn't want you to get interested because I have never told anyone this story."

I thought Fran had a significant problem, now I see Lynda has a bigger one. I also have an immediate problem, because it is my turn to share my story as my dues for this friendship group.

48

I delay by making another cup of Kenya Bold until I can procrastinate no longer. I tell Lynda and Fran the story of Amanda's brief life and my role in her death. It's a lot easier because I told it to Bev and Bill recently. By the time I finish we are all crying, about our own and everyone else's stories.

"Can we see Amanda's room?" Lynda asks, as unafraid as ever.

Part of me wants to say "Yes" and part of me wants to say "No". Instead, I say, "If we climb in the window."

"Aha," Lynda says, "did I not tell you one of my many talents is lock picking? Angeline kept her bedroom door closed. I wanted to see what she was locking me out of. I found a book on lock picking at a second-hand store and kept trying till I cracked it. There was never anything interesting in Angeline's room. However, my skills have proven useful at the Museum for accidentally locked doors in the old buildings, so my penknife has a basic lock picking set on it – voila!"

"Okay," I say. "Let's try the lock, now."

It takes Lynda a few attempts. Then we hear an audible click as the lock barrels shift into position.

Lynda steps away from the door and I crack it open to view Amanda's room for the first time in five years. Robbie has left it tidy, although plenty of dust has accumulated since he moved on.

I find a little carved hedgehog sitting on the dresser. That's odd, I wonder why he left it there. I curl my hand around it and forget it, along with the dust. What I focus on are the walls. Even with all the rips in the plaster, the flower garden I painted is still beautiful; I can see Lynda and Fran admiring it too.

"You are so talented Julia," Lynda says. "I wish I could create like you do. I just repair and preserve textiles."

"Repair and creativity go hand in hand," I say. "We can try making something together and you will see what possibilities you can conjure up."

We stand together contemplating the torn garden. I can see myself repairing the walls and enhancing the patches.

"What do we all think we should do now?" says Fran.

"First," I say, "I need to examine the insides of my mostly bare cupboards to magic up lunch because I am hungry, and I bet Lynda is even hungrier. After that, I have an idea budding in my head which I need you both to help me with."

I dredge up a can of coconut milk and some chilli flakes. We chop up this morning's pumpkin find to make a batch of soup and then eat it in the garden. I need to get two more nice chairs soon, so I can have friends visit in my sitting room.

"What's your idea?" says Lynda.

"We need to tell our stories. We've been carrying them around as huge weights, letting the mass of the past dictate our forward plots. Our stories have made us do strange things to bear them, like keeping objects and behaviours that stop us seeing new ways to move forward. We aren't developing our stories because they are too heavy to shift. We need to lighten our burdens and move our storylines forward. Telling our stories more widely will be part of that journey."

Fran considers this. "There's a branch of counselling called 'narrative therapy', where people describe their lives as a set of linked stories. Stories are how humans make sense of the world, of ourselves, and how we connect with each other – humans are fundamentally narrative beings. We all know stories as something we share and that stories can change over time."

"Yes, I get it too," Lynda says. "Museum practice has changed a lot in the last two decades. It used to be about collecting large numbers of objects, now it's about learning through telling the stories of objects. When curators accept objects into the Museum, we get the people who donate them to tell us their stories and we record them. The display team use the stories to create exhibitions.

"However, there are some things I'm happy to tell people, but not everything. Not my story about Angeline."

"And I'm not telling people about my birth mother," says Fran.

"We'll tell people the parts of our stories we're ready to share. I believe that, as we share more, sharing will get easier. And we are going to get help telling our stories. Lynda, your dolls will help."

"My dolls? What do you mean?"

"We are going to give parts of our stories to dolls, so the dolls can share stories with other people. Then the dolls and their new owners will take the story on, building different futures.

"Lynda, you can create wardrobes for the dolls because you are great with textiles. I fix, create, and make things more beautiful, so I'll mend dolls and make them a set of possessions."

"What do I do?" asks Fran.

"You will help us find friends and homes for the dolls. You work with children, right?"

"Yes, I work with my special children at Linwood High School. I also sometimes assist at other schools, like Linwood Avenue Primary."

"A primary school sounds like a great place to start. I bet there'll be quite a few children who would like a doll, particularly if it comes with lots of interesting things that tell you about its history, what it can do and what it might be able to do in the future. How about an electrician doll who comes with mobile phone cables and a toolbox? A chef doll with bowls, utensils, and cake tins? A climber doll you can raise and lower on a rope and learn about knots with?"

"That's an amazing idea, Julia," says Lynda. "We should celebrate. Where's that bottle of Lindauer sparkling wine, the one I gave you on your birthday? I wouldn't normally have a drink during the day. Not good for my running. But this is a special day."

I pull the Lindauer out of the sitting room cupboard and we toast each other using my growing mismatched mug collection.

We discuss a broad range of ideas around the dolls and debate the afternoon away. Will the dolls come with a written story? This could work for some of Fran's children, but many are not strong readers. Could dolls come with a written story that is also in a sound file, so children can listen to it? How realistic should the doll's stories be? Some of the things we have to say are sad, how would that work with children? How will it work with children who have their own sad and difficult lives?

We develop a plan and a timeline – we give ourselves a month. We will each choose a small number of dolls for whom we will create stories. Lynda will make each doll several sets of clothes, I will make each doll a set of interesting possessions and Fran will write or record their stories, in collaboration with the person who chose the doll. She will also get in touch with Linwood Primary to find children with whom we will share our dolls.

49

NEXT Sunday we meet at Lynda's house to choose dolls. Lynda says she doesn't mind her dolls going to new homes if they are going to a place where they will be loved. However, she isn't sure about giving dolls a new story if they already have their own story. Therefore, she starts by giving Fran and me the choice of dolls without a detailed history.

We work hard on our dolls. The COVID Delta variant is creating new waves of infection around the world and it's hard to imagine it won't reach New Zealand soon. The rest of the world is, once again, employing lockdowns to control the virus so another lockdown feels imminent. We badly want to accomplish something before we get locked down.

Finally, on a Monday morning, we are ready to go to Linwood Primary with Fran. She has approval from the school, talked with the group of children there who she supports and has permission from their caregivers. She announced a special lunchtime session for children interested in getting a new doll as a friend. We will see how many children turn up.

I have butterflies in my stomach eating breakfast. Will any of the children want the dolls? One of them is particularly special for me.

When we reach the school, Fran takes us to a room more like the Sumner Surf Club than classrooms of my memory. There are colourful beanbags on the floor of a warm, sunlit, open space. A group of ten

249

children are chattering and look excited. Fran asks the children to introduce themselves. "Tell us your names and something interesting about yourselves."

"My name is Hossein, and my dad is from Iran and my mum is from New Zealand. We have a dog called Maverick."

"I'm Fiafia, my name means 'be happy'. I'm mostly happy, 'specially when I'm at school."

"Gidday, I'm Fergus and I like playing the trumpet, loudly."

"Hello, my name is Charina, and I came from Manila with my parents when I was a baby. We live in a house with my grandma and grandad and a cat called Charlie."

"I'm Carlos and my mum and dad are from Cuba. I would like to travel there one day because it's warm with yummy tropical fruit to eat."

"Hi, my name is Daiko which means powerful light. My mums say I make their lives shine."

"Hello, I'm Li Kang and I like music and playing with Lego."

"I'm Ruby and my favourite colour is red, so it is good our school uniform is red tops and blue shorts."

"Gidday, I'm Kobus. I have two parents and a twin brother, Johan, but we don't like being in the same school class."

"My name is Aroha because I love to do everything I possibly can. And I have a budgie called Bestie."

"Ata marie children and thank you for those lovely introductions," Fran says. "You are the first special group of children who are going to help some dolls write their stories. Who likes hearing stories?"

"Me, me, me," the children chorus.

"And who likes creating stories?"

"Me ..." There isn't quite the same degree of confidence from the children about creating stories as there was enthusiasm for hearing stories.

"Lynda, Julia, and I are all practising telling each other our stories. We are learning how to do it, like you guys learn things in school. No one is ever too old to learn, and everyone likes hearing stories, not just children. We all have our own stories to tell about our lives. We need friends so we can tell each other our stories, having turns telling and listening. Telling stories is a great way of making our life stories better. Dolls need good stories just like people."

Next, it's Lynda's turn to introduce herself. "Hi, I'm Lynda and I work in the Canterbury Museum."

"Ata marie Lynda," reply the children.

"It's very nice to meet you all today. Some of you might have visited our Museum, with your family or your school. My job is making sure the clothing in the Museum stays looking good. Clothing helps us understand the stories of people who lived before us. Like, did people have nice clothing for special occasions, or did they only have enough money for clothing to work in?

"I have made clothing for your dolls so they can do lots of different activities. But if the stories you create with the dolls mean they need new clothing, so they can go caving, or be a ballerina, I can make new clothing. We could even make new clothing together."

It's my turn. "Hi, I'm Julia."

"Ata marie Julia."

"I am really happy to meet you today, too. My work is for my own business, called 'Broken is Beautiful'. Who thinks broken things can be beautiful?"

The children look confused, and I worry I've started off on the wrong track. Then I bring out my repaired gold filigree teacup together with a large teddy bear who ended up at 'Time and Time Again' and whose bald spots I have covered with an abstract of colourful fabrics. Teddy is down an eye, so I gave him a rakish eye patch. The children look interested and some shuffle forward to get a better look.

"Here's a teddy and a teacup that broke in different ways, and I have re-created. I would never have thought to have roses growing out of the teacup if it hadn't broken. The roses remind me of my Gran, who I used to have tea with. Tea is my favourite drink. What favourite drinks do you have?"

A torrent of answers highlight Coca Cola, milk and hot chocolate, then Fran quietens the children down so I can continue.

"I make sure our dolls have things they need to have fun and interesting lives. Cavers need headlamps and climbing ropes. Ballerinas need barres and mirrors for their practise and a stage on which to perform. If you find your dolls want to do different things with their lives for which they aren't yet equipped, I can help you make those things."

"Thank you, Julia and Lynda," says Fran. "Now it's time for everyone to find a doll who they would like to get to know better. We are going to take turns introducing our dolls to you. Julia, why don't you go first?"

We pull a low table forward into the circle of the children so they can all see. I put my first doll on the table, with her seven sets of clothes the colour of the rainbow, covering multiple activities. Lynda has done a beautiful job, sewing each set out of a fabric with a different flower on it. I have made this doll a bicycle, a surfboard and a tiny brown Temuka tea pot with two little gold-coloured cups.

Aroha throws her arm in the air, bobbing her hand up and down like she wants to leap with it, although she is restrained by her wheelchair. "I love flowers so much and I want to ride a bicycle. Please, please, can she be my doll? What's her name?"

"Her name," I say carefully to keep my voice in check, "is Amanda. She's named after someone I once knew very well. Aroha, it would be lovely if you'll be friends with Amanda. Let's sit down together and read this book about Amanda and how her life began. I'll come back and visit you regularly so we can chat about how you're getting on and the stories you and Amanda are creating together. I'm sure you two will have a great time and I'll be there to help in whatever way I can."

50

LATE JULY–SEPTEMBER 2021

BY the end of July Fran still hasn't reconvened the OA group. The three of us are busy with our doll story project in our spare time, and Fran doesn't have many hours to spare beyond her work and Holly. When we are working on the dolls together, Lynda and I suggest to Fran she can't keep delaying meetings without explaining what's happening. I feel a bit annoyed that she must still be being paid by OA and isn't doing her job.

"Yes, you're right," Fran sighs. "I don't like letting people down. I have rationalised the lack of meetings by thinking we three are working together, the other four are in their pairs and everyone has been progressing. That's what I have told OA in my monthly reports. But I do need to bring everyone back together. I'll send out an email setting the next meeting date."

"Hang on," Lynda says. "What's the story with Matthew? Isn't he the reason you delayed the June meeting? Don't you need to sort that out?"

"I know I have to finish things with him," says Fran. "But I'm worried about how fragile he is and how upset he'll be when I tell him."

"He'll survive," Lynda says. "He's got Monique to support him. He never looked very fragile at meetings."

"He doesn't like to let his vulnerability show. He's a lot softer than his tattooed exterior suggests."

"Fran, you just have to get on and do it," I say.

"Yes, I know I do. I'm just not sure when is the best time."

"You have to *set* a time!" I might be the pot calling the kettle black, but Fran needs an explosive device under her.

"What do you suggest?"

"It's not up to us to suggest a time. But we'll hold you to one that you do suggest."

"Okay, okay. I have to set a meeting and sort things before it. Right?"

"Well, duh," Lynda and I chorus.

We receive Fran's email.

Dear Thursday Group Members

Unfortunately, Holly has been quite unwell and is not recovering quickly, so I'm not currently available to lead a meeting either in person or online. Our next meeting will be 19th August. However, if any of you would like to get together beforehand the Surf Club is available on Thursdays at our regular meeting time. Can you all please reply to this message and tell me if I can share your email address with other group members? Once I receive your replies, I will send a message to everyone comfortable to connect directly.

If anyone would like to chat in the interim, please do give me a call.

Regards

Fran

The only person who sends a reply is Matthew. Over our next shared cup of Kenya Bold Fran revisits her dilemma. "What should I do, girls? I need to reply to Matthew and explain no one else wanted to meet."

"Fran," Lynda sighs. "You know what to do."

When we meet the following week, Fran tells us she has been in touch with Matthew. "I told him our relationship is over. Now I'm getting a stream of calls and messages. I don't know what to do."

"You do know," I say. "Don't reply."

We help Fran hold firm to her resolve to not communicate with Matthew. She gets increasingly stressed as August 19 approaches, when she won't be able to avoid seeing him. However, COVID and the New Zealand Government helpfully solve Fran's dilemma. When the Delta variant takes off in the community mid-August, the Government locks the entire country down again for three weeks and no meetings are possible.

The three of us message regularly through lockdown, planning our next visit to Linwood Primary for whenever lockdown ends and keeping each other's spirits up. My spirits are high because I have both impetus and time to focus on my recreations, and they are going well. Lynda has secured me three slots in a summer craft exhibition at Canterbury Museum and I am deciding what I will show. She is also excitedly generating broader ideas of what we could do with dolls and children. Fran is not so happy because she remains conflicted about the future of our OA group.

> F: Hey girls. Don't think I can do the OA thing any more. It's too much.

> L: If you can't, then don't.

Lynda's directness has not abated in the slightest.

> F: But what about the other group members?

> L: You know the basic First Aid rule. Save yourself first. Injured people can't save other people.

J: You need to think about yourself and Holly, Fran. You have given Lynda and me new skills with which to move forward. I'm sure Monique and Greg and Barry are all in a much better place now too.

F: You're right. I want to work with my children and have time to do things with you two. I will have to get tougher. Lynda, help! Wish I was you!

Lynda and I receive Fran's next email.

Dear Thursday Group Members

I hope you are coping well with this second lockdown and that we aren't locked down for long. I also hope the support relationships you have established in the group are helping.

I am sorry to have to let you know I can no longer facilitate this OA group. I have talked with OA management, and they are happy to provide contact details for existing groups elsewhere in Christchurch that you could join. Unfortunately, this group is too small for them to continue the support contract. Please do get in touch if you would like assistance finding another group.

I apologise for not telling you this in person, but we don't know when lockdown will end, and I wanted to let you know sooner rather than later.

All the best going forward.
Fran

A past me would have been concerned by the crumbling of our OA group but current me hears about its dissolution with equanimity. My friendship with Lynda and Fran will continue outside of OA. I am paying back loan capital with interest every month to Bank Aotearoa. I feel confident I can tell the bank that my support group is no longer operational without repercussion, and I see a not-too distant future where I will no longer have a loan to repay.

51

WHILE Fran wants nothing more to do with Matthew, Lynda and I remain hugely curious about what's going on with him and Monique. Are they still selling their houses and buying one together? Will Matthew find the courage to tell Monique he isn't happy in their relationship and end it? My curiosity might have an unpleasant edge, given my dislike of Monique, but it's unsatisfied, so I persuade Lynda to ask her real estate friend to investigate recent house sales and purchases in Sumner.

Lynda and her friend catch up over a wine to exchange the information. Lynda tells me that both Matthew and Monique's houses have sold for good prices in the post-lockdown real estate frenzy, and they have jointly purchased a property on Scarborough Head, with stunning views over the sea to the Kaikoura Mountains. It's one property above a house that Pa Stout worked on, long ago.

Lynda and I go for a walk on Scarborough Head to check the street out. We peer through the house windows to see it's furnished with Monique's design flair and lined with ply. Monique will no longer have the temptation of plasterboard at home if her addiction rears its head again.

However, only a couple of months later I see the same house on the board in the real estate agent's window by the Supervalue. What happened? In one of those small Christchurch world coincidences, Lynda's hairdresser comes to the rescue. She also proves that you should never trust a hairdresser with any personal information. Lynda repeats the conversation to me over the phone.

"I wish I had blonde hair. The greys wouldn't be as obvious," Lynda said.

"Depends how fussy you are," replied her hairdresser. "I have a blonde client who's a doctor. She must be fifty-five and she's as horrified now by a hint of grey roots as she was by just a few grey strands. She puts a lot of effort into her appearance, and it pays off. Though she's the sort who looks like they don't even try, you know?"

"Funny, there's someone like that in a group I go to. She isn't called Monique, is she?"

"Oh, you know Monique? What a shame about her and Matthew!"

"Yes, isn't it. They got together in our group. Such a pity it didn't last. They seemed a perfect couple. Matthew seemed very pleasant." Lynda was improvising frantically.

"Maybe that's how it looked, but do you know what she discovered?"

"No, what?"

"He was a secret gambler. He'd run up huge gambling debts by taking loans against his house."

"Really? That's terrible." Lynda was indeed surprised. Matthew hid his obsession better than anyone else at OA.

"So when they bought that beautiful new house, he didn't have the money to put into it he'd promised. He told Monique he'd stop gambling. I told her she shouldn't trust him. I mean, what sort of guy hides a secret like that for over a year? What else might he be keeping from you? I advised her to break it off before some other horrible thing appeared out of the woodwork."

"Did you? How did she take it?"

"She ended it shortly afterwards. Said he was getting too clingy anyhow. She should have ended things before they bought the new house. Such a shame having to sell such a beautiful place. But Monique said she's over owing money on a house. She'll buy a small place somewhere closer to her work. She decided to treat herself before it sold and had plastic surgery done to tighten up her face. I know because she asked me to cut her hair to hide the scars while they healed."

"Oh, plastic surgery. Wow."

Lynda and I were both very surprised by Monique having plastic surgery. Had she undergone other procedures in the past that we didn't notice? For someone only recently recovered from wearing drab pinafores, plastic surgery is beyond my realm of comprehension. The message for me from this exchange was to stick with cutting my own hair. For Lynda it was to always wear a mask while visiting the hairdresser as a physical reminder to keep your mouth closed.

52

OCTOBER–DECEMBER 2021

WHEN Fran, Lynda and I get together again at Lynda's house after lockdown ends, she is bouncing with excitement. "It's not coffee. Not just coffee, anyhow. I have so much I want to talk about with you. I want us to start a social enterprise!"

"A social enterprise? What's that?" Fran asks.

"It's a business. But its purpose is helping other people, not making money. It needs to make enough money to run, but its goal is to help children through our dolls."

"We're already doing that," I say.

"Sure we are. But we could do so much more."

"What more?" Both Fran and I are wary, we already have plenty on our plates.

"Here's the bigger picture. We create a limited number of very special dolls. Collectables of the future. We make amazing clothing and accessories and stories to match. We will need to break into the doll collector market, but I've got contacts through my clothing conservator networks. We use the money from high-end doll sales to support expanding our work with children."

"What'd we call it?"

"Easy – 'Dolls with Stories.'"

"And who'd run it?"

"Me," says Lynda happily. "I'd be a great CEO. I've got enough money saved to quit the Museum and try it for a year. I won't have money to travel, but we can't travel now anyhow. Perfect timing. The three of us will be the board of directors. I'll need you both for ideas and support, but I'll make it happen! I'll find secondhand dolls; I see them everywhere I go. I'll recruit volunteers to make clothes and accessories. Another volunteer team will go to schools and co-create stories with children. I know lots about volunteers from the Museum. It runs on volunteers."

"What about the special dolls?" I ask.

"Yes, I'll need you two to help with those. But it'll only be a very small number."

"How will we tell people what we do? I don't know many people to tell," I say.

"We need a website. And to get active on social media. I know who to ask. Barry and Greg were telling stories about Red Zone Cats online. Why don't I get in touch with them? We could meet up!"

I'm not that excited by the idea of meeting with Barry again. And thinking about Greg reminds me that I still don't know what to do about vaccination, despite numerous conversations with Lynda and Fran. However, Lynda's enthusiasm and energy is infectious.

"Let's see if Greg and Barry can help. What do you think, Fran?"

Fran looks nervous. I wonder if she's concerned about remeeting people upset by the rapid demise of our OA group.

"C'mon Fran," says Lynda. "I'll chat with them both first. Check out they're all good. It's a way to keep the best bits of OA going, without you having to run it."

"Okay," says Fran, reluctantly. "I'm willing to give it a try."

"Great, we can have a get-together over coffee. Or Kenya Bold."

"My house is too small for a big group," I say.

"No problem, mine for coffee then." Lynda is on a roll.

53

LYNDA lets us know Greg and Barry are happy to meet up. "They're looking forward to it," she relays. "They have some ideas they want to talk through with us too."

I think Barry is likely to do most of the talking. However, I'm trying to keep my negative thoughts to myself. I have realised, if telling our stories is how we create our own lives, it could be that stories we tell about others shape their lives too.

On a sunny Sunday morning I cycle up to Lynda's house. I would like to say I barely notice the hill climb but that wouldn't be true. However, I no longer need more than one rest and I almost enjoy the ride. Lynda has loaned me her spare road bike. I feel like a fraud riding a road bike. I'm not an athlete. But I am getting good at pretending, wearing my Icebreaker top and Lycra leggings. I did get Lynda to change the weird pedals for normal ones.

Fran gets out of her red hatchback as I arrive, and we go in together. Lynda makes us a coffee while we wait for Barry and Greg; the regular cappuccino with chocolate for me and a flat white with soy milk for Fran. We look at each other when the doorbell rings. Barry and Greg are shuffling on the doorstep, looking as uncomfortable as we feel.

"Hi, Barry and Greg," says Lynda. "Like I said on the phone, we're not here to talk about COVID. Or about vaccines. We're here to talk about business. Right?"

"All good with me," says Barry and Greg nods.

"So, we're thinking of setting up a business and we need to know more about websites and social media."

"No problem talking about that," Barry says. "We've got lots to suggest because we're setting up a business too."

"What sort of business?" I ask.

"We want a better way to support Red Zone Cats than begging for funds. I had the idea of developing a cat food business for easy access to food. And income to pay for volunteers. Maggot farming is taking off internationally. Insect protein's the way of the future. I've persuaded the Christchurch City Council to make some red zone land available for maggot farming in shipping containers."

"You can grow maggots in shipping containers?" Fran's getting drawn in.

"Sure. A woman in Australia has designed containerised maggot farms; I've imported a couple and we're doing a trial. I've got a local pet food company who'll turn maggots into cat food. We'll give the maggot manure to the Council for their fertiliser business. This is a win-win-win."

"What will you call the business?"

"Greg had a brainwave there. Didn't you Greg?"

"Yep. Not sure how good it is – 'Maggots for Moggie.'"

"That's truly excellent Greg," Fran, Lynda and I chorus together.

Greg smiles and transforms himself from a man who disappears into the woodwork into an attractive human being, although his clothes remain brown and grey.

"Greg's going to be our IT guru, right?" says Barry. "He's also been taking an online course in social media since last year. He's a dark horse, aren't you Greg. A dark horse all for the good. His workplace has told him to either get vaccinated or lose his job. Their loss, the cats' gain. He'll work from home and spend more time with Ruby. His missus is well excited too. She got him to go to OA because she wanted him to spend more time out of his Turtle home. 'Maggots for Moggy' is going to get you out of your shell, isn't it Greg?"

"Uh, yes. I think spending time with Ruby is helping a lot."

In a strange way, the Barry-Greg combination works. Barry pushes Greg beyond his comfort zone and Greg sticks his neck out a little more while supporting Barry practically.

"What about your cat food addiction Barry?" asks Lynda. "If you're a cat food producer?"

"No problem there. No way I'm going to eat maggots! My missus is all for this too. She wants me to get away from feeding cats directly and make more money. She believes this is a goer, so she's going to do 'Maggots for Moggy' admin; have work of her own beyond the kids. She trained as an accountant."

"Would you have time to help us with social media, Greg?" Fran asks. "For the social enterprise we are planning – 'Dolls with Stories'. We want to showcase high-end dolls for sale online with their stories. Somewhat like you were doing with cats."

"Sure, I can get you guys going, it's pretty easy. Then you can look for someone to employ and I will train them. Also, there's something you could do for me."

"What's that?" I ask.

"If it's not too much trouble, there's a doll I would like. I'd like a doll called James. Ruby keeps asking about my brother James who died. I thought, maybe, if we had a James doll who could fight with the Turtle team, Ruby and I could write stories about him. Like a super-powered human doll. But not green."

"Absolutely we can do that for you, Greg," I say. "Couldn't we girls?"

Fran and Lynda nod enthusiastic assent and 'Dolls for Stories' and 'Maggots for Moggy' take a significant step forward together.

54

IT'S Sunday and I'm off to Lynda's for coffee, chatting and doll enhancement. Our Sunday meetups have become a regular event. It's not a good day for Fran, she likes to spend quality time with Holly most weekends, so three-way catchups are usually on an evening when Holly can visit with a school friend.

I get to Lynda's house with spare breath, having had no rests on the way up. I'm proud of myself and can't wait to tell Lynda but she isn't home when I knock. That's not like Lynda, she's usually very prompt.

I let myself in with the key Lynda hides in a fake rock by the steps. I'm not yet confident to use the coffee machine so I start working on our showcase doll.

Fran, Lynda, and I had an extensive debate about the first high-end doll we would create. We all had to propose three potential candidates and then voted on them. We agreed to stick with New Zealanders to begin with. Fran suggested Prime Minister Jacinda Ardern, Lorde, as a current international New Zealand performing artist, or Kate Sheppard, who helped New Zealand become the first country in which women got the vote. Lynda suggested former All Black captain Richie McCaw or Sir Edmund Hillary as New Zealand male sporting icons, or Sir Robert Muldoon, who was a horrible former Prime Minister otherwise known as 'Piggy'. I suggested A.J. Hackett, inventor of bungy jumping, Georgina Beyer, New Zealand's first transgender politician, or Ashley Bloomfield, current Director General of Health.

Ashley won the vote, based on his existing popularity as a collectable. Ashley comes across in the media as a very normal person, who has led New Zealand's health response to the worst global pandemic in a century. He's already been immortalised on t-shirts, coffee mugs, face masks, cushion covers, tea towels and in make-your-own kitsets, much to his own surprise. However, our doll will be in a much higher end collectable category.

We've managed to get insider information on Ashley, because one of Lynda's friends married one of Ashley's best mates. He likes running, cycling and played the bagpipes at school so I'm having fun making his accessories. Lynda is challenged by his clothing because he doesn't go in for the flamboyant, but she's having a go at a burlesque party outfit.

I need to finish Ashley for the summer craft show Lynda got me the chance to exhibit at. I'm submitting my teacup with gold roses and Bev and Bill's vase as recreations which profile 'Broken is Beautiful'. Ashley will contribute to the profile of 'Dolls with Stories' and will be credited to Lynda and Fran as well as me.

Lynda bursts in an hour late, when I'm deep in the intricacies of construction of a stethoscope. "Sorry. The lesson ran on."

"Lesson?"

"Yes, I'm learning to mountain bike."

"Is that different to road biking?"

"Very different."

"You're muddy and you have some blood running down the back of your leg."

"I fell off a few times. That's part of learning to mountain bike."

"Don't think it's for me."

We change our meeting time for future Sundays to 11.30am in case mountain bike lessons don't end on time. Lynda manages to go for an early morning run, a mountain bike lesson and still have plenty of energy to work on dolls' clothes. I will always marvel at her energy.

A few weeks later Lynda is late again. This time I brave the coffee machine and make a halfway decent cappuccino though my milk froth is still not as good as Lynda's. I look out the front window as I take my coffee to the table, to see two people cycling towards the driveway. Lynda comes in the front door and the person behinds her pulls off his helmet to reveal springing red curls. It's Robbie!

My instinct is to run but Lynda and Robbie are blocking the door. "What are you doing here? Why did you bring him here?" I ask.

"Because I thought it would be good for you two to meet again, Julia."

"Hi, Julia, it's great to see you again," says Robbie.

"Thanks for the thought but I'd like to go now."

"Stop right there, Julia. We've talked about hanging in there when things get tough. Right? We're friends so we do the hard stuff."

"Yes, but Robbie is not my friend."

"He was your friend. And he could be again."

I take a deep breath and a big mouthful of cappuccino.

"So, how's Rosemary?"

"I wouldn't know, haven't seen her in ages."

"Moved on to someone else then?"

Lynda and Robbie glance at each other and look uncomfortable.

"You have to be kidding me. The two of you? It's definitely time I left!"

"We met mountain biking. And yes, I figured he must be Robbie from your lockdown pretty quickly. I want to get you guys talking again because now you're both my best friends, along with Fran. Do you think you could just have a coffee with Robbie, Julia? Then you can leave."

I have two choices. I can storm out like after our vaccine conversation, which seems an eternity ago, or I can stay and make the best of things. I shove my pride out of the way and opt to stay.

Lynda makes coffee for her and Robbie, then another for me. She's bought my favourite brownies.

Looking at Robbie still makes my heart twist a little, but I will have to live with that feeling. Robbie and Lynda make sense together. They are much closer in age, and in interests, than Robbie and me.

"Robbie, I'm sorry how things ended. I made a mistake. I would like to be friends if it works for both of us."

"Thanks Julia. I am still so grateful I got to stay at your house during lockdown. Did you find the hedgehog I left you?"

Hedgehog? Oh yes, I remember the hedgehog that I thought Robbie must have accidentally left behind. "You left it for me?"

"It was a present I was meaning to give you, rather than just leave in the room. Things ended a bit suddenly, didn't they?"

"Why a hedgehog?"

Robbie looks a little embarrassed. "I whittle animals for people with my Da's old knife, it's my way of expressing creativity, beyond putting flowers on coffees. I try to choose an animal that suits the person."

Now I see why Robbie's embarrassed. He thinks I am like a hedgehog? However, my pride and my prickles need to stay down.

"Your carving is great; you could do more of it. Maybe sell things?"

"I'd never considered it, but maybe I should," says Robbie. "I hear from Lynda that you two are doing great things with your Dolls in Schools."

"With Fran," we both chip in.

"Yes, I'm looking forward to meeting Fran too. Perhaps I can help you. You never know when you might need a builder. Or a barista? How about I make us all another round of coffee?"

55

JANUARY–MARCH 2022

LYNDA is totally focused on 'Dolls with Stories' and our enterprise is growing rapidly, assisted by an expanding team of volunteers. Ashley won the visitor's vote at the Museum craft show and Greg is helping us organise an online Ashley auction, with lots of publicity. It's going to be fun and nail-biting. How much money might we raise for this phase of 'Dolls with Stories'?

My phone is ringing hot with people wanting re-creations. Robbie has informally taken over my repair business because he doesn't yet have a work visa that will allow him to apply for a job. Robbie's visa was tied to Coffee Culture, and they don't need baristas because the growing Omicron wave is making New Zealanders reluctant to eat out. I'm still the front but Robbie does all the repairing.

Fran and Lynda and I are working on the next collectable doll; we decided to push our limits and try Georgina Beyer.

I visit with Aroha at Linwood Primary once a month. We are writing an Amanda book and she is illustrating it. She's very good at drawing and I am helping her with writing. Fran is organising a meet-up next month with Aroha's aunty; Aroha lives with her aunty and three cousins. I'm looking forward to getting to know more of her family.

There's something big I had to do to keep seeing Aroha, I had to get vaccinated. Actually, it wasn't nearly as big a deal as I thought it would be. The Government introduced vaccine mandates in late

2021. People working in schools and healthcare had to be vaccinated. You had to show a vaccine pass to go into most businesses. Anyone participating in extracurricular activities at Aroha's school had to be vaccinated to reduce transmission of COVID to the children. Anyone included me.

I was gutted when Fran first told me about the vaccine requirement. I still didn't want to be forced to get vaccinated. I wasn't nearly as strongly opposed to getting vaccinated as I'd been earlier in 2021. The passion I felt when reading all those articles online dwindled away as my life became more populated with real people and activities and my time on social media shrank. But changing my mind felt like admitting I was wrong.

Fran, Lynda and I talked about vaccines a lot in that latter part of 2021. I managed not to yell or storm out. They listened to me and heard that I was scared. They admitted sometimes they still had little niggles in the backs of their minds, although Fran lined up for her six-month booster shot as soon as she could.

"Think about all the food we eat and products we use and don't consider in depth," Fran said. "Do you look at the list of chemicals in your shampoo or toothpaste? How often do you read all the ingredients on packets in the supermarket?" She had a good point there.

I finally caved in and bought glasses from the $2 Shop, but I often forget to take them shopping so can't read the labels. My new wardrobe is much more stylish than my pinafores, but I miss my big pocket on the front where I could keep all sorts of things.

"Life's such a juggling act," said Lynda. "Not much is sure. But you do what you have to in order to keep on running. And we trust in Ashley. Right?"

I wanted to keep seeing Aroha and Fran said she'd go with me to the vaccination. The chemist in Sumner was doing vaccinations so, one Saturday morning, we met there. There was no queue. The friendly pharmacist asked for my name and birth date and a few questions about my medical history. They asked if I had any questions. It turned out I had no more questions. They stuck a needle in my arm, so small I couldn't feel it, put a bandaid on, gave me an info sheet and made me wait fifteen minutes. After that I went home to see if felt sick or turned into a two-headed monster. Neither of those two things happened. Maybe I will get sick later, but a vaccinated me can hang out with Aroha, be less likely to make her ill, and that's the story I'm writing now.

56

WITH my recreations, dolls and Aroha, I'm hugely busy and haven't got around to calling Mum for a while; it's a surprise to hear my mobile ring and see she is calling me.

"Hi, Julia."

"Hi Mum, how are you? Sorry I haven't called in so long. Things are going really well. I've been snowed under with work."

"It's been a bit tough, actually Julia. I haven't been well and Brucey, Brucey is—" Mum's voice breaks up into sobs.

"Oh no. What's happened, Mum?"

"He died. Brucey died."

"I'm so sorry. What did he die of?"

"We both got Omicron. From Shirleen. She'd been to bowls when I told her it wasn't safe, but she missed her mates. She didn't tell us she'd gone to bowls because she was embarrassed. She and Ray came for drinks three days after bowls then the next day she was sick and two days later Brucey and I got ill. I thought we'd be okay because we'd been vaccinated. I talked to Wendy, and she said she'd get someone to keep an eye on us. But then Wendy got sick too and no one rang us. So many people were ill at the same time. Brucey was having trouble breathing but I didn't want to bother anyone, they all sounded so stressed. Then he just died. He died!" Mum breaks down in tears again.

"Will there be a funeral?"

"We will have a little celebration of Brucey's life in March. There's too much COVID around right now and Ray and Shirleen and I are all feeling too tired. Do you think you might be able to come, Julia?"

"I'd love to come Mum. I will be there with bells on." Does one attend a funeral with bells on? Probably not but it sounds better than, "I'll be there in black."

"That will be lovely Julia. There's plenty of room in Brucey's house for you to stay."

There's something else I know I need to do but have been putting off with the excuse I am too busy. Mum's call has yanked the something else out of its box in my brain. I need to try to reconnect with Johnno. If he doesn't want to connect with me that's okay but I need to try. I considered looking for him back when I was investigating Robbie, then my downward slide boxed Johnno away again. I've thought about Johnno frequently recently, but used the excuse of my multiplicity of other commitments to stall. Brucey's death is my reminder you never know when time will run out.

It doesn't take a lot of internet investigation to find where Johnno is living and his current contact details. He's working for Babbage Consultants in Sydney and has been for several years. Why didn't he come home when he was so close? However, it doesn't matter, what matters is that he comes home now.

I take a deep breath and dial Johnno's mobile. I don't know how much this will cost me, but I can afford a phone call. I have to afford a phone call. "Hi, Johnno, it's me, Julia."

"Julia, I can't believe it's you. It's been so long since we talked. I know I should have got in touch. I have been thinking about you the last two years. All that time I could have visited before COVID and then I start thinking about you when no one can travel. You were so angry when Gran died that I didn't think there was any point visiting. Do you remember how you yelled at me over the phone? Told me I was useless and didn't

274

care about any of you? That you hated me and never wanted to see me again? That I should just stay overseas?"

I don't remember any of this.

"I had to go, Julia. I had to make my own life. A life I could be proud of. I needed to forget growing up in a party house with a mother who couldn't remember our birthdays. I thought that meant I had to forget everything and make a new life. But I still missed you. I just couldn't say it."

Tears are running down my face and Johnno's voice is breaking up.

"I miss you too Johnno. Do you think it's time to come home for a visit? Mum's partner, Brucey, just died and they are going to have a memorial in March."

"Brucey, was that loser still around? Mum never stayed with anyone for so long!"

"Not still around. They were apart for ages. But Brucey got very sick two years ago and Mum helped him till he died."

"Do you think Mum would want me to come?"

"I'm sure she does. And I want you to come too."

57

JOHNNO lets me know when he'll arrive in Christchurch and books a rental car for us to drive up to Golden Bay together. The Government helps out by allowing vaccinated travellers to enter New Zealand without isolation from early March. Johnno tells me he's vaccinated without it appearing like he has considered the issue in any depth, and I just say, "Me too."

I take a bus to meet Johnno off the plane. I recognise him instantly when he comes through with the flood of passengers, even with a mask on. How could I have thought I might not recognise him? He's part of me and that can never change.

It's like thirty years have rolled away and we are two children in bed telling each other stories again.

"What happened …?"

"And then you …"

"Do you remember when …"

"Wasn't that funny …"

"When Gran caught us …"

Our drive to Golden Bay is the first long-distance road trip we have ever done together. Luckily, we are well past the "His finger is on my side of the seat," and "She poked me," phase of life. Although we do have battles over the radio station. Johnno's music taste is more at the heavy metal end, and he expresses disgust at the thought of listening to a country station. I want to economise by making sandwiches on the fly while he doesn't want to get the rental car dirty and demands a good coffee regularly.

We find Brucey's house in Takaka; neither of us is good at navigating so we take several wrong turns in a town with only one main street. Mum must have been watching for us because she comes to the door in a red and orange caftan. She looks frail and thin in the voluminous fabric, but her arms are outstretched to welcome us, and we share a hug that, at least temporarily, washes away the anger and frustration and disappointments and suggests the possibility of new beginnings at any age or stage of life.

She shows us to a room with sagging twin beds, orange candlewick bedspreads, a flowered carpet and abstract wallpaper patterns that are a time travel head trip. Then we share a cup of Kenya Bold tea because I brought my own, in case Mum didn't yet subscribe to Kenya Bold, and because Johnno and I are coffeed-up to the max from our drive.

Brucey's memorial is an open day at his house. Many people pass through, and Mum is the centre of attention. She revels in the spotlight and offers everyone a glass of punch as they arrive. Mum says the punch is non-alcoholic, but it seems to make people very happy. We are all exhausted by the end of the day and are grateful that Shirleen and Ray help clean up.

Over coffee the next morning – Johnno has investigated Takaka cafés and returned with three keep cups full of excellent coffee – our conversations turn more serious. Mum's talking about Brucey. "It was tough, you know. Looking after him when his mind was going."

"Yes, I do know Mum. I very much remember how it felt looking after Gran when she got dementia. I should have been exploring the world in my twenties but instead I was at home looking after an old person."

"I'm sorry, Julia. I know I wasn't great as a mother or as a daughter. And I know an apology can't make up for what I didn't do. I excused myself as a daughter when I saw what a great job you were doing. I excused myself as a mother because I thought Gran was filling in the gaps, but now I know that wasn't enough.

"I was so excited to have you at the beginning. I thought having babies in a communal household would make everything fun and easy. Everyone would want to share raising two little delights. And you were both lovely babies. However, communal living isn't all it's cracked up to be; when shit needs cleaning up there aren't many people who volunteer."

"I have a way you can help make up now," I say.

Mum looks nervous. "I'm a bit old to be looking after children, dear."

"No Mum," I laugh, "I would hardly be pregnant at fifty, would I! I'm talking about helping lots of children, through the business that Fran and Lynda and I have set up – 'Dolls with Stories'. You could be part of setting up a branch in Golden Bay."

"That sounds interesting, Julia. Tell me more."

I explain the 'Dolls with Stories' model. Mum says she knows a young immigrant who, like Robbie, is waiting for a new work visa so she can be legally employed. She's trained as a kindergarten teacher but is keen to keep herself occupied at present so has been helping Mum with the garden for cash. We meet with Frauke; she's very excited by the potential of 'Dolls with Stories' because she worked with special needs children in her hometown in Germany. Golden Bay can become the first branch of 'Dolls with Stories' outside Christchurch and I already see how to spread further. Lynda will be thrilled.

Johnno's keen to help out too. He offers a large donation to support Lynda's salary. He says that, since he became a partner in the engineering consultancy, he hasn't known what to do with his surplus income, but now it's obvious.

Fran, Lynda, and I agree to have a get-together in Takaka after six months to check in on progress and that Johnno will join us as a director if he likes the direction the enterprise is headed in.

Life's going well but I know it won't always be a bouquet of golden roses. My relationship with the internet remains infused with caution. I never again want to be sucked back into the depths of the web and the plethora of conflicting information that I could spend my whole existence unravelling without discovering anything about reality. What I do want is to be present in this physical world, with friends who feed each other pumpkin soup from their unruly gardens, glue their lives together with cups of Kenya Bold and coffee, and create shared stories.

Thanks for reading *Broken is Beautiful*. I hope you enjoyed it.

If you are wondering what might happen to Julia, Lynda and Fran in the future, sign up for updates on when *Threads of Connection* will be published at:

www.janeshearer.com

THREADS OF CONNECTION

Life in 2030 is challenging. The sea is tearing off mouthfuls of land, toilets hurl their contents into houses, the council is letting the city disintegrate, and energy quotas are keeping people home. Julia, Lynda and Fran are running 'Humans with Stories' workshops, helping isolated adults find commonality through story-telling. Can the group spin threads which are strong enough to weather the storms threatening their community?

ABOUT THIS BOOK

Broken is Beautiful is set in Christchurch, New Zealand, during the COVID pandemic. For people in Christchurch, 'broken' has been part of life since the Canterbury Earthquakes struck the city in 2010 and 2011. Civil emergencies became a regular occurrence during the earthquakes. When the first COVID lockdown was announced in New Zealand, in late March 2020, there was a feeling of déjà vu.

When COVID arrived in New Zealand, our country closed its borders – it was easy to close borders on an island. We then remained largely isolated from the world for the period *Broken is Beautiful* covers – March 2020 to March 2022. Isolation has so many effects on how people and communities behave and COVID isolated people at many levels.

Broken is Beautiful is the story of a group of people who have pre-existing problems and join a support group just before the pandemic takes off. The characters' trajectories are, of course, influenced by the New Zealand response to COVID – who in the world wasn't affected by their country's response? In particular, vaccination and vaccination mandates became a fraught issue in New Zealand, dividing families and friends between those strongly supporting vaccination and those concerned about it. Mandating of vaccine passports for all adults, together with vaccination for numerous occupations, exacerbated the situation.

A core question during the pandemic was, why do people choose their vaccination stances and will they change their positions? A question that still occupies people's minds is how to be friends when you have different views regarding vaccination. However, this isn't a problem restricted to vaccination. Can people remain friends and colleagues when they differ on important matters? The Obsessives Associated group at the centre of *Broken is Beautiful* is one depiction of the whys and hows of such a situation, with a hopeful take on the challenges.

ACKNOWLEDGMENTS

Thank you to everyone whose stories have inspired this book, both personal and anecdotal. Please keep telling them to me. Thanks to my beta readers, Ann Shearer, Chris Nelson, Rew Shearer, Cleone Blomfield, June Baptista, Sue Harcombe. It's a lot easier to believe in a book when other people engage with the story. Terri and Lynne, your houses gave me my mental images of Julia's home, though not of her boxes! Thanks to Lesley Marshall for her assessment and Rew Shearer specifically for putting me on the right track with dialogue. Thanks to Holly Dunn who did a superb job on my cover and to Stephanie McConchie for her thoughtful and detailed editing. Special thanks to Chris for cooking dinner so I can get on with writing, and all his support in everything I do. Thanks to Sarah Nelson for being the future. Don't we all tell stories to share our past with the future?

www.ingramcontent.com/pod-product-compliance
Lightning Source LLC
Chambersburg PA
CBHW010703100726
47900CB00010B/2768